GARDEN OF THE DEAD

The new novel from the best-selling storyteller

Randy Quinn took over his father's position as manager of an exclusive cemetery, despite the negative opinions of his friends and contemporaries about the job. Still unmarried, and living in his parents' house after their passing, he is worried about grave-robbers when the relatives of a wealthy man insist on burying him with expensive jewellery. But when, as he feared, the grave is disturbed, he uncovers the coffin and makes a shocking discovery...

Recent Titles by Andrew Neiderman

DEADLY VERDICT
LIFE SENTENCE

GARDEN OF THE DEAD

Andrew Neiderman

Severn House Large Print
London & New York

This first large print edition published 2012
in Great Britain and the USA by
SEVERN HOUSE PUBLISHERS LTD of
9-15 High Street, Sutton, Surrey, SM1 1DF.
First world regular print edition published 2010 by
Severn House Publishers Ltd., London and New York.

British Library Cataloguing in Publication Data

Neiderman, Andrew.
  Garden of the dead.
  1. Cemetery managers--Fiction. 2. Grave robbing--Fiction.
  3. Suspense fiction. 4. Large type books.
  I. Title
  813.5'4-dc23

ISBN-13: 978-0-7278-9937-8

Severn House Publishers support The Forest Stewardship
Council [FSC], the leading international forest certification
organisation. All our titles that are printed on Greenpeace-
approved FSC-certified paper carry the FSC logo.

MIX
Paper from
responsible sources
FSC® C018575

Printed and bound in Great Britain by the
MPG Books Group, Bodmin, Cornwall.

For my wife Diane.
I am the words; she is the music.
Together, we sing on.

PROLOGUE

He had never felt uncomfortable in the darkness. Even as a little boy, he didn't ask that a light be kept on or cry when the door of his bedroom was closed. In fact, he welcomed the darkness. It was in the darkness that he was able to think deeper thoughts, thoughts he wouldn't want anyone else to hear or to know.

Some people could look at your face and read your thoughts no matter how good you were at hiding them. In the dark that wasn't a worry.

He even disliked the stars and certainly disliked the moon because of how unmasked their light made him feel.

When he was twelve, he found this coffin-like cabinet on their property and tested himself by climbing into it and letting it close over him. It was warped enough to permit all the air he needed, and he never went into it during hot weather.

At first it was admittedly difficult. What if the lid jammed? No one might hear his screams and he would starve or become dehydrated and die in the darkness he cherished so much. After a while, however, he was very comfortable. It was a great escape, even better than tree houses or caves. He didn't have to share his hideout with anyone and in it he could plan and plot without anyone criticizing him or offering any opposition.

And then there was Lazarus.

He had heard that story enough times to memorize every word. He didn't believe in the story, but it was always fascinating, and now when he climbed out of the cabinet he thought of himself as resurrected every time but in a far different way. Every time he was resurrected, he was sure he had grown more powerful, more self-confident. It was in the darkness that he could leave the heavy baggage others imposed on him. So that when the time came to make a very important decision, one surely most men his age would retreat from making, he could do it easily.

So easily in fact that he never heard a peep from his conscience.

Actually, he believed that when he climbed out of the cabinet for the last time, he had left his conscience completely in there. It wasn't his conscience anyway. Church, school, parents and government had forced it on him.

Getting rid of it was a relief.

Now he could be who he always wanted to be without the slightest pang of guilt, especially now.

ONE

Carving out a grave perfectly was an artistic endeavor to Quinn.

He used a backhoe, of course, but after he had the hole deep and wide enough, he would lower himself into it and, with a small hand shovel, sculpt it into a perfect rectangle with a smooth floor. Except for Jack Waller, who co-owned and operated the Sandburg Cemetery in what was now an exclusive residential community in the upstate New York area once famous for its summer resorts, no one seemed to take any particular notice of the graves Quinn dug. Most mourners avoided looking down into a grave, and few in the eye of the storm of grief would pause to compliment anyone for such a thing anyway.

Quinn had a suspicion that the dead appreciated his extra efforts, but he wouldn't ever say such a thing. Most people thought he was weird enough as it was, especially since he had been digging graves since he was fourteen, working with his father first and then taking over when his father was too sick to work. He insisted on helping dig his father's grave. It was one of his last opportunities to do something he considered significant for him. He and his father had dug his mother's. Neither was buried in the Sandburg Cemetery. It was a relatively new cemetery.

Waller and his partner Richard Valentine bought the tract of land twelve years ago and made it something special with the elaborate landscaping, tiled walkways, and fountains adorned with angels, birds and flowers. They built a state-of-the-art, full service funeral home with a mortuary and reposing and slumber rooms with expensive furnishings and beautiful paintings of tranquil scenes. The home included a non-denominational chapel that could easily become a Catholic, Protestant, or Jewish sanctuary in minutes. There was even a small theater for video remembrances accompanied by music.

They couldn't discriminate against any race, but to make it even more exclusive they charged four times the price any other cemetery would charge for any grave-site and maintenance. They had very restrictive rules on what kind of monuments to permit, its size, shape and cost. There was nothing inexpensive. When someone said, 'You can't take your money with you,' Quinn would think metaphorically that *the dead in the Sandburg cemetery certainly took a significant part of their wealth with them.*

Today was the first time he had an opportunity to literally believe it. He was in Jack Waller's adjoining office waiting for instructions. The door was slightly ajar. Waller kept one well appointed and furnished office for greeting his bereaved and making the arrangements, and another for his detailed business work. That office was Spartan, practical and, to Quinn, a bit dreary with its Venetian shades instead of curtains, bland dark-gray walls, tightly woven light gray rug and fluorescent lighting. It was always untidy. It reminded him of the detention room in high school, not that he was in that room much at all.

Quinn was tired this morning because he had been suffering from insomnia lately and as a remedy thought he would stay up watching television until he was too exhausted to keep his eyes open. Unfortunately, he got hooked in a thriller and was unable to turn it off. He battled sleep until the film ended and then fell asleep quickly. He would have overslept, but Waller woke him to tell him to come to the funeral home. There was an immediate assignment. Matthew Kitchen had died and arrangements were being made quickly, so quickly in fact that 'It's almost as if his children wanted to get started as soon as possible on forgetting him.' That was the dry humor of Jack Waller.

Quinn would be there and not only because it was Matthew Kitchen, one of the wealthiest and most influential men in the community, and not only because he had once had a serious crush on Kitchen's daughter Evelyn in high school. He would be there quickly because Waller paid him too well for him to jeopardize his job. He was the only yearly salaried employee for Sandburg Cemetery, which under his title of cemetery manager included overseeing and maintaining the landscaping, snow plowing the long driveway in the winter, de-icing the walkways and servicing any electrical or plumbing issues. He had an ever changing roster of part-time assistants, ever changing and part-time simply because it was difficult holding on to anyone for this sort of work. They either got drunk and didn't show up or moved on to better paying labor.

Quinn had fallen asleep in his clothes so he just had to wash his face with cold water, brush his hair and leave for the funeral home. It wasn't the first time he was roused and rushed out without breakfast or putting on fresh clothing. There was no one else at his home to care.

At twenty-eight, he still lived alone in his father and mother's house, an eighteen hundred square foot two story Queen Anne with twelve acres of surrounding forest, none of which had ever been cleared. The house was paid for so all he had was its maintenance and the real estate taxes. There was always some talk about housing developments being started adjacent to his property, which made the prospects for its appreciation very good. A quarter of a mile in on the west, there was a small creek that trickled into the larger Sandburg Creek. He had a productive submersible well and good leeching ditches for sewerage.

Bachelorhood wasn't difficult for him. He was self-reliant from his early teen years and since then had always looked after his own things, washing his own clothes and cleaning his own room with the same compulsive immaculate behavior his father evinced with everything he did. His mother wasn't as neat and was never much of a homemaker. Life itself seemed exhausting and overwhelming to her. He loved her dearly, but he had no emotional cataracts when it came to seeing her for whom and what she was ... lazy.

Working beside his father, he cared for the property, took pride in its pristine appearance, learned how to plumb, do electric work, automobile maintenance and carpentry. He poured cement and improved the sidewalk, repaired any equipment, helped his father add on a room for them to use as a den to house their television and a pool table, laid carpet and wood floors and cut firewood for their self-made, fieldstone fireplace. There never seemed to be an hour lacking something to do.

Quinn slept in the room he had slept in since he was three years old. In fact, as silly as it seemed, he still had the pictures of comic book heroes on his walls and still had old baseball and football stars' pictures hanging where they had first been hung. It gave him a sense of security, a feeling that he hadn't lost the magic of family. Years had gone by; his parents, who had him late in life, were gone, but he remained safely encased in his cocoon.

Sometimes, at night, when he heard a creak that sounded like footsteps, he would imagine it was only his mother getting up to get herself a glass of milk. She said it helped her sleep. If he heard what sounded like a pickup truck nearby, he would imagine it was his father coming home from work.

There was no obvious reason for him to be a loner. Randy Quinn wasn't an ugly man by any means. He was six feet two inches tall with broad shoulders and a lean, muscular body firmed by years of manual labor. He had played football in high school, but he was always too slow to be more than a defensive lineman and despite his strength and size, he was really never aggressive enough to suit his coach. Because his father had some health problems and he had to complete his work more often, Quinn never played during his senior year, which was probably the year he should have played the most.

With deep set dark blue eyes, a shock of thick light brown hair, male model high cheek bones, a Romanesque nose and firm, strong lips, he also should have been a heartthrob, especially in his senior year, but he was attending a small school with a K-12 population of barely more than one thousand students. Everyone's family, business and sibling history was well known. No one had to spill his or her intimate details on a talk show here. It was as if the community had its own nerve endings through which news of a marital crisis, the criminal action of a relative, the unwanted pregnancy of a teenage girl or simply a serious illness shot through the community's spine with the electric speed of a reflex. What that unfortunately meant was Quinn could not disguise the work he did or avoid the negative connotations associated with it.

He was nicknamed Corpsey early on in junior high, and the name stuck. Everyone knew what his father did for a living and everyone knew what he did on his summers and holidays and weekends. The fact that he had little or no contact with any corpse didn't seem to matter. Anyone in any way attached to a cemetery and a funeral home was smeared with the same brush. It was as if they were infected by death and others thought they might infect them.

Often the subject of jokes, he retreated from much social contact with other students. He did well enough in school, but saw graduation almost the way an inmate viewed his prison release. He had some interest in going to college. However, his father didn't encourage him and by now his mother was in an alcoholic retreat, slowly closing the lid of her own coffin with gin and cigarettes. He toyed with enlisting in the army, but was afraid of joining any organization from which he couldn't make an instantaneous retreat and with the Iraq war still raging, he envisioned once they had discovered what work he had done as a civilian, he'd be assigned to escort the dead.

Just recently, in fact, he had dug the grave of one of his former high school classmates, Nick Reuben, killed in Iraq. Usually, he didn't know the people that he buried in this cemetery that well. They had traveled in more exclusive circles. He knew who some of them were and occasionally knew their relatives, but he hadn't had the same sort of close contact with any of them that he had with Nick. Nick had sat two desks behind him in math and next to him in English literature.

When Nick's coffin was being lowered into the perfect grave, Quinn thought about the time they had read Hamlet and Nick had teased him with some of the gravedigger's speeches. He would follow him through the hallway quoting lines like 'Whose grave is this? Mine sir. How long hast thou been a gravedigger? How long will a man lie in the earth ere he rot?'

Quinn would walk faster, but once, tired of it when Nick followed him on to the school

16

bus and continued quoting and teasing him to show off for some girls, he turned and punched him just under his nose, loosening some of his teeth and causing a nosebleed. Quinn was suspended for a week and in detention for two days, but Nick never teased him again.

Two years after their high school graduation, Nick actually apologized to him for the incident in junior high. Since he had enlisted, Nick had become surprisingly mild, careful, and generous. It was as if he were trying to stack his good side to strengthen his chances of making it back in one piece. Quinn bore him no malice and wished him good luck. He had worked extra hard to make Nick's grave perfect, smoothing the sides and leveling the floor as if his old classmate were actually going to live in it.

Right now, still half asleep, he waited in the adjoining office and barely paid attention to the voices in the arrangements office, but then the voices made him sit up, especially the female's voice. He recognized Evelyn Kitchen. Sometimes, even now, he would pause no matter what he was doing and recall her walking through the high school hallways. To him it was more like she was floating. Her steps were that soft, her body that lithe. She had an angelic glow about her. He had noticed her before, of course, but in her senior year, she seemed to bloom like a flower that had waited for just the right

17

amount of pure sunshine.

When he got up enough nerve to approach her, he felt himself tremble, his voice crack. She was friendly in a polite and proper way, but disappointingly aloof. He felt as if he had been dismissed. To the rest of the students, especially the boys who also had been rejected, and the girls who were dying of envy, Evelyn and her fraternal twin brother Stuart were the epitome of snobbery. Neither had much to do with the other students, and neither participated in any extra-curricular activities. The story was that Matthew Kitchen insisted they attend a public school to develop their character, but they were friends only with students their age who attended private schools. Perhaps that was the only way they could show their father defiance.

In Quinn's mind, maybe hopefully so, Stuart was far more of a snob than Evelyn. He had a slim, almost feminine body with small shoulders, thin wrists and a narrow waist. Quinn had a suspicion Stuart spent just as much time on his complexion and hair as Evelyn did. He was admittedly very bright, but usually sardonic to a fault and when he was pushed too hard or when he pushed hard enough to rile up someone, he usually effected a quick retreat. The other guys called him Hit and Run Kitchen. Everyone said that if his father wasn't so important and influential, he'd be dead.

Matthew Kitchen had built a small empire

with his brilliant real estate acquisitions, and then he parlayed the money into other ventures like racetracks, festival sites, and successful restaurant chains. County politicians wined and dined him. His influence was said to have reached deeply into the state capital and even the governor's office no matter who the governor was or what party was in power.

However, it wasn't only the sound of Evelyn's voice that stirred Quinn even though he had expected some lawyer or assistant would be handling the funeral arrangements. It was what he overheard Stuart and Evelyn say. The requests they were making sounded absolutely stupid.

Jack Waller tugged on his right earlobe as would Humphrey Bogart in many of his films to indicate he didn't understand something someone had said. The fifty-two-year-old businessman had sold the auto dealership he had co-owned with his partner Richard Valentine and then together they had invested in the cemetery. The concept had taken hold quickly. He was right on with his theory that people cared as much about where they would reside after death as they did in life, especially the wealthy who had owned elaborate, beautiful and expensive homes. They refused to believe death could end it all, and one of the best ways to show that was to move their remains into expensive real estate and construct opulent monuments.

'Let me completely understand what you two are telling me,' Jack said.

He couldn't help talking to his cemetery customers with the same somewhat artificially friendly manner and slick smile he had employed as an automobile salesman. With his smooth coffee-black thick hair, his perennial suntan, almond bright brown eyes and capped teeth, he looked like someone a Hollywood director had cast in the role.

He gazed down at the jewelry that had been set before him on his desk.

'You want your father buried with his Rolex, gold necklace, gold bracelet and diamond wedding ring? That's how you want him dressed?'

'It's what my father wanted,' Stuart Kitchen said. He stood in front of Jack's dark-cherrywood desk and folded his arms across his chest. He wore a light-gray pinstriped suit and dark-gray matching tie, but Jack thought the suit was at least a size too big. He had the amusing thought that Matthew Kitchen's son wasn't just trying to step into his father's shoes, but slip into his father's clothes as well. He knew, as well as most people, that Matthew Kitchen hadn't given his son much authority. He assigned most of what he didn't oversee himself to his trusted attorney, Liam Duncan. Just recently, he had appointed Liam to the position of CEO of

20

his corporation and given him a majority position, ensuring that Stuart wouldn't have the power to blunder and destroy what he had built.

Jack looked at Evelyn Kitchen. She remained seated, her beauty so exquisite that she reminded him of the perfect cameo pin his grandmother had handed down to him through his mother. Her looks were that classic.

'But to leave those things on the deceased and bury them, too? I mean, forget about the value for a moment. Isn't there any sentiment attached, something you'd want to pass on to your children?'

He realized as soon as he had asked the question that it was pointless, since neither Stuart nor Evelyn was married or, as far as Jack knew, even engaged.

'My brother just told you, Mr Waller. It's what my father wanted,' Evelyn repeated, but without Stuart's aggressive tone.

Waller was quiet a moment.

'OK.' He shrugged. 'Of course we'll arrange for that if that's what you want.'

'It's not what we want. Didn't you hear my sister? It's what my father told me he wanted,' Stuart said more sharply. 'Is there a problem?'

'No, no problem. As I said, we'll do as you ask.'

'You have the suit we want him to wear, including the shirt, socks and shoes. After you're finished with Dad, we want the coffin delivered to the house for our private wake.'

'A-huh.'

'We'll take care of permanently sealing the coffin,' Stuart added. The implication was clear. They wanted to be sure that no one in Jack's company lifted the jewelry off their father's body.

'How do you mean to permanently seal it?' Jack asked. He wanted to add, what are you going to do, drive in nails, screws, or use super glue?

'Leave that concern to us.'

'Fine,' Jack said. 'Whatever you want.'

'Of course, that's why it will be closed for the more public service here in the morning,' Stuart said.

'No problem,' Jack said. He thought to ease the tension and added, 'Your father chose the best sites in the cemetery for your mother and himself and...' He hesitated and then simply added, 'Any other family members. No rain in sight. I'll have the preparations begun today. Let me just check with my cemetery manager to see if there's anything else to consider. He should be here by now. Can I get either of you something to drink? Coffee, juice, water?'

'No. We don't have any time to waste. We have other things to do today,' Stuart replied.

Jack looked at Evelyn. Her gaze went toward the floor and she lowered her head

22

just a bit. He rose quickly.

'Be just a moment,' he said and walked out and into his adjoining Spartan office.

Quinn sat back, trying to appear as if he hadn't heard a word. He loved how Waller refused to call him a gravedigger. Cemetery manager sounded even more important than he was. He played no part in any major financial decision or any future planning except when he asked for additional tools or new machinery. He folded his arms across his chest and closed his eyes just before Jack Waller entered the room and closed the door softly behind him.

'You hear any of that?'

'What?'

Jack lowered his voice.

'Always thought those two were queer anyway. Nevertheless, this is going to be a sizeable and impressive funeral. We buried his wife four years ago and had an overflow crowd, remember? People were standing outside the chapel. You had to hook up those external speakers for the service. Limousines were lining the road from here to kingdom come.'

'I remember,' Quinn said.

How could he ever forget that day? Even in her grief, Evelyn looked beautiful to him, maybe even more so. She took her mother's death hard, he recalled. He couldn't even get her to look at him with any recognition. Why should she remember me anyway, he had thought? We barely spoke to each other when we were kids. Back in school, he had been too shy even to wave a hello, and if her eyes met his after the formal and dismissive way she had responded to his initial greeting, he quickly looked away. He had simply placed her on too high a pedestal. She was not only beyond his reach, she was beyond his words and looks.

'Yeah, well, do one of your best jobs, not that you do any that aren't very good,' Jack said.

Waller scratched his head and looked at the door adjoining the two offices. To Quinn it was obvious he wanted to come in here simply to get away from Kitchen's son and daughter. He knew Jack didn't have to check on him. He just wanted to take a short intermission.

Quinn often thought that Jack wasn't really suited for this work. He avoided going near the corpse as much as he could. He and Richard had hired a former mortician who had owned a smaller funeral home with a much longer history, Curt Marcus. Curt was hired not only to embalm the bodies, but also to dress them and carry out whatever cosmetic work was required. He was capable of the whole nine yards or, as Richard liked to joke, 'the whole six feet.' They pulled him out of retirement with an offer the sixty-four year old couldn't refuse.

However, Quinn knew that regardless of what went on here right now, Jack would be quite nervous and irritable all day, all week in fact. His wife had finally confronted him about his adulterous affair, and they were just starting a nasty divorce. Fortunately, they had no children. Although it wasn't his business, Quinn gathered that was because of his wife's infertility, not Jack's.

'OK,' Quinn said leaning forward and poised to get up quickly and go to work. Waller, however, still stood there in front of him.

'Those two are very weird,' he muttered and gestured at the adjoining door and then lowered his voice into a loud whisper. 'Both in their late twenties and as far as I know, not involved with anyone of the opposite sex. The rumor always was that they were gay. It's easier to believe it about Stuart, I suppose. She doesn't look like a dyke, but these days, you can't tell about anyone.'

Quinn knew all that, of course. The rumor about Evelyn especially had its origin in high school, not because anyone knew of her relationship with another girl, but because she was so disinterested in any of the boys. It was probably because of his idolization of her, but he wouldn't accept the characterization.

'I don't think that's true about Evelyn,' he said. 'But I wouldn't trust Stuart in the shower.'

'Whatever. I'm sure Matthew Kitchen was

25

hoping to see a grandchild or two before he passed on. They're twins, you know.'

'Yeah, Jack. I know. They were both in my high school class.'

'Oh. Right, right. I forgot they attended public school here. You're their age, but you seem older to me.'

'Thanks, I guess.'

'Are you sure they weren't both queer then?' Jack asked.

'I didn't have much to do with them,' Quinn said. 'No one did.'

Ordinarily he hated nasty gossip, but his distaste for anything negative about Evelyn was instantly resurrected as well.

'Makes sense being their twins. If one's queer, the other would be.'

'Dad once told me he had buried four sets of twins in his time and each had died within two years of the other,' Quinn said to get off the topic.

'Yeah, your father would remember little things like that. People used to think he had the ear of the Grim Reaper and could have private conversations with him anytime.'

Quinn shrugged.

'He took what he did seriously. I don't think anyone knew as much about the cemeteries around here and who is buried in them.'

'Right, right.' Waller rubbed his hands together and shook his head again when he looked at the doorway. He turned sharply at

Quinn, his eyes narrowing suspiciously. 'You heard what they said. Don't bullshit a bull-shitter.'

'I hear and don't hear,' Quinn said. 'It's not my business. What goes on in there is your business, Jack.'

'Yeah? Well, those two want to bury their father with more than one hundred thousand dollars in jewelry, maybe two hundred. Who the hell knows what else in his pockets? His personal jewelry. Can you imagine? Word gets out we're liable to have some grave robbers here digging him up and leaving us with some ugly mess. The place will look like a war zone or something.'

The idea of one of his perfect graves being ruined brought the blood into Quinn's face. The whole cemetery was his and his father's creation. It was more than simple religious sacrilege. It was an attack on him and his father's memory. Some men were proud of the houses they had built; he was proud of the graves he had dug. After all, whose house lasts longer? Not that graves and the monuments he and his father had set didn't sink, collapse with time and water. His father had shown him enough of those, especially the historic graves in the area, graves of men who had fought in the War of 1812 in fact, much less the Civil War and two World Wars, Korea and Vietnam. One had sunk so deeply, he claimed they were standing on the dead man's actual remains.

'They want to seal the coffin at home. Whoever heard of such shenanigans?'

Quinn smiled at the use of the word. It was one of his father's favorite words. Funny, how that came to him at this moment. We really remember people in an accumulation of tiny things, he thought, small remembrances … like his mother's shuffling through the house at night to get her glass of milk or the way his father would sneeze and then pound his fist on his thigh as if his body had committed a small betrayal. Things like that were always more vivid and resurrected the dead faster and more completely than mere photographs. These sorts of memories brought aromas with them, or sounds.

Quinn often envisioned a new kind of grave stone, one that had a small screen on it and buttons that would start a memory video but also emit the deceased's favorite cologne or perfume. Maybe children would visit their parents' graves more if there were things like that, or maybe they wouldn't. Maybe it would be too painful. Maybe it was easier to look at a cold stone with some carved numbers and words, drop some flowers, put some rocks on it or just stare and leave.

He went to his own parents' graves from time to time, but he never felt fulfilled. *They are not here,* he thought. *This whole thing is an illusion. It's like a hand trick. First you see them and then you don't. Why in hell would a soul want to remain down there in the cold, dank earth when it could wander about in the fresh air?*

And yet, they demanded and required respect and a decent burial. The dead were, after all, the most helpless and vulnerable. Waller was right. If Kitchen wanted his valuables with him down there, he could have them, but it only made him more vulnerable.

'I suppose they want to seal it themselves because they're putting in all those valuables. Well, I'm not saying anything about it to anyone,' Quinn said rising. 'Don't worry about me, Jack.'

'I'm not. I'm worried about them. Idiots. They'll surely tell someone else, maybe lots of someone elses and it won't be long before the whole damn community hears of it.'

'I'm sure nothing will come of it,' Quinn said hopefully. 'Dad did tell me that from time to time he believed the bodies in the coffins had valuable things still on them. None of his graves have been disturbed.'

'Those cemeteries don't come close to this one.'

'So?'

'So? So? You ever hear what Willy Sutton, the famous bank robber replied when he was asked why he robbed banks?'

'Can't recall.'

'He said because that's where the money is. This cemetery is where the money is, Randy.'

Jack always referred to him by his given

name when he was trying to impress him or complain about something he had done, not that he did that much wrong. Otherwise, like everyone else practically, he would call him 'Quinn.'

'What do you want me to do, dig it deeper?'

'I don't know,' Jack said. 'Awwww...' He waved at the air between them and went back into his nicer office. Minutes later, he returned and told him to start to prepare the gravesite. 'I'm not about to argue about anything with the bereaved,' he said.

On his way out to get to his backhoe, Quinn heard voices and looked back to see the Kitchen twins leaving the funeral home. Evelyn looked a little taller than her twin brother. They were fraternal twins anyway, Quinn thought. They didn't have to look exactly alike in all ways. Both had reddish-brown hair that was a little more on the ruby side when the sunlight slapped down over them as they passed through the beautifully tree-lined walkway to their gray Mercedes sedan.

At the car, as if she could feel his gaze on her, Evelyn Kitchen turned sharply to look his way. She was wearing a light blue skirt and a little darker blue knit sweater. He couldn't make out her face in very great detail, but he easily resurrected his high school memory of it. He always thought that if she wanted to, she could have easily been a famous model.

She held her gaze on him almost as long as he was holding his on her and he felt sure, although he would blame it on the sunlight later, there was something odd about her expression, the way her lips twisted. It wasn't a smile exactly. It was more like a grimace of pain, a reach for some sympathy. Did she remember him after all? Was she calling to him, asking him to help her? Help her do what? Get over the sorrow? Did she think that just because he was awash in it so often that he knew some secret, some way to escape the pain?

Her brother got into the car quickly, but she held the door open and continued to look his way until her brother obviously said something to her. Then she got in. He watched them drive off, but he wasn't able to get any better look at either of them because of the way the driveway turned to the left.

He continued on to the garage, started up the backhoe and headed out to the gravesite. He'd be at that and the rest of his work for most of the day. He wasn't sleepy anymore either, but something gnawed at him as he rode along toward the gravel road that crisscrossed the cemetery. He wasn't sure what it was.

He hit the brake, turned and looked back at where Evelyn Kitchen stood when she looked his way. It was as if he could conjure her up again.

And he wanted to do that vividly. Just hearing her voice and seeing her had restored his energy. There she stood, he thought, looking at me.

She had looked like she was ready to call out to him just before her brother called out to her.

He wondered what she wanted.

Because whatever it was, he very much wanted to give it to her.

TWO

When Evelyn spoke to Stuart now, she felt as if she were tiptoeing through a minefield. It wasn't only what she said that he reacted to, but also how she said it. He was so sensitive to every nuance in her voice that she was extra careful where she would put accents and where she would raise and lower her volume. The most innocent thing she could say would suddenly be viewed as negative, critical or even threatening.

Stuart would hone in on her with those piercing paranoid eyes, focusing like a skeptical X-ray machine refusing to accept negative results. In his mind something was always on the verge of emerging, something ugly and threatening, something that would destroy their relationship and love for each other.

As he had said literally hundreds of times during their adolescence and still said to her now, even after all this, 'you are, after all, your father's daughter.' The implication was clear. Evil was part of her nature. She could not help it or even prevent it. Only he could do that, and only if she listened to him and obeyed him.

'Are you sure this is a smart thing to do, Stuart?' she asked softly, keeping her eyes forward.

So much time passed that she didn't think he was going to respond. He was capable of that. He could close himself off so tightly that a bomb could explode and he would barely wince. Even when they were much younger, she imagined him shrinking inside of himself until his outer body was merely a shell. He was especially good at doing that when their father chastised him or simply criticized him. In those days his father, frustrated, would seize him at the shoulders and shake him so hard that she was convinced he would snap his spine. But Stuart wouldn't change expression, wouldn't shift his gaze and certainly wouldn't speak. He was practically catatonic.

In the end their father would throw up his hands and tell their mother to try to do something with him, but she was even more incapable of controlling Stuart. In fact, Evelyn thought their mother was actually afraid of her own son. Perhaps because she was his mother, she knew he was capable of things far worse than those things of which his father disapproved. Both she and her mother knew how vengeful he could be.

What made it all even more dangerous was the fact that Stuart was brilliant. Despite their father's dissatisfaction with him, he was unable to find fault with his school grades. Arguing with him was frustrating because Stuart always had good answers. All that would happen was that their father grew more frustrated. She could see the disgust and displeasure sinking into their father's face.

What could possibly be worse for a father than for him to find his own son distasteful? She could not recall a single instance when either had embraced the other with any sign of affection. Even when he was a very little boy, Stuart avoided their father's attempts to be loving. He would turn away his head, look down or walk away. When he was older, he treated their mother the same way. The only one he had ever come to for any sympathy or love was to her. She was very aware of it and sensitive to it and knew if she rejected him or disappointed him even in the slightest way, he would go into a deep funk that could last days. Once he spoke to no one for nearly a week.

'Smart?' he finally said out of the corner of his mouth.

'I know what Mr Waller was worrying about, even though he didn't come right out and say it, Stuart.'

He turned to her and gave her that smile she detested, the sharp, condescending grin.

'Really? What was it he was afraid to say?'

'Someone might come around afterward

and dig up Daddy's grave to steal the jewelry.'

'You don't think Daddy would let that happen, do you?' he asked, still grinning.

'I'm serious, Stuart.'

'So am I,' he said turning back to look at the road ahead. 'Didn't you ever notice how his so-called trusted assistants and two-face friends behaved around him? How they treated him as if he were some divine being, usually with their eyes down, their faces so full of hope and prayer. If only he would lay his hand on one of them or grant him some wish. They practically knelt before his desk and kissed his ring.'

'A ring you want to put in that coffin,' she reminded him.

He turned very slowly, moving in his typical robotic fashion, his eyes like two cannons being adjusted before firing.

'Don't you remember him once telling us that it was a magical ring?'

'He was just trying to be a father and ease our fears when we were younger, Stuart.'

'I took it seriously,' he said.

'Stop it.'

'I did. Once, when he had taken it off and he wasn't around, I put it on my finger to see if I felt any stronger, any safer. I concluded it worked only for him.'

She took a chance and just said it.

'He never told you to bury all that with him.'

36

Stuart didn't respond.

'Did he?' she followed.

'I know what I'm doing. And you very well know why, too. Stop questioning it.' He looked at her quickly and sharply this time. 'You know I'm doing it all for you.'

'I wish you would consider a different way,' she said softly.

'I have. This is the best way. Don't I always do what's best for you, Evelyn? Isn't your welfare, your happiness my highest concern? Well?'

'Yes, Stuart.'

'So don't ask about it anymore. Just let me handle it all.'

She looked out the side window at the blur of scenery. Her eyes had a film of tears over them now.

'I love you,' he continued, 'but you're not lily white when it comes to all this either and you know it, Evelyn. I don't expect you to lather me with thank you kisses, but I do want to see some appreciation.'

She lowered her head. No one could whip her with words as well as he could.

'Soon it will all be over,' he continued. 'And after it is, I'll help you bury it all so deeply that you'll wonder if any of it actually ever happened. You'll see. You can't over-estimate what I can do for you, for us. Just continue to cooperate, continue to be my sister, and continue to stand at my side. You will, won't you, Evelyn?'

He didn't sound threatening. He sounded a lot like he used to sound when they were eleven or twelve, hoping she believed in him and cared for him as much as he cared for her. That was when he was most vulnerable, when he needed her affection and devotion. She never doubted that without it, he would wither and die.

'Yes, Stuart,' she said. 'I will.'

'Good. I see good things ahead for us. We'll make up for all the sorrow. We can go on a trip, buy new cars. You need new clothes.'

'No, I don't.'

'Yes, you do. You need to get rid of anything and everything that ties you to bad memories. Throw it out or give it to Alice Chapman for her pet charity.'

She nearly laughed.

'That's Animal Samaritans, Stuart. I can't see any dogs or cats wearing my clothes.'

He did laugh.

'Well, you know how I am with our help, even someone who's been with us since we were children. Besides, I always thought Father treated her too much like a relative and not a servant.'

'She was more dedicated to him than any servant we've had, Stuart.'

'That's not good,' he snapped. 'Without the proper distance, your employees take advantage.'

She wanted to disagree, but didn't.

'Let's not think about any of that. You have

to think of tomorrow as the first day of your new life, Evelyn, otherwise you will not recover. That's what I'm going to do. We're going to be reborn. Why, we'll even change our birthday,' he said. 'How's that?'

'Stop fooling, Stuart.'

'I'm not fooling. I'm dead serious. It will be like a Papal edict or something. We'll pick the new day and declare it and it will be observed.'

She looked at him to be sure he wasn't being sardonic. He looked deadly serious.

'Change our birthday? Really?'

'Why not? There's nothing we can't do together, Evelyn, not now. We're free. I was always freer than you were, of course, but now we're both free.'

He turned on his favorite CD and sat back. She looked at him a moment. He appeared to have sunk into his own cocoon, his own little world again and if she spoke, he probably wouldn't answer. He wouldn't hear her. The music played on, but she was in her own silence now, too.

It would be a long silence, a silence that might never end.

She imagined herself in the coffin with her father, embracing him, holding on as the lid was closed and the darkness sent her reeling backward, through her adolescence, through her childhood, through her birth and gestation until she was once again forming in her mother's womb beside Stuart.

And in this imagined scene, he was staring at her, his eyes wide open, his face frozen in amazement.

Jack carried Matthew Kitchen's clothing and the jewelry to the embalming room. Keeping his eyes turned away from the corpse on the table, he hung up the suit, shirt and tie, put the socks and shoes on a counter and signaled to Curt Marcus, who paused in his work and approached.

'No underwear?' he asked with a smile. What amazed Jack was Curt's morbid sense of humor. It seemed to fit well with his narrow face, thin nose and mealy mouth. His thin gray hair had gone into a full retreat and was standing its ground only around his temples and the back of his head. The crest was splattered with age spots and old freckles. It looked like someone had flipped a paintbrush in his direction while he was bending over.

'No, but we've got this stuff instead to put on him,' Jack said and emptied the blue velvet bag of its jeweled contents on the counter.

'What the hell ... that worth anything?'

'This is a very special Rolex, Curt.' He turned it over to show him the inscription.

'From the governor?'

'Kitchen was instrumental in getting him elected and who knows what else. I checked on this watch just before I came in here as soon as his children left. I was told this model with what's in it would sell for around one hundred and sixty thousand without the inscription. It was anyone's guess how much it would go for in an auction, but the feeling was it would be something significant.'

'No shit,' Curt said turning it over and studying the workmanship. 'We're just putting it on him for the wake, is that it?'

'No, Curt. This isn't going to be a public viewing. They insist he be buried with it all. They claim he left instructions for them to do just that.'

'Buried with it?'

'You heard me.'

'Well, I've seen loved ones leave costume jewelry on their deceased, and even some much, much less expensive real stuff, but this is madness. What about this gold bracelet? It has diamonds in it and with the price of gold today ... this is thick, Jack.' He bounced it in the palm of his hand. 'I bet this is worth something like a hundred thousand as well. And this ring and this gold necklace...'

'All of it goes six feet under. It's what they asked for, Curt. When you're done, they want him delivered to their home for a private wake. They'll check on the jewelry. You can be sure of that, and then they want to seal the coffin themselves for the public ceremony here.'

'I think I'll take a few pictures of this one,'

41

Curt said. 'I've got a few albums, you know.'

'I'd rather not know,' Jack said.

Curt laughed and Jack shook his head and left. The phone started ringing in his office just as he stepped back into it. It was Paula. For some reason, from the moment they had begun his extramarital affair, she called him Jacky instead of Jack.

'What's up, Babe?' he asked.

'I can't stand it here any more, Jacky. I don't feel well and that quack you hired isn't listening to me.'

'You don't have much longer, Paula.'

'It's easy for you to say that. You're not locked up like some errant girl in a nunnery.'

'It's not what I wanted you to do,' he reminded her.

'Yeah, yeah.'

'I don't get this contradictory morality, Paula. You are willing to have an affair with a married man, but not abort the fetus.'

'I don't want to argue this again, Jacky. Besides, it's too late anyway.'

'It's never too late, from what I hear.'

'Stop it, Jacky.'

'All right.' He looked at his watch. 'I've got a few things I have to do this afternoon, but I'll take a ride up to see you.'

'Whoop tee do.'

'Don't you want me to come see you?'

'You'd better and I want those chocolate covered strawberries.'

'Will do.'

'How's the divorce going?'

'It just started, Paula. It's not going to be a walk in the park. I had no idea she had hired a detective.'

'I promise you I won't,' she said.

He was silent.

'Jacky?'

'I know you wouldn't. We trust each other. The two Musketeers.'

'Soon three,' she said.

He wiped his face with his free hand. Somehow, some way, he had to find a good exit, he thought. He couldn't help this sinking feeling telling him he had jumped from the frying pan into the fire.

His other line began to ring.

'I got another call. I'll see you later.'

'I hope so,' she said. 'I told you, I'm not feeling well. I need you,' she whined.

He pressed the button for the other line and said hello.

'I hooked a real fish this time,' his partner said.

'What do you mean, Richard?'

'Investor for the parcel. I've already approached Morton's attorney again, but with an offer he won't refuse. We can afford it now'

'Now you're the Godfather?'

'It's looking good. I'm setting up a meeting.'

'Who's the investor?'

'He's out of Westchester, Tom Biglow. They

43

call him the real estate king down there.'

'And he wants this?'

'He dabbles. My cousin hooked us up. Be happy, will you. We'll finally turn this project into some fast track cash cow instead of a service for the very rich, and from what you tell me is going on in your life, you'll need it.'

'Thanks.'

'What are partners for?' Richard said and laughed.

Evelyn got out and went into the house ahead of Stuart. She was actually trembling and she didn't want him to see it. Everything about this solution felt so wrong. It was as if she had stepped into quicksand and instead of her brother throwing her a line to help her out, he was putting his hands on her shoulders to push her down into it.

The house was so quiet. Even before her father's death, it was quiet, but the silence seemed to be deeper now, more like the silence between people who knew some dark secret and had agreed to keep it between them. That silence was in their eyes. They still heard the unspoken words, and when they looked at each other, they acknowledged them. They couldn't be buried under the weight of other memories, other thoughts. They were too strong.

We'll never look at each other and not hear these words, she thought. And if I try to avoid looking at him, even for an instant, he

44

will know why and that will anger him. Besides, now he wanted to do even more together. What she had thought would release her, free her to be her own person, had trapped and imprisoned her even more than she had been before.

'Oh, you're back,' Miss Chapman said as Evelyn started toward the stairway.

'Yes, Miss Chapman.'

She could see that their father's longest serving employee still had red eyes. For the moment at least, her father's death trumped any other thought, not that she was incapable of ignoring or burying other unpleasant things, especially if they involved any of the Kitchens. Still, Evelyn was afraid from day one that she would look at her with such distaste that they would have to get rid of her. Of course, as long as her father was alive, she wouldn't dare have even the slightest criticism in her look or voice. What would happen now, Evelyn wondered, and especially after the funeral?

She was confident Stuart wouldn't fire her, despite how loyal and devoted she was to their father. He wouldn't permit her to go out in the world and risk her telling strangers their secrets. With regards to Miss Chapman, Stuart was fond of quoting the Godfather. 'Keep your friends close, but your enemies closer.' She told him she could never think of Miss Chapman as being any sort of enemy.

'That's because you're too naive and trusting,' he replied. And now he blamed everything on her being too naive and trusting. Maybe he was right.

'I remember how hard it was when I had to make arrangements for my sister,' Miss Chapman said. 'Would you like me to bring you some tea, something to eat?'

'No, I'm fine, Miss Chapman.'

'I've been packing your father's things. It's not easy. I can't believe he's gone,' she said.

'Packing his things? What things?'

'Your brother told me to get all his clothing ready to be given away. He had some suits and shirts that were barely worn, you know. After your mother passed, he permitted me to lay out his clothing for the day.' She smiled and added, 'As your mother would say, he could be so occupied in his mind, he'd wear two different socks or even two different shoes if it were left up to him.'

'Right,' Evelyn said forcing a small smile.

The heavy silence between them was loaded with the weight of what they both knew, the horror of it. It passed. Evelyn headed for the stairway again and Miss Chapman went to oversee the preparations for the private wake. They would hold it in their large living room, and Stuart had already given orders as to how he wanted the furniture rearranged and what to display and what to put away.

She climbed the stairway slowly and then paused at her father's bedroom door. It was closed. Her fingers actually trembled when she went to open it. She stood there looking in. The bed had been stripped and all the pictures of her father and mother had been taken from the dresser. Even their blown-up wedding picture had been taken from the wall.

She heard Stuart coming up the stairway and turned on him. He paused, anticipating.

'Why did you have all of his things, Mother's things, removed?'

'First,' he began approaching her, 'I don't want to see it turned into a shrine, and second, I'm taking that bedroom now.'

'Why?'

'I'll be closer to you,' he said smiling. 'It's the master bedroom, Evelyn. It should be mine now. Does that disturb you?'

She felt every muscle in her body tighten.

'No,' she said. 'I'm tired. I need to lay down a while.'

'Of course. It's understandable,' he said. 'I'll be going over to the office in a while.'

'So soon?'

'Father might have manipulated me into a weaker position, but that's only temporary,' he said. 'For now, however, I want them to understand I'm not in any retreat.'

She said nothing. Her gaze went to the guest bedroom just down the hall. That door was not only shut, but she knew it was locked.

'Don't think about that,' he said.

Sometimes, Stuart could read her thoughts. Was that belief that twins, identical or fraternal, could get into each other's minds valid? It frightened her to think it was possible, but there were many times when she believed it. She blamed it on her windowpane face, at least a windowpane when it came to Stuart.

'That's impossible,' she muttered and went to her room. She looked back from her doorway.

He was still standing there looking after her, and for a moment, she saw him as a little boy again, disappointed in her decision to be alone.

He once told her he had a nightmare that he was left behind in their mother's womb. In the dream he was jealous of the air she breathed without him.

'I'd like always to be a part of anything you do, Evelyn,' he told her. He made it sound as if he would die the moment she had.

Maybe that was why he was able to do what he had done, and why he didn't see it as anything but good.

THREE

Most of the day, Quinn couldn't stop thinking about Evelyn Kitchen. Finally, he paused
and began to lecture to himself as if he were
really two people. He had been talking to
himself at home more than he would like.
Now he was doing it at the cemetery.

What are you getting so excited about anyway,
he asked himself. Maybe she was looking
past him toward the cemetery. If it were a
smile, maybe she was smiling at the shape of
a cloud or a pretty bird.

When he really gave it thought, he realized
it was only on the rare occasions like the one
with Nick that he had any contact with the
bereaved who buried their loved ones in
Sandburg Cemetery. Most of the time, he
was invisible to the mourners. He saw the
way people looked at him whenever he waited off to the side for the services at the burial
site to end. When they did see him, most
turned away instantly. He was too much of a
reminder of what would next be done. If any
gazed at him longer than a few seconds, they
looked like they were looking right through
him anyway. No one acknowledged him,

except of course Jack. No one smiled or nodded. It was truly as if he was Death's ambassador here on earth, and who wants anything to do with that representative?

In traditional Jewish funerals, the mourners would wash their hands before going home or to someone's house. His father told him they do it because they were close to death. After that, he wondered if any of his Jewish friends washed their hands after they had shaken his or even touched him. He couldn't help but believe they felt soiled. Was everything he or his father had touched viewed as morbidly stained? In his eyes, people didn't have to be Jewish to behave this way toward his father and him. He tried to put it out of his mind, but it wasn't easy growing up with these thoughts.

There were girls in high school beside Evelyn Kitchen that he wanted to ask on dates, but he wasn't just shy; he was terrified of being rejected. He saw how some looked at him with some sexual interest, but then, as if they had lost their minds for a moment, quickly snapped out of it and ignored him as did the others.

His closest buddy in high school, Barry Palmer, was always advising him to do different work.

'Get a job with a building contractor or a plumber, for Christ sakes, Randy. You can do that easily and you'll make just as much money and not be so scary and distasteful to the girls. I can get you an after school and weekend job with some of the people who hired me.'

He was tempted to do just that, but he always felt it would be like rejecting his father, and he loved his father too much to do that. His father always gave him the option. He didn't have to work with him, but Quinn never said no. Neither of his parents made a big thing of his poor high school social life anyway. They had this faith that some day he would break out, start dating, find a nice girl, get married and have his own children. It was as inevitable as rain. For now, they thought, there was a bit of a drought in his young life, but he'd wake up one day and start to seed his future. In any case, it wasn't worth worrying about or doting upon too much. When you ignored something unpleasant enough, it either faded or was just forgotten.

After high school, he had a few short romances, but nothing amounted to anything. The closest he had come to a committed relationship lately was with Scarlet Moore, the oldest of three sisters. She was a waitress at the Centerville diner now. She was divorced after four years of a bad marriage and had a three-year-old daughter. She lived at home with her widowed mother who shared the care of her grandchild, thus permitting Scarlet to work and have something of a social life. Her two sisters were married and living in the West, one in Oregon and one in Northern California.

The chance meeting, love affair and eventual marriage of Scarlet's parents reinforced his own personal philosophy about life. So much of it was random, just chance at the start, but afterward, when you had an opportunity to take a breath and look back, it all suddenly made sense. What for example, in Scarlet's case, would bring a Southern debutante from Atlanta to the Catskills to meet a small town bureaucrat who oversaw the county's water reservoir? What was logical about that?

Scarlet, who had beautiful shoulder-length strawberry blonde hair always tied up at work, told him her mother was on a tour with other beauty contestants. It brought them to one of the Catskills' better-known resorts, the Browns, and at an event at which local politicians and government officials were invited, her mother met her father.

'He was smitten with her from the get-go,' Scarlet said, obviously relating the story the way her father or her mother had told it to her and her sisters, most likely many times. She wasn't smitten with him, but he was persistent. The day after she arrived home in Atlanta, he rang her doorbell. 'Your father won me over with good old-fashioned persistence,' her mother had claimed.

'My mother said her father had told her that any man who couldn't eat or breathe without her was a good bet. My father was also a damn good looking, personable man whose great-grandmother just happened to be from South Carolina. There was no argument about naming me Scarlet. And yes, I always say, "I'll worry about it tomorrow."'

Not a bad philosophy to have these days he thought as he walked to the garage: worry about it tomorrow.

Alice Chapman cringed at the sight of the coffin coming up the long, circular driveway. She had come out on the portico. A moment later, Stuart was beside her. Ever since he was a little boy he could sneak up on her like that. It was as if he metamorphosed from a shadow. It always took her by surprise and left her cold.

'His last trip home,' Stuart remarked.

'Yes,' she said. Without further comment, she turned and re-entered the house.

Stuart watched the hearse pull as close to the steps as it could. The driver and his assistant got out quickly.

'I'll get two of my groundsmen,' Stuart shouted to them. He went to the side of the house and signaled to the men he had told to be available. They dropped their brush clippers and hurried to the front.

The coffin he and Evelyn had chosen was one of the most expensive and one of the thickest and more elaborate. It would take at least four men to bring it up the steps and into the living room. He nodded toward the hearse and the two workers joined the driver and his assistant. With his arms folded, he watched them slide the coffin out and then lift it. He could see it was heavy, but if he had chosen anything much cheaper, it would not do. Some very important people would attend his father's funeral. He told himself that at this point, he was doing it more for himself than for his father. That made him feel better about it.

He stepped back so quickly as they approached that it seemed he didn't want to make any contact with the coffin. Alice Chapman was waiting just inside the entry-way to direct them. He followed a few feet behind and watched them carefully place the casket on the casket rack previously set-up. Then they stepped back.

'You can go back to work,' he told the groundsmen. They nodded and left quickly.

The driver hesitated and then started to open the casket.

'Leave it,' Stuart said sharply.

'Well, we always...'

'I don't care what you always do. That's fine. Thanks. What time will you be here tomorrow?'

'Mr Waller told us ten.'

'Good. I'll see you then. We won't have official pall-bearers until we're at the funeral parlor, however,' Stuart added. 'I'll have those two here to help get the coffin back into the hearse.'

'Very good,' the driver said, glanced at his assistant and then with some awkwardness, nodded and started out. Stuart followed them to the front door. They paused, nodded at him again and left.

When he turned, Alice Chapman was standing there watching him.

'I'd like to have a private moment with him for my goodbye, Stuart,' she said.

He smiled.

'You are a loyal employee, Alice. I hope you'll remain so.'

'That goes without asking,' she said sharply. She never refrained from facing him down, no matter how unpleasant he was to her. His mother had often left her in charge of both him and Evelyn when they were young children.

'I'll open the coffin for you,' he said. 'Then you can make your private goodbye while I go up to get my sister.'

He went into the living room. She followed but remained a good half a dozen feet away, watching. Carefully, he lifted the lid and set it back. For a few moments, he stood there looking at his father.

'They did a good job on him,' he said without turning to her. 'He looks better than he did when he was alive.'

'Oh my God, Stuart.'

He turned to her with his sardonic grin.

'He does, Alice. Come look.'

She shook her head and approached. He watched with great interest in the way her face revealed her emotions, her deep sadness. She must have been in love with him, he thought. Nothing else would explain how easily she accepted him now. He was always curious about the devotion and loyalty people showed his father. He told himself it was simply because he could do so much for them, but there were people who didn't depend on him for anything, but still had that devotion. It was either their weakness or blindness, he thought. What other reason could there be?

He stepped back.

'He's all yours,' he said and headed out and up the stairs.

Evelyn's door was closed, but he knew she never locked it. He opened it slowly and peered in. She was in bed and looked dead asleep, as peacefully asleep as their father below in the living room, in fact. For a split moment, he had a terrific surge of terror. What if she took her own life, swallowed too many pills or something? He could feel the hot surge of blood and the thumping in his chest.

'Evelyn,' he called before he approached her bed.

Her eyelids fluttered and then opened. She looked at him as if she didn't recognize him.

'Are you all right?'

'Exhausted,' she said.

56

'Of course, of course. You should be. I don't know how you've had the strength to do what you've done. I didn't mean to disturb you.'

'What is it?' she asked struggling to sit up. He put his hand on her shoulder.

'No, just rest, Evelyn. They brought him,' he said. 'He's in the living room.'

'Oh. I should...'

'I left Alice with him. She wanted some private time. Can you imagine?'

She stared at him a moment and then let herself fall back. Her hair spread over the pillow. He smiled.

'You are so beautiful, Evelyn, even when you're this exhausted. I know,' he added quickly before she could respond, 'you're going to say that's egotistical of me since we're twins.'

She shook her head.

'I haven't said that for a long time, Stuart.'

'I know. I miss your joking with me.'

She pressed her lips together.

'Don't cry, Evelyn. You know if you cry, I'll hate myself for having anything at all to do with it.'

She nodded.

'I'll come down in a while.'

'No rush. He's not going anywhere,' Stuart said. He took her hand and then leaned over to kiss her on the forehead. He stroked her hair once and left.

Alice was still standing by the casket when

he returned to the living room.

'That's a long goodbye,' he said.

She turned, glanced at him with fury in her eyes and walked out.

He watched her leave and then looked at the casket.

Even dead he could turn people against me, Stuart thought.

But that won't last much longer.

It was that thought that filled him with renewed hope. Soon things would return to the way they used to be. He'd be happy again.

They'd both be happy again.

And the dead would haunt only themselves.

He was going to see to that.

Quinn really didn't expect Evelyn Kitchen to turn away from her father's service at the grave site two days later and then give him what he imagined was another one of those soft, almost angelic smiles. She didn't do it when her mother was buried. But he couldn't help hoping for it this time, the confirmation that what he thought he had imagined that morning in front of the funeral home was real. However, when after the last words were said and she did turn away and looked in his direction, she looked at him just the way the others did, as if he weren't there.

His heart sank with disappointment. He

watched the bereaved friends and family slowly make their way back to their waiting limousines and cars. The funeral service had gone on much longer than anticipated. There was another overflow crowd and some dignitaries were to attend and speak. The congressman from the district was apparently held up because of some transportation snag. Finally, he arrived, but the delay pushed back the funeral nearly another hour.

Fall had come slinking in this year, meek and embarrassed, but then, as if it had realized it was pussyfooting around, charged over the terrain with a sudden vengeance. Almost overnight, leaves went from fading green to yellow and brown. The air was dry. The leaves broke from their branches and sailed like the earth's errant teardrops floating over roads and lawns and the graves Quinn had recently dug. It annoyed him. Before the funeral party had arrived, he had lowered himself into Matthew Kitchen's grave to scoop up the leaves that the wind had driven along as if it were playing golf on his cemetery.

It was cool and the sky had an appropriately sooty gray layer of clouds galloping in from the north-west. No movie director could have designed a better scene for a burial, Quinn thought. When the Kitchen family arrived at the grave-site with their friends, he approached the service and stood much closer than usual. Often, these days he didn't come out of the funeral parlor until the mourners had all left.

Evelyn Kitchen looked Jackie O dignified and beautiful. She had the same royal demeanor, carrying sorrow gracefully and serving as a guide for the bereaved. Even the children of relatives and friends looked up at her and tried to emulate her dignity. He saw them correct their posture and stabilize their lips and eyes as if they were all posing for a family portrait.

To Quinn, again maybe because he was seeing what he wanted to see, Evelyn Kitchen looked far stronger than her brother Stuart. He seemed nervous, his handshakes quick bursts of groping fingers, his eyes in flight from the faces of the sorrowful and sympathetic. Unlike so many sons Quinn had seen at their father's burials, Stuart looked impatient and eager to flee. He didn't want to prolong it, to hang on to anything, to hope for a miraculous resurrection. He wanted to close doors, shut off lights, and hang up phones.

Fall helped him along. Twilight was abbreviated now, a one-sentence prologue to what had been paragraphs during the summer. Both his parents loved summer twilights the most and enjoyed sitting on the rear porch watching the solar globe take on its own unique red as it sunk below the tree line, making the forest look on fire. Never did he feel more like part of what his parents had created together than he did during those precious but too rare wonderful twilights. All three of them spoke softer then and tried to touch each other warmly with their eyes, their words and their hands.

The better burials occurred at twilight, Quinn thought. They paralleled laying the day to rest. Maybe Matthew Kitchen lucked out with all the delays. Nature had set the table for a feast of beloved parting. This was about as good as it gets.

It was almost completely dark by the time he finished his work, including putting up the grave marker. All the while he had this empty, sinking feeling in the bottom of his stomach. One small smile from Evelyn Kitchen would have given him ... given him what?

Hope?

Was he naive enough to believe that just because a woman smiles at you, she wants to know you better? And why after all these years anyway? He chided himself for having such an idea in the first place. It reminded him of something his father had told him: 'People see what they want to see, hear what they want to hear. It'll never change.'

His father loved repeating this, especially after or while they were in one of the booze troughs, as he liked to call Stack's Bar or Whiskey Town. Each competed with the other for the business from manual laborers, trades people and those on disability income. There were no high rollers here, not even legal assistants, much less actual attorneys. They went to bars that served more mixed drinks than draft or bottled beers. A sports jacket and tie or even a cleanly pressed shirt would stop conversations at Stack's or Whiskey Town.

Inevitably, when Quinn and his father went there 'to cool down our hot juices,' as his father liked to say, they would walk in on a fiery conversation about one political issue or another, the verbal combatants already with faces crimson from raging, each trying to out-shout or out-talk his opponent.

'There's another informed democratic debate,' his father would say through the side of his mouth.

Quinn was only in his early twenties then and still feeding like a calf off his father's wisdom. Unlike his contemporaries – and maybe this was another reason he felt alienated from them and they from him – he never had the characteristic teenager's disdain for older, wiser minds, nor the rebellious strain of his peers that enabled them to push the envelope, drive too fast, stay out too late, drink alcohol whenever possible, get stoned whenever possible and challenge authority. The worst accusation leveled against him wasn't that he was a square or a nerd or any such thing. He was simply accused of being too old for his age. Somehow, he had skipped the 'best' years.

'No matter what either one says, the other will see or hear what he believes,' his father explained. 'That's why you'll never see me having a halfway intelligent conversation in here.'

His father's answer when someone tried to bait him into one of those discussions was, 'Don't know enough about it.'

'Well, I'm telling you.'

'Thanks. Appreciate it,' his father would say and turn back to the ball game he pretended to watch.

He stood there, remembering. He loved recalling those conversations. He was so lost in his reminiscing that he didn't hear Jack Waller step up beside him.

'Well, that's that,' Jack said.

'Yeah,' Quinn said. 'You were right. Quite a crowd.'

Jack stared down at the grave as if he had Superman's X-ray eyes and could see through the earth and into the coffin.

'You know what I'm thinking?'

'I can guess.'

'Gold diggers used to spend months, years even, sifting through streams or digging up hills for a tenth of what's down there.'

'I would have won the prize for the right guess,' Quinn said throwing his tools on to the box at the rear of the backhoe.

Jack laughed.

'Richard wanted to suggest that they pour

six feet of cement over and around the coffin and then fill in the grave. He's carrying on about our not constructing the building for the vaults.'

'Some people believe in dust on to dust,' Quinn said. 'I know my father did.'

'Yeah. Well, good job,' Jack said and began to walk away.

Quinn started the backhoe and headed for the garage. He couldn't shake off his depression tonight. He didn't want to rush home and throw together some dinner for himself and then fall asleep watching television. If ever he missed his father, it was now, at these times, when they would take a breath and go to Stack's or Whiskey Town.

After he closed up the garage, he decided he would go to Stack's. He could get a nice roast beef sandwich and some vegetables and fries at the bar. He hadn't been there for months, but wanted to be there very much tonight. He craved noise, laughter, even those hot political arguments, anything and everything to remind him that even though he worked among the dead, he walked among the living.

What he didn't know was because of this night, he would end up blaming himself, and where that would take him was something he couldn't even imagine.

FOUR

Stack's was just outside of Monticello, one of the bigger villages in the county and the county seat. The bar and restaurant were constructed out of a large garage that had been used for buses nearly forty years ago. Barry Stack's father, Leonard Stack, not only built a hard wood floor tavern, but a two bedroom apartment behind it in which Barry and his wife Tina now lived with Barry's widowed mother Estelle, who up until recently worked in the bar as well. Barry and Tina had sons, both in the army. One was in Iraq, the other, luckier, was in Germany.

Like Whiskey Town, Stack's had its regulars, most of whom were locals, high school graduates who had remained in the area, some who had been through the armed services but had returned to find work where they had family. Just about everyone, local or not, knew who Randy Quinn was and what Randy Quinn did for a living. There were a few there who did the same work, but at other cemeteries. To Quinn's surprise and delight, Barry Palmer was there this particular evening. They had lost touch when Barry had gone to Dallas to work for his uncle in a tool manufacturing plant.

'I was going to call you tomorrow first thing,' Barry said the moment Quinn saw him.

'How long have you been back?' Quinn said as they hugged hello.

'Just a day or so.'

No one looking at the two together would believe they had been in the same high school class. Barry had aged decades, it seemed. Once a slim, dark-brown-haired boy with features so dainty they were more feminine, Barry was now forty pounds heavier with dark rings around his eyes, deep lines in his once soft, nearly alabaster face, a face that looked ravaged by whatever lifestyle he had while living in Dallas. Smoking, drinking, working in a drearier environment, perhaps all of it together had taken its toll.

In contrast Randy Quinn seemed only to have blossomed over the intervening years. He had a virile outdoors-man's complexion, was still as fit looking as he was in high school, but filled out and matured in the right increments so that he looked even more handsome and more vibrant. There was nothing in his face to reveal depression or unhappiness.

'You still working in the garden of the dead?' Barry asked after he saw to Quinn getting his beer and after Quinn quickly ordered his food.

'Yeah, I'm still tilling the ground, only now I'm in charge of the whole farm. Cemetery manager.'

'What's that?' Barry asked and Quinn explained how he had become chief cook and bottle washer for the exclusive Sandburg Cemetery.

'Dad was there at the start, but only part-time. He helped create it, design it. As it grew and Dad slowed down, I took on more and more and eventually the owners offered me the position.'

Barry nodded and smiled.

'Still single, too?'

'And my pockets still jingle. You?'

'I was married for nearly two and a half years,' Barry said, pronouncing the words as though each had the taste of sour milk.

'What happened? You screwed around?'

'Didn't get the chance. She beat me to it. I was going to have kids with her, too.'

'Lucky you found out in time.'

'I didn't really find out in time,' Barry said swirling the beer in his glass. 'One day she came home to me to tell me she was pregnant with someone else's baby. The guy wanted her and the baby so she didn't lie about it.'

'What did you do?'

'Shrugged and changed the channel. It was a lousy movie. So was my marriage, it seemed.'

'Too bad.'

'Right. Soon after my uncle lost his company,' he added. 'That's why I came home.'

'Really? What happened there?'

Estelle Stack served Quinn his meal.

'You sure you don't want to eat anything?' Quinn asked.

'Naw. I had some beef jerky an hour ago.'

'What the hell kind of a dinner is that? So, what happened to your uncle's business?' Quinn asked and bit into his roast beef sandwich.

'Seems he was cheating on his taxes and the IRS came swooping in. He still might go to jail. I don't know. One day I was there. The next day I was out with no salary. Could have stayed in Dallas, I suppose, but just had this urge to come home, tail between my legs or not.'

'What are you going to do?'

'Dunno.'

'I can offer you some part-time work if you want,' Quinn said. He smiled. 'On a cemetery. Even though it's not good for your sexual and social life,' he added recalling how Barry would lecture him about finding new work so he could get laid.

Barry laughed.

'I don't think I'm worrying about the girls liking me as much. Might take you up on it ... just until I find something.'

'Fine. You can come around tomorrow.'

'Look at you. Hiring people. You've become quite the big shot, eh?'

Quinn shrugged.

'Don't think of myself as any sort of executive, if that's what you mean. I do what has to be done. That's all.'

Barry nodded, but Quinn could see that the situation still seemed to upset him. Quinn was supposed to have become the real loser, unattractive to most girls because of what he and his father did for a living, stuck in a small hometown, living at home with his parents and still doing work more distasteful to most than even digging and cleaning septic tanks. But it was Barry who felt like the failure with work and with women. Not only that, he could clearly see how healthy and strong Quinn was, and there wasn't a morning he didn't look in the mirror now and wonder what the hell had happened.

He drained his beer and ordered another. Fortunately for him, his anger at how things turned out didn't find voice in the conversation they continued to have. Barry found solace in describing the good things he once had, the new friends he had made and the places he had been. He particularly stressed the latter because from what he gleaned of their conversation, it was clear Quinn had not been out of the area for a vacation, not even to visit any relatives.

He could see that some of what he was saying took hold. Quinn's indifference about what he missed began to wane. He looked sadder, more thoughtful and admitted that there had been many times when he had felt sorry for himself, times when he was convinced he might have made a mistake not going into the army and maybe seeing more of this world. Barry readily agreed, but now that he had gotten the conversation and mood turned more his way, he changed the topic to remembrances of the good times they had together when they were in high school.

Inevitably, their thoughts returned to one girl in high school with whom everyone on male hormones had fallen in love, Lillian Clarkson who was a senior when they were both sophomores. She was sexy as far back as the seventh grade. What ever happened to Lillian Clarkson, the brunette who had what they both thought was a doll's face with a Mariah Carey body? Barry wanted to know.

'If she blessed you with a little smile or flirtation, you forgot what bothered or depressed you that day.'

'Yes,' Quinn said, but he was really thinking more of Evelyn Kitchen.

'Remember how we used to count the freckles on her cheeks and argue who was closer to the actual number?'

'Neither of us got close enough to confirm our guesses,' Quinn said.

'Don't tell me she married that asshole Corny Blocker.'

Corny, shortened from Cornelius, was one of the best looking boys in the senior class at the time. He was a star on the basketball team. His father was a very successful attorney so the Blockers were one of the wealthiest families in their class. Quinn used to say Corny can't help but be an arrogant bastard; it's in his blood. But he did admire him and had to admit to himself that he and Lillian made the perfect Hollywood couple, easily winning King and Queen of their prom.

'No, she didn't,' Quinn told him. 'They broke up during their first year in college. She ended up marrying an attorney though, lives in Oregon. Corny works in his father's firm and married a girl from Michigan he met on a case he had in New York City. He's made quite a name for himself already as a trial attorney. One of these days, he might run for district attorney.'

'How do you know this gossip shit?' Barry asked. 'I thought you hated gossip.'

'Still do, but people always talked about each other around here. You know that. I can't help but hear things.'

'At the cemetery??' Barry asked half joking.

'Sometimes.'

Quinn never brought Evelyn Kitchen into their conversation. He had never let anyone know how deeply she had touched him. Not even Barry, who was his best friend, knew how much he had longed for her to smile at

71

him. His infatuation with her embarrassed him even more back then. Let someone like Barry know it and he'd kid him forever.

They both continued to laugh at some of their memories and then decided to go over to Whiskey Town just for kicks. Barry wanted to see if he'd recognize any of the regulars and sure enough, he did. Quinn surprised himself by agreeing to go. Something was eating at him in places he usually kept off-limits. He needed more distractions and distractions they were. The night went longer than either thought it would. Reminiscing seemed to be soothing for them both after a while. It was the balm to cure all present depression. By the time they were ready to call it quits, Quinn, who was barely holding his own, advised Barry that he wasn't in shape to drive.

'Just come over to my place tonight,' Quinn told him. 'Leave your car here.'

Even if he wanted to, Barry wasn't capable of putting up an argument. He got into Quinn's truck and proceeded to fall asleep almost immediately. Driving sobered Quinn up quickly. Although it was late and the roads were practically devoid of any traffic, he drove with extra care. He and his father had buried too many victims of automobile accidents. One year, it had been like a motorized epidemic, five teenagers and four community college kids alone. Winter set a trap for those who drank too much and were reckless. Death laid itself out on the icy roads like a welcoming carpet.

When they arrived, he had to wake Barry up to get him into the house and into the guest bedroom that was last used when his father's younger brother, Frank appeared unexpectedly on his return from a trip to Canada. He was five years younger than Quinn's father, but he died three years earlier after he lost a battle with lung cancer.

Barry was incapable of undressing himself. Quinn just took off his shoes and dropped him in the bed. He was still curled up like a baby when Quinn woke at six thirty as usual and started to make coffee. He went out to get the morning paper that was left in a box beside his mailbox and returned to have some breakfast. He had the paper out and was reading an article on Matthew Kitchen. He hadn't realized just how extensive the man's holdings had become. From what the writer was describing, there apparently were articles and obituaries in a number of state papers. Kitchen's influence was significant when it came to some national political figures as well as those in the state.

He looked up when Barry stumbled into the kitchen, wiping his face with a cold wet cloth.

'Didn't expect you to be up,' Quinn said.

'Jesus. How much did I drink?'

'Lost count,' Quinn said. 'Have some coffee.'

Barry flopped into a chair at the table and waited while Quinn poured the coffee. After a few sips, he took a deep breath and then just laughed.

'I feel like shit, but it was the best time I've had for a while,' he said.

'Me too,' Quinn confessed. 'You want some eggs?'

'Whatever you have,' Barry said and turned the newspaper to see what Quinn had been reading. 'Yeah, I remember this guy. Remember his daughter was a looker, but queer, right?'

'I don't think so.'

'Yeah, believe me, she was not interested in men.'

'How would you know?'

'Some girl I was dating was friends with her.'

'She had no friends in our school. She and her brother hung out with kids who went to private schools.'

'Yeah, I know, but this girl ... Lois Feldman ... right, Lois, she went to one of those private schools. Her father was a lawyer and did some work for Kitchen. She was at the house a few times when I went over to see Lois.'

'You never told me about that.'

'Wasn't that proud of the attempt to date and screw Lois. She wasn't a great looker, but she had a reputation. Anyway, I got the feeling she resented me taking up Lois's time, know what I mean? I talked to her, but

74

it was always a pretty short conversation. She'd leave soon after I arrived, but it gave me a creepy feeling about Lois, too. Evelyn and that brother of hers were weird. They were twins, right?'

'Still are,' Quinn said. He could feel the irritation in his own voice.

'You did this burial?'

'Yep.' He cracked some eggs and dropped in some milk. 'Scrambled all right?'

'Sure. I remember you could cook.'

'Eggs isn't cooking. You should taste my meatloaf. That's cooking.'

Barry laughed and continued perusing the full-page article.

'What a big shot he was! Really rich, but as they say, you can't take it with you,' Barry offered. He said it like most people said it, Quinn thought, almost a justification for being poor.

'Yeah, well he did. Some of it anyway.'

The words came out before he could stop them. He was still a little annoyed that Barry had known Evelyn Kitchen more intimately than he had.

'What's that mean?'

'Nothing.'

'You don't say nothing, Randy. C'mon. What's it mean?'

'Can you keep it to yourself?'

'I'm not exactly going on the radio here. So?'

'They buried him with valuable jewelry.

75

His kids said that was what he wanted.'

'Bull shit.'

Quinn turned and raised his hand and then went back to the eggs. He threw some bacon around them and it all began to sizzle.

Barry continued to read the article.

'How much you think it was worth?'

'What?'

'The jewelry.'

'Jack Waller checked on the items. He thinks easily more than two, two hundred and fifty thousand dollars,' Quinn said. 'Maybe more. Matthew Kitchen didn't spare any change when he bought things for himself and he liked expensive things. They have a twenty thousand square foot house.'

'I remember,' Barry said. 'Lois and I were going to go there, but I broke it off before we could.' He looked at the article again and shook his head. 'Thousands of dollars in jewelry six feet under. What good that do his kids?'

'Read on. They don't need it,' Quinn said.

'They don't need it?' Barry looked at the pictures of Evelyn and Stuart. 'Well, one thing's for sure.'

'Yeah, what's that?' Quinn said bringing the eggs and bacon to the table.

'He don't need it neither.'

'Maybe he did,' Quinn said sitting and starting on his eggs.

'How's that?'

'The Greeks used to bury their dead with a

coin in their mouth.'

'Huh?'

'They believed the dead needed it to pay Charon, the ferryman who carried people across the river Styx to the Underworld. Maybe the price's gone up,' Quinn added, smiled and ate.

Barry grimaced.

'Figures you'd know everything about burying people everywhere,' he said and then started on his eggs and bacon.

'After breakfast, I'll take you back to your car. Go home and get yourself cleaned up,' Quinn told him. 'Come over to the cemetery about ten. I'll introduce you to Jack Waller and tell him you're hired on for a while.'

'To do what, dig?'

'Not today. We'll have to clean up the place, leaves, some trimming maybe. There's always lots to do. Good hard, outdoor manual work.'

'Haven't done that for a while,' Barry said. 'If I cut grass, do I cut over the graves?'

'Yep and around them. Graves is what's in cemeteries, Barry.'

Barry didn't look too happy about it.

'It's not bad work. You'll get used to it. Oh,' he said. 'You'll see Nick Reuben's grave, I'm afraid.'

'Nick?'

'Yep. Killed in Iraq. I took special care with that one,' Quinn said.

Barry sat there for a moment with his fork

77

in the air, his mouth partly opened. Then he shook his head.

'Special care? You make it sound more like you're building them a house.'

'It is a house, a house for the dead.'

'You look like you believe it.'

'I do.'

Barry stared at him a moment and then shook his head again before continuing to eat.

'I'm not sure I can do this,' he said.

'Well,' Quinn said, 'if you're there at ten, I'll know you can.'

FIVE

Quinn wondered if there had ever been a time, even a moment when he had considered whether or not he could do this work, too. Most young people aren't interested in cemeteries and some were outright afraid of them. Being near or around the dead was too much of a reminder about your own mortality.

The short answer was he never hesitated and never regretted doing the work. He never had a nightmare about it either. Maybe it was because of his father and the fact that his father had been doing the work a long time and showed no signs of regret or displeasure. It was good, honest labor and like any good laborer, he took pride in the quality of the work he did.

The first time he confronted anything negative about it was when he was in the fourth grade. His memory of that day remained vivid. Because the school system was so small, the elementary school building also housed students in the seventh and eighth grades. There was another building in another hamlet to service nine-through-twelve, and that was also where the ball fields were located and the gymnasium for the basketball games.

Elementary children were still too young to care about or characterize each other on the basis of what their parents did or didn't do, especially when the children were in the first four grades. After all, a fourth-grader was only nine years old. Prejudices hadn't yet taken firm hold. They repeated or thought about the things they heard at home, but rarely did they act them out at so young an age.

The classes were brought to a cafeteria for lunch and their teachers monitored them. Usually, the contact with the older students in the seventh and eighth grades was minimal. The students liked to segregate themselves, the older ones avoiding sitting too close to or near the younger ones. Junior high students viewed themselves as far more mature. It was as if they had taken a giant leap from the sixth grade to the seventh, and crossed the Grand Canyon. Physically, the girls were maturing faster than the boys and there were even some eighth graders who had become pregnant.

On this particular day, three of the seventh grade boys had targeted Quinn, either to look older in front of the girls or to fulfill some mean impulse. They bore down on him as he carried his tray to his table and surrounded him. He looked up with surprise as the first boy on his right said, 'Your father buries people.'

He tried to ignore them, but they stayed right alongside him.

'You ever see a dead person?' the boy on his left said.

He paused, shook his head and continued toward his table, but they followed.

'Dead people stink,' the first boy told him. 'Your father come home stinking like dead people?'

The others in his class who sat at the table looked up surprised.

'No,' Quinn said and opened his container of chocolate milk.

'You're probably too used to the stink to know,' the second boy said. He sniffed him. 'Ouch,' he followed. 'He does smell like a corpse.'

The others pretended to sniff and smell the odor as well and hold their nose. Quinn looked up helplessly as they performed their dumb show, pretending to gag and throw up. He was happy they finally became bored and left, but when he looked at his classmates, he saw the change in their faces and he knew he would carry the non-existent stench with him for a long time, maybe forever.

Despite this, despite the way his friends and classmates began to peal off and away, he never blamed his father or resented the work he did. So he was the community's most famous gravedigger. So what? He made a living doing that and caring for cemeteries and grave-sites. They had a nice home and he lacked for nothing. He simply closed himself off like a clam and lived comfortably in the security and strength his father provided. Maybe he was suited for the isolation. Maybe he was too independent to be dependent upon friendships. Maybe what they really resented was his inner strength and his clear vision of who and what he was.

Yes, he was too old for his age, but he resisted making the effort to fight back to regain the popularity and acceptability he had when he was in grade school. If they didn't want him for who he was, he didn't want them. That was the way he thought then, but was it the way he thought now? Was he ready to admit that he had indeed missed a lot?

Despite his youth and good health, he couldn't help thinking that time wore us all down, chipped away continually. It never took a day off, no holidays, not even a pause to catch its breath. It was as if time had finally managed to break through the walls he had built up around himself. It wasn't that he was peering out at the world he had so successfully avoided; it was as if that world were now peering in at him.

'You ever think you're hiding behind a tombstone?' Allan Goldstein asked him once. He overheard Barry who was nagging him again about getting different work, doing something more attractive to the girls.

'How do you mean?' he asked Allan, who happened to be destined for class valedictorian. Somehow, despite his being labeled everything from Egghead to Nerd, Allan managed to date some nice looking girls through their high school years. He was in Washington, D.C. now, working in the National Health Institute.

'You're afraid of girls. Anything to keep them away,' Allan suggested. He shrugged. 'Maybe you're just shy, but it's convenient to have them avoid you.'

'That's bullshit,' he said, but Barry just nodded and smiled.

'Hiding in a cemetery.'

Was that where he still was, he wondered, hiding in a cemetery?

Other than the normal, regular maintenance, there was nothing much more to do at the cemetery today. Jack just gave him a short wave and nod when he arrived in the morning. Colder fall days had slowed the grass and begun to dry and paint the blades a light yellow at their tips. The surrounding forest was losing its last breath of color. Naked branches no longer hid the trees deeper inside the pockets of woods. As he had told Barry, there was more sweeping up to do than anything. Some graves were already overrun with the crisp, dead leaves. They had leaf blowers, but for most of the grave-sites, he'd use the rakes. It was a matter of bringing the tractor and wagon around to load them in and then later in the day, burn them off in the great barrels they had for that purpose.

He was still thinking about Evelyn Kitchen, replaying the whole cemetery service in his mind when he heard Barry call to him. Quinn never heard him drive up. He was that deep in thought. Barry got out of his truck and waved. Quinn smiled to himself, happy to see him. If he ever wanted to avoid this work, today was the day. Barry would take his place. He dropped the rake and walked over to him.

'Sure you're up to it?'

'No, but what else is there to do?' Barry replied.

Quinn nodded.

'I'll introduce you to Jack. He likes to know who I hire, and then you can start raking up those leaves. The grass won't need cutting until the end of the week. It might be the last time the way this winter's rushing at us. After this it's just pruning the landscaping, white washing and polishing.'

'You mean as long as no one else dies to get in here,' Barry said.

They walked into the office. It took only a few minutes for Barry to fill out the paperwork for his social security number, address and phone number. Jack glanced at it and nodded quickly. He was on the phone with his divorce attorney.

84

'He didn't seem to care very much,' Barry commented when they left.

'He trusts me and he's pretty buried right now in his divorce. He's had a woman on the side for nearly a year and his wife found out. Marriage can be tough on some.'

Barry's face darkened.

'Sorry,' Quinn said remembering Barry's marital woes.

'Forget it. I did.'

'We'll work to dusk,' Quinn told him. 'Break for lunch in two hours.'

'Gotcha. Where's Nick's grave?'

Quinn pointed to it. Barry nodded, took a breath and started to work.

Ever since Quinn began working with his father, his mother always made them lunch. It was the one thing she wouldn't avoid doing. She always bagged his lunch for school as well, and after they were both gone, he continued the tradition and prepared his own lunch and brought it to work in an old-fashioned black lunch pail. He prepared an extra meatloaf sandwich and another soft drink in anticipation of Barry coming to the cemetery. He was afraid that if Barry left for lunch, he might very well have too many beers and not make it back, or if he did make it back, not give much more toward a day's work.

'You're like somebody's old mother,' Barry said when Quinn offered it to him. 'I never been good at any of that domestic stuff.'

'In the long run, it's easier,' Quinn said.

'Yeah, well, if I take a lunch break, I'd like it to be somewhere beside a cemetery. You mind if I don't join you?'

'Suit yourself.' Quinn checked his watch. 'Take two hours. That'll leave us about three to get in the rest of the day before it gets too dark.' He smiled. 'I don't think you want to be here in the dark.'

'Very funny. See you in two. Kayfield's still there?'

'Yeah, but new owners. Food's OK,' Quinn shouted after him.

'How would you know? You make your own you hermit,' Barry shouted back.

'Not always,' he yelled. Barry shook his head, got into his truck and drove off.

Quinn watched him go and then went inside to eat his lunch in the small kitchen Waller and Valentine had installed when they first built the funeral home. Maybe it wasn't quite the most appetizing place to have lunch, but it was quiet and clean. There was a television set behind a counter so he could catch up on some world news.

Jack stuck his head in on his way out.

'How's your new guy working out?'

'Good enough,' Quinn said.

'I'm off to meet Dick. We're having dinner in Westchester with a possible new investor.'

'Investor? For what?'

'Richard still wants to buy Mortman's old farm.'

'How many times have the family turned you guys down?'

'Four counting the offer we made through a shell corporation. Richard won't give up. He has this idea that dying might continue and our place should expand. He says he heard Teddy Morton's in some financial trouble and might be more willing to sell.'

'He owns it with his sister, right? She's not in financial trouble. Her husband's truck and bulldozer dealerships are going strong.'

'Whatever. As I said, he's got someone interested in going in with us and making an offer they won't refuse. Notice, I said won't, not can't.'

Quinn laughed.

'If we get it, he wants to talk about lowering prices for the new section. The plan is to keep it well segregated and offer it for some of the county welfare business. We're not making money fast enough to satisfy him.'

'Partners are hell,' Quinn said.

'Tell me about it.' Jack said, but Quinn had the feeling he was talking about a marriage partner and not a business one. He waved and left.

To Quinn's happy surprise, Barry was back fifteen minutes early and at the work enthusiastically. In fact, it was he who had to call it quits.

'Nice work. We should have the place looking good end of the day tomorrow. How you feel?'

'Tired. I guess combining it with the hell we raised last night is a good reminder we ain't eighteen,' Barry said

'Oh, that's lots of those reminders coming around.'

'Yeah, thanks for reminding me. OK. I'll see you about the same time?'

'Right,' Quinn said. He took the tools to the shed and watched Barry get in his truck and drive off.

The sight of him leaving, the dead silence that followed and the eternal posture of the tombstones and monuments suddenly filled him with depression. It was as if that mental photo, the picture of Evelyn Kitchen had awakened him to his utter loneliness. It was something he heretofore convinced himself was desirable, but like the Emperor Who Had No Clothes, it now looked just plain naked.

He made a command decision and decided to go to the Centerville diner for dinner tonight. Most nights it serviced local families and sometimes he liked to stay off to the side and watch them. The banter between siblings and their parents brought back some of his own family memories. To him seeing a husband and a wife cooing over their sons and daughters was like sitting before a warm fire. It was quite relaxing.

And he wanted to see and talk to Scarlet. Maybe he'd wait around for her to get off work. They'd had two trysts up to now, both

88

at his house. The time between them was long enough to keep her from thinking there was any hope of anything lasting, but she seemed OK with that. She wasn't all that eager to get attached to someone so quickly again anyway, and she recognized that Quinn was so set in his ways, she would have to make considerable compromises. Still, there was something attracting them both to each other, something strong enough to keep the meter running.

Maybe it was because of that deep, dark feeling in the pit of his stomach tonight, but he thought she looked especially inviting. He always thought she had a nice face, maybe not drop dead beautiful, but full of a sweetness and peacefulness that in and of itself was more important. Her smile was soothing and her soft kiss on his cheek felt like an inoculation against loneliness.

'You're looking like prime cut tonight,' he said. Her eyes twinkled.

'Going to wait around until ten?'

'Some things are worth waiting for,' he replied. She laughed and he made it a point to take as long as possible to eat his turkey dinner. Afterward, he indulged in pie à la mode with coffee. The diner was busy. Scarlet and the other waitress, Shirley Roland, never stopped until close to nine thirty.

'Shirley's cleaning up tonight. I took her turn last night,' Scarlet told him. 'Be just fifteen more minutes. I'll call my mother and let her know not to keep the light on.'

'No rush. What I have isn't going away.'

'In case you didn't notice, it's different for a woman, especially today. Check out television, the movies and magazine covers. Youth has even replaced greed. They're getting facelifts at the age of thirty. I know some women who'd rather fight cancer than wrinkles.'

He laughed. She had a great sense of humor, self-deprecating, full of resignation with only a trace of ego. She would make someone a good wife. Her first husband was a total idiot, he thought. Twenty years from now, he'd be sitting somewhere alone and regretting his role as horse's ass and missing his daughter as well.

He looked out the windows. The diner had a well-lit parking lot, but just beyond it was a sea of thick night. It was fully overcast, too, so the heavens were of no assistance. These roads outside of the small villages were not well lit. Beside the cost, there was a stubbornness about keeping it looking rural.

It would be good to go home with someone as warm and loving as Scarlet Moore tonight, he thought as she emerged from the kitchen, her apron off, her hair now down. She had put on her light blue jacket. He thought that despite how long and hard she had worked tonight, she still held on to that young, vibrant look that kept her spirit lit.

She's a lighthouse, he thought, a beacon to

guide him into a soft bed of comforting sleep. He smiled, but as she approached him, his cell phone vibrated and then did the little Irish ditty he had downloaded as a ring tone. He shrugged his shoulders and looked surprised. She stood back as he flipped it open and said, 'Quinn.'

'Hey, Randy, where are you?'

It was Jack.

'Centerville diner. What's up?'

'I need a favor. I'm down in Westchester with Richard. I left an important piece of paper in the office on the right hand side of the desk. Need it for this negotiation in the morning. Can you get over there and fax it to me? I'll give you the number.'

'Sure. It's on the way back,' he said looking at Scarlet and wagging his head. Jack gave him the fax number and thanked him. He flipped the phone closed. 'Small favor I have to do for Jack Waller. Got to stop at the funeral home. You have a problem with that?'

'Only if I'm in a hearse,' she said and he roared.

This was going to be a great night, despite the small interruption.

On the way over, he talked about meeting and hiring Barry Palmer. It gave him a chance to reminisce about his high school days. As he described them, it sunk in more and more in his own mind how much of an outsider he had been. Everything he described seemed to be from the perspective of someone looking in, an observer rather than a participant.

'Barry and I were two peas in a pod, although he was a little more outgoing. He actually went to a few school dances and was on the cross-country team. Did pretty well, too. I played football, but not with a full heart and missed most of the games in my senior year when my father was ill. I guess I was like some shadow moving through the building most of the time,' he told her.

He turned and smiled.

'I didn't have much chance being elected class president.'

'I wasn't much different,' Scarlet said. 'If you saw my picture in the yearbook, you'd think I was anorexic, scrawny and big-eyed like some starving kid in Africa. There was only one credit next to my picture. It was pathetic.'

'What was that?'

'Glee Club.'

'Oh, so you sing.'

'Yeah, when I'm with fifty others,' she said and he laughed.

'Here we are,' he announced as he drove through the entrance to the funeral home and cemetery. He noticed a driveway light was out. 'Got to fix that tomorrow. Don't want ghosts bumping into each other.'

She laughed. He gazed at her in the ambient light from the otherwise well-lit drive-way. She didn't look a bit nervous about coming to a cemetery at night. She was calm and even a bit curious. He liked that.

'Won't be long,' he said and pulled his truck into his usual parking space even though he could easily have pulled right up to the front entrance of the funeral home. Old habits die hard, he thought. 'Want to come in?'

'Sure,' she said and then added, 'but not because I'm afraid to stay alone out here.'

'I believe it.' He laughed and went around to help her get out.

'Bit noisy,' she kidded. Somewhere off in the distance, an owl was complaining about something.

'You should see the place on Halloween Eve.'

She laughed and he took her hand. They started for the front of the building, but something caught his eye and he suddenly stopped and turned to his right.

'What?'

'The garage door,' he said letting go of her hand.

'What about it?'

'It's not quite shut and I know I shut it when I left.'

'Uh-oh, thieves.'

'Maybe,' he said hurrying over. He stood there looking at the door for a moment. It was a good two feet from the ground. Whoever had opened it had not closed it properly.

'Isn't it locked?' she asked.

'Damn right. Was,' he said.

'Maybe Jack came by.'

'No, he left for Westchester at the end of the day and that's where he called from. He left before I did.'

He continued to stand there a moment and then he turned to her.

'Come back to the truck with me for a moment,' he said.

'Why?'

'Just come back,' he said a little more forcefully. He didn't want to say it, but there was a possibility that whoever was stealing stuff was still in there.

When they reached the truck, he opened the passenger door.

'Just sit in here until I check it out. The keys are in the ignition and the doors will be locked. Something happens, you can drive off to get help.'

'You heard someone in there?'

'No, but who knows, right?'

She nodded and got into the truck. He surprised her again by walking around to his door, opening it and reaching under his seat.

'What...'

He produced a thirty-eight snub nose pistol.

'Truck insurance,' he said. 'Lock the doors.' He closed the door and started back

94

to the garage. He glanced back at her and then he lifted the garage door with his left hand, holding his pistol with his right.

No one came at him nor did he hear anyone. Slowly, he went to the left and flipped the light switch. It took only a few moments to be sure that no one was in there. He checked some of the equipment, tested the locked boxes and then stood there a moment looking around.

The realization struck him like a swift kick in the groin, it was that painful a possibility. He went to a shelf and got his most powerful lantern. Then he started back to the truck. She opened the door before he reached it.

'Anything missing?'

'No,' he said.

'Oh, that's good. Then maybe you forgot to lock it and didn't close it completely.'

'No. I saw where the door was forced open, probably with a crowbar.'

'But you said nothing's missing.'

'Not in here,' he said.

'I don't understand, Randy.'

'The backhoe...'

'It's there. I see it.'

'It was used,' he said. 'After I put it in the garage.' He turned toward the cemetery plots.

'How do you know?'

'The way it's parked and the wheels are turned.'

'Well, what are you going to do?' she asked.

'I have to go look at a grave,' he said.

'Look at a grave? Why?'

He didn't answer. Whatever the reason was, she thought, it had turned him into someone she had never seen.

SIX

'Maybe you should wait at the truck,' he said when she got out to follow.

'Now, I do mind being alone here,' she replied. He nodded and waited for her to catch up. 'Why are you so upset? If nothing's missing, what do you suspect went on here?' she asked. 'Teenage vandalism?'

He didn't answer. He turned into the main walkway that snaked up through the different sections of monuments.

'Randy?'

'Not sure yet,' he replied.

She glanced around.

'I've never been to a funeral at this cemetery. Never knew anyone rich enough who died, I guess,' she said.

'Jack and his partner want to develop a low income section just beyond those newly planted Evergreens. That's why they're in Westchester meeting with an investor.'

'Different kind of low income housing,' she said. 'Poverty follows you to the grave.'

'It does that,' he said. 'They're hoping to dig up some of the county welfare business.'

'Dig up doesn't sound right in here,' she joked.

She could feel the tension in him and hoped to lighten things up a bit. He just nodded. She could see something very bad was gnawing away at him. There was an intensity about him that she had never seen, a tone in his voice that made him sound like someone else. Wasn't he the one who had told her that there was a stranger living inside us all?

He turned right and took her down another walkway, holding his beam steady. Then he stopped at the Matthew Kitchen's grave-site.

'Why are we stopping here?' she asked. She saw there was no monument yet, just a marker to indicate who was down there.

Quinn hadn't said it, but he had expected to see an uncovered coffin. It wasn't, but that didn't satisfy him. He ran his beam slowly over the fresh earth and then paused and went to his knees.

'What are you looking for, Randy?'

He didn't reply. She watched him sift some of the dirt through his fingers.

'Shit,' he finally said, obviously coming to some conclusion.

'What?'

'This grave's been dug up and then filled in tonight.'

'Tonight? How do you know? It looks fine to me.'

98

'I can tell. I know my ground, every inch, every bump in the earth here. If you look, you can see it has been very recently uncovered. Feel it,' he said holding up a fistful.

She opened her hands and he dropped the soil into her palms. She shook her head and tossed it to her right. The glow from the flashlight made his face ghoulish. She was beginning to get the jitters.

'I'd never be able to tell the difference,' she said. 'What you're saying doesn't make any sense anyway. Why would anyone dig up a grave and then fill it in again, Randy? One final morbid look or something?'

He stood up and put his hands on his hips as he nodded at the marker.

'There is or probably was some very valuable jewelry in this coffin. That's Matthew Kitchen,' he said and directed the beam of light on the marker so she could read.

'Matthew Kitchen? Oh. Yes, I know who he was. I saw the news articles on him yesterday. One of the wealthiest men in the county.'

'Right,' he said standing.

'Why was there jewelry in the grave?'

'Matthew Kitchen supposedly left orders to be buried with it. Jack gave it to Curt Marcus, our mortician, to dress on the corpse.'

'Ugh,' she said. 'When you look at a cemetery, you usually don't think of the corpse and all that.'

He nodded.

'The Kitchens insisted on the coffin being locked shut at their home before it was returned to the funeral home and prepared for the public mourning.'

'So no one could steal the jewelry?'

'That was my and Jack's conclusion.'

'So, you knew this had happened, that someone had come over here and dug up this grave, just from looking at your backhoe?'

'First thing that came to mind. As I said, it wasn't exactly where I left it and the wheels were turned too far to the right. I knew someone else had parked it and there's no one else working here who would drive it.'

'You are a detail guy.'

He looked at her and nodded.

'With some things.'

'What are you going to do?'

He looked at the grave.

'I have to call Jack and tell him about this. We'll need to get permission to dig it up.'

'Dig it up?'

'Disinterred.'

'Really?'

'There's no other way to see if the corpse was robbed.'

'You're not going to do this tonight?' she asked, the note of alarm clear in her voice as she looked back at the marker.

'I don't know. Jack will have to call Kitchen's son and daughter to get formal permission.' He checked his watch. 'Getting late, but...'

She nodded.

'It would be a first for me, seeing a coffin dug up. How long will it take you?'

'Oh, not long. The backhoe scoops it out pretty quickly.'

'Why don't I hang around then, hold the light or something and help. You'll get done faster.'

'You sure?'

'Well, it wasn't exactly what I had in mind when I left the diner, but this is what makes life interesting, the unexpected.'

'I'll take the expected,' he said. 'Oh, crap. I'd better get Jack's paperwork faxed first. He's waiting for it. C'mon,' he said turning and walking quickly.

She glanced back at the marker and then she skipped a few steps to catch up with him. She wasn't going to stay too far behind, not in this place, not now. She was afraid to look back or even to the side. It was all suddenly too ghoulish for her, but she wouldn't start complaining.

'Actually, we don't have to call anyone. I could just dig it up myself and check,' he muttered.

'But you just said he had to get permission from Mr Kitchen's children. Isn't that illegal?'

'Yeah.'

'I mean, you could check and then cover it

up again and then get permission, but then you'd have to reveal that you dug it up and then...'

'You're right. You're right,' he said and walked faster.

'You act like you have some suspect in mind,' she said catching up.

'I do.'

'You do? Who?'

He paused.

'Could be Barry Palmer.'

'Barry Palmer? Your friend from high school?'

'Yes. He's back. As I told you, I gave him a part-time job here yesterday. The night before, however, I opened my big mouth and told him about the jewelry down there in the coffin. So this could all be my fault.'

'Oh. But why do you suspect him if he was your friend?'

'He's hit some hard times, wife cheated on him, his uncle in Texas who had given him work went bankrupt. He's back living with his aunt. Both his parents died years ago.' He shook his head. 'Barry worked construction when he was in high school. He can work that backhoe almost as well as I can.'

'It's one thing to dig, but do you really think he could come here in the middle of the night and open a coffin?'

'"Desperate people do desperate things," my father used to say.'

He continued walking. He opened the

funeral parlor door and turned on lights as he led her toward Jack's office.

'It's a beautiful place,' she said looking around as they walked through, 'but it's creepy, too.'

'Is it?' he asked as though anyone having that thought really did surprise him.

She nearly laughed.

'Yes, Randy. It's very late at night. You think a grave was dug up and we're in a funeral parlor. It's creepy.'

He nodded and opened Jack's work office door, flipped on some lights and went to the desk where he found the document.

'First things first,' he said. 'I know Jack. He's probably cursing about me taking so long.'

He loaded the fax, tapped in the number Jack gave him and waited while it went through. Then he sat behind his desk, looked at Scarlet and lifted the receiver to call Jack's cell phone.

'There's a kitchen through there,' he said pointing at a door. 'Can you get us some water? There are cold bottles in the fridge,' he added.

She nodded and went off while he paused for a moment to calm himself. Then he punched out Jack's cell phone number.

'I got the fax,' Jack said seeing the call was coming from his office. 'Thanks.'

'I'm not calling about the fax,' Randy said. He heard a few men talking loudly in the background, but he began his story from the moment he had driven up and thought something was wrong about the garage door until now. During his description of events, he realized Jack had moved into a quieter area. He didn't speak until Randy concluded and even then seemed speechless.

'Jack? You still there?'

'You think you can tell that by looking at the ground at night?'

'I had a light and I know when ground's been recently turned, Jack. It doesn't take Sherlock Holmes. Someone used the backhoe, for sure after I did. You know I can tell that. Believe me. That grave's been dug up.'

Again, Waller was dead silent.

'Jack?'

'I'm trying to figure out whether I'm dreaming this conversation or really having it,' Jack Waller said. 'Did you call the police?'

'Not yet. I thought you'd want to call the Kitchens first. There are legal things you have to do to dig up a grave and open a coffin,' he said as Scarlet returned. She handed him a bottle. 'Thanks.'

She stepped back sipping hers.

'This would be the first time for me and Richard.' He was silent a moment and then said, 'Well, I'm not calling the Kitchens now. It's nearly eleven, Randy and at the moment I have nothing more than your suspicions, no matter how positive you are about all this. We'll check it out again in the morning when we can all look at the site. It can't make that much difference now.'

'Whatever you think.'

'Yeah. Geeze, I had a bad feeling about this from the start, remember? They must have told a dozen of their friends or something or maybe the service people at their estate found out. Or maybe, you're wrong,' Jack said hopefully.

Quinn thought it was too soon to suggest Barry. Maybe Jack was right. Maybe it was the Kitchens' fault. They had been the ones to talk too much or one of their employees saw the jewelry go into the coffin.'

'You know I'm not wrong about it, Jack.'

'Damn, if I had only remembered the paperwork and didn't ask you to go back there tonight,' he added.

Quinn thought that was an odd thing to say.

'I would have noticed in the morning anyway, Jack.'

'Yeah, yeah, but you wouldn't have ruined the rest of my miserable evening. I'll see you in the morning.'

He hung up.

'What?' Scarlet asked.

'He wants to wait until morning.'

'Makes sense, doesn't it? It is kind of late and the coffin's not going anywhere tonight anyway, Randy,' she said.

He looked up at her as if he had just realized she was standing there, nodded, took another swig of his water and stood.

'OK, we might as well head out.'

'You'll get no argument from me,' she said. He was missing all her attempts at humor. He didn't even smile.

She followed him as he turned off the lights and locked the door of the funeral home. Then he returned to the garage, adjusted the door to close as best it could before turning for the truck. Scarlet already had gotten into the truck cab and was waiting.

When he got in, he just sat there a moment. He wondered how the Kitchens were going to react to this, especially Evelyn. A frightening thought crossed his mind.

'If you just want to take me back, Randy...'

'What? Oh, no. I wasn't thinking of you.'

'Thanks for the compliment,' she said.

He shook his head.

'I didn't mean it that way. Something just occurred to me, something not very pleasant.'

'Barry again?'

'No, me.'

'You? How so?'

'What if they suspect me? Who has a better opportunity to do it?'

'Why would you call it in then?'

'What better cover-up could I create?' he replied. She stared at him. 'I even have a witness now for my scenario. You.'

'I don't know as that would make any

sense at all, Randy. If you did do such a thing, why would you think anyone would ever find out? They'd have to have a suspicion out of the blue and then get the coffin dug up.'

'Yeah,' he said nodding. 'You're right. I'd have to be some kind of paranoid to do it and then prepare for the possibility of someone suspecting the grave was robbed.'

He didn't want to tell her that his motivation for worry was his concern that Evelyn Kitchen might think ill of him, as remote a possibility as that was.

For a moment she was silent and then she shook her head.

'Well, if you did do it, Randy, you could at least have the decency to cut me in.'

Finally, he laughed. Then he started the engine and pulled away.

He tried hard to get his mind off what he knew had occurred, but it wouldn't let him go. He was even off somewhere when they got into his bed and began to make love. He went through the motions, but as soon as it ended, Scarlet sat up and groaned.

'You really are obsessing about this thing, aren't you?' she asked. 'Either that or I've lost my feminine magic.'

'Sorry,' he said. 'I can't help it. I feel like an idiot. I promised Jack I wouldn't be the one to let out about the jewelry in the coffin and then I go and do it.'

'But you're sure it was Barry, and besides,

you spoke with someone you trusted,' she said.

'Doesn't matter. I was the big mouth and as for him, I haven't seen him in years. I can't vouch for him. Didn't matter that we were best buddies in high school. People change daily as it is. I should have known better.'

'Tell me about it,' she said. 'I have a marriage as evidence.'

'I guess so,' he said.

'Look, Randy, there's nothing you can do about it right now, is there? Well?'

'I guess not.'

'Maybe it would be smart then for you to just get some sleep,' she said and started to get out of the bed.

'Can't you stay? I'm better in the morning. It's late. Don't go.'

'I'll stay, but everything looks different in the morning. So keep your eyes off me,' she said.

He smiled, reached over to bring her closer and kiss her.

'I'll make up for it,' he said.

'Guys who leave me lousy tips usually say that, but they don't come back.'

'I'll be back. I promise.' He kissed her again. 'In the morning, bright light or no.'

'OK. I'll call my mother. She doesn't sleep much anyway, so I won't be waking her. Besides, she'll probably think it's a good thing. She has me reading the personals looking for dates, and she's someone who was with only one man her whole life.'

He laughed.

When she hung up the phone, she looked at him. He hadn't moved a muscle. He just lay there looking up at the ceiling.

'Randy,' she said. 'You're still obsessing.'

He turned over and closed his eyes. In the morning he did make up for it and it wasn't just to please her. His restlessness took the form of sexual energy. She actually gave him a compliment.

'I feel either you resurrected me or I resurrected you. Either way, you lived up to your promise.'

He laughed and rose to shower. Afterward, she made breakfast and then he took her back to her own car which was still at the diner.

'Call me later?' she said. 'Tell me how this all works out, even if you were wrong.'

'Absolutely. Thanks for putting up with me,' he said.

'Well, there were some benefits,' she told him with a wink. He laughed.

That might be the only time I laugh today, he thought as he started out of the diner parking lot and made his way back to the cemetery.

SEVEN

When he drove in, Quinn saw Jack's SUV and Richard Valentine's old Buick in the parking lot. It was over fifteen years old. Jack said Valentine was like that, using everything he owned until it was worn to a frazzle before replacing it. Something had finally brought Valentine out to the funeral home this month, Quinn thought. He hadn't even attended the Kitchen funeral. Quinn could count on his fingers how many times he had seen him here. If he had such distaste for being in a funeral home, why did he invest in it?

They were both waiting for him in Jack's Spartan office. From the looks on their faces, he knew something wasn't going right.

'What's happening?' he asked and nodded at Richard Valentine, a stout man who still had his college wrestler's build. Even as a young man, he had dark puffy eyes. This morning they looked like two inkwells. He was pressing his lips so firmly that it sent a ripple through his cheeks and emphasized his sharp, bony chin.

'We looked at the site,' Jack said. 'I don't

110

know how you can tell it was disturbed.'

'Believe me, I can tell, and besides, Jack, someone broke into the garage and used the backhoe. What else would they use it for and...'

'It doesn't matter anyway,' Richard said.

'Why not?'

'Stuart Kitchen doesn't want the grave touched,' Jack said.

'What? Didn't you tell him what we think all this means?'

'Sit down, Randy,' Jack said. 'Relax, will ya.'

Quinn dropped into the yellowing wooden chair and waited.

'It's a good thing Kitchen feels that way, too,' Valentine said.

'What? Why?'

'Who needs this kind of publicity? The people who bury their dead here think it's first class non-stop to Heaven.'

'That grave was dug up and for sure those valuables were taken off the corpse,' Quinn insisted.

'If the Kitchens don't give a shit, why should we?' Valentine asked.

'Integrity,' Quinn said.

'Huh?'

'The integrity of our cemetery has been compromised. A grave is sacred ground.'

'That ground, those plots belong to the Kitchen family now,' Jack said softly. 'If they so choose to overlook the possible thievery, they so choose. Over and done with, Randy. Put it to rest.'

'It doesn't make any sense to me,' Quinn said. 'They took great pains to ensure that the jewelry wouldn't be removed. They sealed the coffin. They told you,' he added before either owner could respond, 'that this was what their father wanted. They made a big deal of it, Jack. I heard it.'

'I thought you said you weren't listening.'

'Yeah, well I was.'

Valentine just stared at him, but Jack shrugged.

'I told you rich kids are crazier, especially those two. We appreciate your concern for the cemetery, Randy. We really do, but that's that. Let's move on.'

'Don't either of you even care to know who might be the thief? Hell, it would bother me plenty to know someone like that was on my property.'

'Jack's said it. He didn't take anything from us,' Valentine said.

It was Quinn's turn to stare. The man had no values, he thought, no pride.

'Anyway, thanks for getting right on it, Randy,' Jack said. It was clearly said with a tone of *I move to adjourn*.

Quinn nodded and stood.

'By the way, we both want to do more here than just say thanks, right Dick?'

'Absolutely.'

'You'll find a nice bonus in your next

112

check,' Jack said.

Quinn barely nodded, turned and walked out.

'Man, he is a bit anal about his work here,' Valentine said as soon as Quinn was gone.

'He's worth every penny and more to us. It's chiefly because of him that this place looks the way it does.'

Valentine smiled.

'We lucked out with Stuart Kitchen. This place could have become a circus because of who his father was.'

'Right.' Jack rose.

'You lucked out twice this week, Jack. You're one lucky son of a bitch,' Valentine said.

'Don't ever tell Paula that,' Jack said going to the file cabinet. He paused and turned to him. 'You didn't say anything to Mary, did you?'

'No.'

'The whole point in having Paula go away for the last two months was to keep it as quiet as we could.'

Valentine nodded.

'How were you going to deal with it if she didn't have the miscarriage, Jack?'

'Marry her. What did you think?'

'And now?'

'Let's just say I'm having second thoughts.'

Valentine laughed.

'Helen will never take you back, not with her Irish temper.'

'So I'll be a bachelor again.'

'And poorer.'

'And poorer,' Jack agreed.

'How did you handle it?' Richard asked.

'Believe me, you don't want to hear the grisly details, Dick.'

'Yeah, yeah. Let's change the subject. I've worked up a projection of the income we could enjoy from the welfare department burials. We'll have to grease a few palms to get more than our fair share, but it's doable.'

Jack nodded, but sifted through some papers in a file.

'You paying attention?'

'I hear what you're saying.'

Valentine studied him a moment. They had been partners in one business after another for nearly thirty–five years now. He always felt they were more like brothers. He disliked his two younger brothers anyway. Both were personal injury lawyers and telegraphed their feelings of superiority whenever the family got together. Recently, Teddy won an award of one million eight-hundred thousand. He couldn't help but feel left in their dust, and he always resented how his mother favored them over him. Her refrain was 'You're too much like your father.' The implication was clear. They were more like her.

'Don't go into it, Jack, but I can see it was rough, wasn't it?'

'Yeah, it was rough. I didn't expect to be there when it happened, Dick.'

114

'Right,' Valentine said. 'Let's change the subject.'

Quinn couldn't stand the helplessness he felt after leaving Jack's office. Those two had no sense of responsibility. The dead were commodities to them and nothing more. A grave was just a hole in the ground. Obligations to loved ones ended with the maintenance agreements. The only religious icon in their chapel was the almighty dollar.

He checked his watch. It was nearly ten thirty and Barry hadn't shown. When he opened the garage door and looked at what he had to do to repair it so it would lock properly again, his temper began to simmer. He gazed at the cemetery entrance, looked at the backhoe, and then went to the phone in the garage and called Barry's aunt, Lily Palmer.

Barry's father's sister had never married, and was now close to eighty-five if she was a day. She had lived alone most of her life and was still quite independent. Remarkably, she was physically capable of doing her own driving, shopping and housekeeping, better in fact than women twenty years her junior. He recalled how fond of her his father was. She was one of the few old-timers who remembered the nickname his grandfather had given his father, Spike. She would call him nothing else and even referred to Quinn as Spike's boy.

'This is Lily Palmer,' she said in her formal, Emily Post manner.

'Hello, Miss Palmer. It's Randy Quinn.'

'Yes, how are you?' she asked. Before he could ask anything else, she added, 'And Barry, I suppose, slept at your home again last night?'

'No, Miss Palmer. Barry didn't sleep over. I haven't seen him since the end of work yesterday. That's why I was calling you. He hasn't reported for work this morning. You say he didn't come home last night? You're sure?'

It was possible he was still asleep in his bed and she didn't realize it. Quinn remembered the Palmer's house well.

'Work? Barry got work? What kind of work?'

'With me, Miss Palmer, at the cemetery.'

'Oh. Well, that boy never mentioned it. Unfortunately, he takes after my brother. I had to be there wiping his nose even after he was married twenty years. My sister-in-law, God rest her soul, was as selfish as a fox.'

Quinn knew she was about to burst into one illustration after another.

'When was the last time you heard from him?' he asked quickly.

'Heard from him? He was here for a little while late in the afternoon yesterday, but he wouldn't stay to dinner last night, and I had prepared a pork roast. He's had a very hard time of it since he left home, you know.'

116

'Yes, ma'am, I know.'

'And according to him, he had a harlot for a wife. I don't know if he told you much about that, but...'

'Yes, ma'am, he did,' Quinn said quickly. 'If you hear from him, would you tell him to call me. It's very important.'

'Yes, I will. How have you been, Randy?' she asked as if the conversation had just begun. He knew she would remember his father's stock answer to that question.

'Pretty good if I count in tips, Miss Palmer.'

She laughed.

'I miss Spike,' she said. 'As I'm sure you do, too.'

'Thank you, Miss Palmer. Please be sure to tell Barry I'm looking for him.'

'OK,' she said. He could hear the disappointment in her voice because he was cutting the conversation so short.

'Goodbye,' he said.

'Yes, goodbye, Randy.' Her voice seemed to trail off with his name, dissipate like smoke in a stiff breeze. It had the sound of a final goodbye and struck a note of sadness in him that resonated in his bones.

That son of a bitch, he thought. It irked him that Waller and Valentine would just sit in that office and take the viol-ation, but why would Stuart Kitchen refuse to permit the inspection of the coffin? Why would he make such a big deal of it all and then just slough it off like this? From what he overheard in his voice when he was in the arrangements room, he did seem to feel his father's presence and fear disobeying his final wishes. Did he now feel free of him and able to defy him since he was six feet under?

He recalled how firmly Evelyn had stated those wishes, too. Was it possible that Stuart had made the decision without first conferring with her? Between Jack and Valentine's silence and Stuart Kitchen's not telling her, the whole thing would be swept under the carpet. She'd never know. No one else but him and Scarlet Moore would know what had gone on here.

Meanwhile, somewhere out there, Barry Palmer was driving along and whistling, dreaming of the money he was going to raise selling the jewelry.

The bastard had dug up one of his graves, violated one of his sites, and a promise made to a dying man and all because of my own big mouth, Quinn thought, now convinced it had to be Barry and not anyone associated with the Kitchens.

He slammed a wrench against the wall and stood there staring at the backhoe. A thought came to him. He could lose his job doing this, but he wouldn't sleep or stop thinking about it if he didn't.

He returned to his work, but kept an eye on the funeral home and saw when Richard Valentine left and then when Jack drove off at the end of his day which was growing earlier and earlier. It was nearly the end of his workday anyway. Every day now, night clawed a little farther into daylight. Soon, he'd be going home every day in the dark.

He picked up his lantern, shovel and large brush and got on the backhoe, but then he hesitated. He could start one helluva horet's nest. Was it really worth it? Were Valentine and Waller right? It was the Kitchens' business and if they didn't care, why should he or they?

What would his father do? He wondered and looked at the driveway in front of him as if his father's ghost stood there.

'Start that engine,' he heard him say.

And he did.

'What's wrong, Stuart?' Evelyn asked.

He was sitting behind his father's desk in his father's den-office. He looked up sharply. It didn't surprise him that she had come in to ask that question. Just as he believed he could feel her every mood, he believed she could feel his as well. It was what made them so special. Too bad their father didn't realize how special they really were together.

'You should be resting, Evelyn. I'm sorry if anything's disturbed you.'

'What's disturbing you, Stuart?'

'I'm just a little annoyed,' he said. 'Maybe, more than a little otherwise you wouldn't have come in here.'

'No, it's not just this, whatever it is. I haven't seen you all day and you left abruptly last night and didn't get back until very late. What can you be doing so soon after Father's funeral?'

'My goodness,' he said. 'You're worse than Alice Chapman when it comes to keeping track of my whereabouts and movements in this house.'

'I couldn't sleep last night so I heard you come home. I wasn't waiting up for you or keeping tabs on you,' she said even though she knew he wasn't being critical. He was smiling at her.

'I know that,' he said. She stood there waiting. 'Fact is, I like that, like that you asked,' he continued. 'You're still concerned about me.'

'I never stopped being concerned about you, Stuart, but you're not answering my initial question. Why are you annoyed right now? What's happened? Does it have something to do with business?'

He spun the chair to his left just the way his father would and gazed out of the bay windows that faced the stable. Flicker and Diamond, their two black Arabians, would be almost indistinguishable from this distance if it weren't for Diamond's white spot on his forehead, which shaped like a diamond gave him his name.

'I hope we can go riding again soon,' he muttered. 'I like when we do things together

120

without everyone around us.'

'Stuart, please,' she insisted, stepping closer. He turned to her.

'Jack Waller called me to tell me his cemetery manager suspected that Father's grave had been uncovered, that the coffin might have been opened and the jewelry taken. They wanted to disinter the coffin and have the police examine it. At no expense to us, of course.'

Evelyn brought her hand to her mouth to smother a gasp.

'What did you tell him?'

'I told him I didn't want the grave disturbed. I made a point of saying neither you nor I had mentioned the jewelry to anyone, that only his people knew what was in that coffin.'

'Well ... he's saying it was disturbed already, isn't he?'

'No. He's saying some gravedigger suspects that it was. Something about him knowing his dirt. I told him frankly the jewelry was my father's and my father would get anyone who took it from him.'

'You didn't really say that, did you?'

'Well, something like it.'

She continued to look at him skeptically.

'It's all right,' he said. 'I warned him that if someone working for him touched our father's grave, we would sue him. He got the point.'

'But if someone already has...'

121

'Stop it,' he snapped. Then he smiled. 'Don't I always take care of things, Evelyn? Haven't I always been dependable and responsible?'

'Yes, Stuart.'

'Then don't start obsessing over this and get yourself sick or something. You insisted on knowing, so I told you. Leave it at that. Oh,' he said rising quickly and going to the file cabinet on the left. 'I have something to show you.'

He knelt and pulled open the bottom drawer to take out a thick folder.

'Look at what he had, what he kept,' he said holding it up for her.

She stepped over and took the folder. Then she sat in the bullet red-leather chair and explored the folder's contents.

'All my school tests and homework papers back in grade school,' she said. 'Even my kindergarten papers. He never said he had all this.'

Stuart nodded.

'I found only yours,' he said. 'I haven't found any of mine.'

She looked at him.

'You know he was proud of your academic accomplishments, Stuart.'

'Proud for himself, not for me. It was always his side of the family that enabled me to do anything significant. It's a wonder he didn't demand we genuflect every time we encountered him.'

She looked down. There was no sense arguing with him about it and really no reason to any more.

'You're really not concerned about what Jack Waller called to tell you?' she asked softly.

'Evelyn ... I said forget it,' he replied harshly, his eyes flashing sparks of rage. 'I said it's over. It's over.'

She took a deep breath, nodded, stood up and handed him the folder.

'You keep it,' he said. 'No point in leaving it in this file cabinet. I'm going to get rid of most of his personal accolades. He designed this place so it would remain a monument or something. Maybe he thought we'd turn it into a museum.'

She didn't reply. She nodded and started out.

'Just get your strength back, Evelyn. We have so much to do. So much to make up for,' he added, but she was already gone.

Anyway, he was saying it to himself.

EIGHT

He didn't hear her come up behind him. He had just begun the digging when he sensed someone nearby. How he did that, he couldn't explain. Maybe it came from living alone so long. He got so he could sense a garter snake long before he saw it. He paused and turned. Then he shut off the backhoe.

'Where's everyone else?' Scarlet asked looking around.

'What are you doing here?'

'What am I doing here? You never called me. I waited all day. I even listened to chatter and the news on the local radio expecting to hear something that way, but there was nothing. I called your house and then took a chance you might still be at work or maybe something was going on here so I left the diner and drove over. I saw your light and heard the backhoe. Why are you doing this alone?' she asked looking around. 'Shouldn't the police be here?'

'Stuart Kitchen didn't want to dig up the coffin, even after Jack explained what I believed happened.'

'So? It should have been over then, should-n't it? You told me it wasn't legal to go around digging up coffins without permission. What are you doing, Randy?' she asked stepping up to the backhoe.

'This grave was dug up and I'm sure the jewelry is gone,' he said jabbing his right forefinger toward the ground.

'But it wasn't you who might have been robbed,' she said softly. 'Or your father's grave, Randy.'

'That's what Jack and Richard say, but yes, I was. Look, it's like I built you a safe and assured you what you put in it was sacrosanct and then someone robs it because I idiotically revealed what was in the safe.'

'But Stuart Kitchen you said...'

'Stuart Kitchen wasn't robbed. He was robbed,' Quinn said nearly shouting and nodding at the grave marker. She just stared up at him. 'My promise was made to him, not to his son or daughter.' He relaxed, realizing he might be frightening her with his passion. 'Look, it's probably not easy for you to understand...'

'No, I do,' she said stepping back. She walked over to where he had placed the lantern and held it up so the light fell over more of the ground. 'Go ahead,' she said. 'I'll help you do what has to be done.'

He nodded at her, started the engine and began to dig again.

'How do you know how far down to go?'

she shouted over the sound of the engine.

'Oh, I know,' he said. 'I could do this with my eyes closed, but keep the light on it nevertheless.'

She nodded and was quiet until he slowed down and a few moments later turned off the backhoe entirely. Then he reached back and grabbed his shovel and the brush. He dropped the brush at the edge of the grave and lowered himself down.

'The detail work,' he said looking up at her and offering a smile. He could practically feel her trembling.

She didn't expect it, but her heart was pounding. She felt her throat tightening, too. Holding the light above him, she saw how carefully he gently continued removing dirt until he had uncovered the coffin. It was as if he were taking the blanket off a burn victim. Then he reached up on the edge of the grave and found his brush. He meticulously cleaned off the top of the coffin and around the edges of the lid.

'Don't want to get any dirt in there,' he muttered just loud enough to hear. She wasn't sure whether he was talking to her or to himself.

He paused and looked up at her.

'All right. I'm going to do this. You can hand the light down to me, Scarlet and step back, if you want.'

'I'm OK,' she said.

'If you're sure, step a little closer, but be

careful. Don't fall in.'

'Oh, I won't do that. I've fallen into a few deep holes in my life, but not this one,' she replied and brought the full impact of the beam on the coffin.

He played with the lid and when he began to lift it, he looked up at her.

'This was supposedly permanently sealed so it's either been opened or never was permanently sealed.'

'Maybe he's not in there any more,' she said. She was making a joke, but the possibility lingered between them as if the words were echoing.

He turned and slowly lifted the lid completely. She leaned forward with the light.

And then she screamed.

It was such a piercing scream that Quinn felt his own bones shudder. He thought it was loud enough to wake the dead. Quinn half-expected Matthew Kitchen would sit up. He gaped at the contents of the coffin.

The naked baby's eyes looked like two tiny pink marbles. Its torso was shrunken and wrinkled like an old beige sock. The umbilical cord had been cut. He could see it had been a boy. The baby was folded into a fetal position and placed on Matthew Kitchen's stomach. Its dark-brown hair looked painted on. Matthew Kitchen's hands were folded just an inch or so away from the baby's head. His face was more purple now and oddly his eyes were wide open making it look like he had died in a state of shock or perhaps was shocked when the baby's body was placed on him.

Eyes are not usually kept open, Quinn thought. He stepped back.

'Jesus Christ,' he said.

'What is that, Randy?' she asked, her voice in a hoarse whisper.

'A baby.'

'I know, but is it supposed to be in there?'

'Hell no,' he said. 'Bring more light on it, Scarlet.'

She leaned over and he stepped up to the coffin again and gently moved the baby. He touched its hair and looked closely at its fingers.

'I know enough about dead bodies to tell you this baby was put in here recently.'

'You mean that's why someone dug up the grave?'

He shook his head.

'I'm not sure. It would need someone from forensics to tell you that, I suppose. In any case this doesn't make any sense. Why not give the baby its own burial? Even if it was something illicit, why dig up a grave unless...'

'Unless what?'

He reached in to push up Matthew Kitchen's suit jacket sleeves.

'No watch,' he said. He looked at Kitchen's fingers. 'No ring either and no bracelets.' To complete the search, he pulled down on the shirt collar and the tie. 'No necklace. The corpse has been robbed as well,' he said. 'Man, this is pretty weird.'

Scarlet wasn't able to speak. Her gaze was fixed on the dead baby. She didn't even hear what Quinn was saying. When he moved to get out of the grave, she backed up. Then, to reconfirm what she saw, she stepped forward and directed the light on the two corpses.

'That's not an aborted fetus, Randy. It looks full term to me or close to it. The umbilical cord was tied.'

He gazed back and nodded.

'It was a boy,' he said and sat staring down at the coffin.

'What are you going to do?'

'Call Jack first,' he said, 'and then the police, I guess.'

'But this was illegal, this digging up of the grave. Isn't it like an unlawful search or something? I've seen enough courtroom drama on television to know that keeps evidence from being considered.'

'I don't know how this all plays out. I know that baby isn't supposed to be in there and I know the jewelry is gone. That I do know.' He slipped back into the grave and closed the coffin. 'This is going to be another late night. I should have sent you back to your car.'

'I should have run to it myself. I'll have nightmares forever,' she said.

'C'mon. There's a lot to do,' he said.

129

He started away. She glanced back at the coffin and stepped quickly to catch up with him.

'What a horrible thing to find. You sure there wasn't anything said about a dead child?'

'Nothing. No, that child was put in the coffin after everything was done with Matthew Kitchen's corpse here at the funeral home. Curt Marcus would have had to be told. We'd all know. I mean, there are death certificates to have processed, medical examiner's reports, whatever. It's a whole lot of procedure nowadays. You don't just decide to bury someone because it's convenient.'

'You really believe it's possible someone dug up the grave, opened the coffin, stole the jewelry and put the baby in there? You suspect Barry. Whose baby would he have put in? Could he have done something like this?'

'I don't know. Maybe.'

'I can't imagine anyone doing such a thing.'

After another silent moment, she seized his arm and he stopped walking.

'What?'

'The baby could have been put in before the coffin was returned to the funeral home for the wake, Randy.'

'You mean ... the Kitchens?'

She shrugged.

'You said Stuart Kitchen refused Jack's offer to dig up the grave and check the

130

coffin.'

'Yes.'

'Then Barry could have come here, dug that up, saw the baby but robbed the corpse anyway? Of course, he wouldn't say anything since he robbed the corpse.'

'I suppose,' he said. 'There's a lot to assume with that theory. Damn. Well, first things first,' he said and they walked on.

'This is really déjà vu,' Scarlet said when they entered the funeral home and he put on all the lights.

'Yeah, well, it might be my last time. When Jack and his partner learn what I did ... even with this discovery ... I'm probably gone.'

'You sure you want to do this then? I'll have no trouble rewinding the tape and erasing what I just witnessed. You just have to go back there and fill it in again.'

'No, I think it's too late,' he said. 'It's like un-ringing a bell.'

'Putting the toothpaste back in the tube?'

'Yeah. I don't think either of us would sleep well at night if I did that.'

'I know. Damn. No one's safe any more,' she said. 'Not even after they die.'

Quinn nodded.

'Maybe least of all when they die,' he said.

'Water again?' she asked when he sat behind Jack Waller's desk.

'You know it.'

She nodded and left. He took a breath and then lifted the receiver. Just as he put his finger to a number, he thought of another idea. He hung up and went to Jack's file cabinet, searching through to locate the Kitchens' home phone number.

'What did he say?' Scarlet asked as he turned with the file in his hand.

'I didn't call him yet. I want to do something else first,' he said.

'What?'

'Call the Kitchens and tell them what I've found.'

'Why, Randy?'

'Because we'll be able to tell from their reaction whether or not they're involved in this,' he said.

She sat.

'That's not your job, Randy. That's the job of the police. Call your boss first like you planned. And then let him be the one to call the police. You've done enough. You don't want to get any more deeply involved in this.'

'It's not how I'm built. Maybe you should get out of here now, Scarlet? You're seriously involved here. I'm not certain about all the legal ramifications.'

'What do you mean?'

'As you pointed out before, you participated in an illegal act, digging up that grave, and now you're going to be called in as a witness as well. There's no need for you to be involved in all that. Just go home.'

'Are you serious?'

'Dead serious. I'll call you. I promise this

time. You've got your little girl to think about. I can tell you first hand what it was like growing up here with a graveyard stigma attached. Who knows how your customers will react once they hear about this Halloween event? You can't account for how people see you. They'll start thinking you're ghoulish.'

'But don't you need me?'

'For what? They'll come. They'll see the baby and that the jewelry is gone and that will be it. What you say or even what I say won't be as important.'

She thought a moment and nodded. He was making sense and she was afraid.

'I hate leaving you alone here,' she said.

He smiled.

'I've been alone here many times, Scarlet.'

'Not with something like this out there,' she said. 'Right?'

'Right, but I can handle it, Scarlet.'

'OK, but you better call me this time, Randy. I mean it. I want to know what's happening.'

He raised his right hand. She thought a moment and then stood, started to turn and hesitated.

'I can't help feeling like I'm deserting you.'

'Don't,' he said, 'you're not. I'm sorry I let you become involved in it at all. Think. People would even have a hard time with you at the diner. You could lose your job.'

She nodded, started out, hesitated at the

door and then left. He went to the window and watched her get into her car. As soon as he saw her drive off, he returned to the desk. For nearly a good minute, he sat there doing nothing, just staring at the phone. Then he lifted the receiver and tapped out the Kitchens' phone number.

'Hello,' Evelyn Kitchen said.

When he heard her voice, he nearly lost his, considering what he was preparing to tell her. He swallowed and spoke slowly.

'Miss Kitchen?'

'Yes, who's calling?'

'This is Randy Quinn. I don't know if you remember me, but...'

'Yes, of course I do. I know exactly who you are,' she said.

He felt himself blush, but it felt good.

'I'm sorry to have to call you to tell you this, but I had reason to dig up your father's grave.'

'What? Why?'

Don't you know? He thought. Jack said he had called the Kitchens. Clearly Stuart hadn't told her.

'Well, I knew that you had him buried with some very valuable jewelry. Last night, when I stopped by the funeral home to do my boss a favor, I noticed someone had used my backhoe. I was suspicious so I checked your father's plot and saw it had been dug up.'

She was silent for a moment. He wondered if she had covered the mouthpiece and was talking to her brother.

'Go on,' she said.

'I told my boss and this morning he called your house and I guess spoke with your brother?'

'Yes.'

'And he said he didn't want the coffin checked.'

'That's correct,' she said.

She had known. He felt the disappointment fall around his shoulders like a cold towel.

'Well, I felt guilty about it.'

'You did? Why? You didn't...'

'No. What I did do, however, was tell someone about the jewelry, someone who I had just hired to work here, and after I saw that the backhoe had been used, I suspected he had done it. It got me pretty angry. To make a long story short here, I just dug up the grave and I checked your father's coffin.'

'You opened my father's coffin?'

'I know. It sounds terrible, but...'

'It is terrible. That's why we didn't want it done.'

'Yes, but...'

'My brother is going to be very, very upset. I wouldn't be surprised if he calls the police,' she said, her voice sharp, angry and as formal as he recalled it could be.

'He doesn't have to,' Quinn said calmly. 'I'm calling them.'

'Well you should and rightly so.'

'But not because of what I did, but because of what I found.'

'I don't understand.'

'Your father's jewelry was gone all right. Worse, there was a baby boy on his chest.'

'What?'

'There's an infant's corpse in there as well.'

She was silent.

'Miss Kitchen?'

'This is a bizarre phone call, Randy.'

'I know. Believe me, I am not enjoying it. Anyway, I'm sorry,' he said not knowing what else to say.

'We'll be right there,' she told him and hung up. The click sounded like a gunshot. He held the receiver for a moment away from his ear.

I've done it now, he thought. Did I do it for the reasons I expressed to Jack and Richard or did I do it just to hear her voice and see her face? In the end it might not make the slightest difference, except to him.

He called Jack's mobile.

'Now what?' Jack answered, seeing Randy was again calling him from his office. 'What the hell are you still doing there this time of the day?'

'I'm sorry, Jack, but I had to check that coffin.'

'Check? What do you mean, check?'

'Uncover it and open it.'

'Are you crazy? You can't do that. You should know what's required to uncover and open a coffin. We told you...'

'You're not listening, Jack. I already did it.'

'What? You mean you've uncovered it?'

'And opened it. There'd be no sense not to once I uncovered it, Jack.'

He was silent.

'Jack?'

'If the Kitchens find out what you did...'

'They already found out.'

'How?'

'I had to tell them,' he said.

'What the fuck. You called the Kitchens before you called me?'

'I thought I should. The jewelry's gone.'

'I told you. We don't give a shit about the damn jewelry. You had no legal right to do that. Now they'll sue the hell out of us.'

'I don't think so, Jack.'

'Oh, you don't think so, huh? And why's that, genius?'

'There's a dead baby in there with Kitchen,' he said.

'Huh? What dead baby?'

'I don't know, Jack, but I told Evelyn Kitchen and she said she and her brother would be on their way over here.'

'Jesus. What have you done to us?'

'Didn't you hear what I said? It's a dead baby, Jack, a dead baby in there with Matthew Kitchen.'

'I heard you. Don't do anything else. Don't breathe too loudly in fact. I'll call Lou Siegman. You sit tight. He'll know best how to handle it,' Jack said. 'Lucky he plays poker with us. I have his home number.'

Lou Siegman was the township's chief of police, but Quinn thought it was going to involve more than the local law enforcement.

'We'll try to keep it quiet for as long as possible,' Jack continued. 'I gotta call Richard. He's gonna be raging mad and fit to be hogtied. I don't see how I can save your ass after this.'

He hung up.

Quinn sat there again for a moment with the receiver in his hand. Why should Jack's insensitivity to the fact that there was a dead baby in the coffin amaze him, he asked himself? We sit and watch women and children, innocents all over the world destroyed as a result of people looking to build their net worth. It's easy to watch it on television. Somehow, the horrible events and the tragedy merge with the fiction, the more and more realistic dramas are taken right out of the news, and then we go to sleep embraced by the comfort parents have given children after they woke screaming from nightmares since time began: 'It's not real.'

Maybe this isn't real. Maybe he could walk back out there and look into the open coffin and see Matthew Kitchen's corpse bedecked with the expensive jewelry and nothing else. He could close the lid and backhoe back the earth over the coffin. He could call Scarlet and tell her it was all a dream. They could meet again and continue on to his house to make love and fall asleep to wake up with a real hunger, not only for more sex, but a Sunday morning breakfast.

He kept expecting himself to wince and wake up, but that didn't happen and the dirt on his hands and in his fingernails drove home the reality. This was all happening and what might seem like a nightmare now, could easily become something far worse.

When he rose from Jack's desk chair this time, he felt like Lazarus standing up in his own grave.

And he'd ask himself the same question.

How could he live knowing what the living did not know about the darkness beneath their feet?

NINE

Quinn couldn't sit still. He paced about the funeral home and then he went outside and waited. It was closer to twenty-five minutes before he saw a pair of headlights and then a car turn off the road and head for the cemetery entrance. He stepped back in the shadows and watched as the Kitchens' Mercedes sedan pulled into a parking space. Stuart shut off the lights and got out first. For a moment Quinn thought only he had come. Then Evelyn emerged. They looked at each other and started toward the funeral home. Quinn stepped forward, held up his hand and called to them so they could see where he waited.

'The police should be on their way,' he said as they drew closer. 'Jack Waller called Lou Siegman, the chief of police.'

Stuart paused and Evelyn stopped beside him. She was wearing a black jacket with a hood and a pair of black jeans. In the cloud filtered moonlight her face looked like the face of a Kabuki dancer. Stuart wasn't wearing a coat over his suit jacket. His hair fell loosely over his forehead.

140

'Why did you dig up my father's grave if I refused permission to do so?' he asked.

Quinn had never realized how nasal Stuart Kitchen sounded normally. He wasn't someone he had much to do with in high school and rarely, if ever, saw him since.

'I realized it had been dug up since your father's internment,' Quinn said. He looked to Evelyn. Hadn't she explained why?

'That was what Jack Waller told me you suspected, but I specifically told him to leave it be. I was very clear about it, and without our permission or the police getting a court order to do so, that was illegal.'

Quinn saw Evelyn put her hand on her brother's left forearm as a controlling gesture.

'I told your sister that I thought that if your father's coffin was robbed, it was my fault,' Quinn continued. 'I had told someone who I hired to work here what you had buried with your father and I suspected he had dug up that grave and stolen the jewelry.'

'Whom did you tell about my father's jewelry?' Stuart asked.

'Barry Palmer,' Quinn said.

Evelyn took her hand off Stuart's arm.

'Barry Palmer?' she asked. 'From our school?'

Our school? Quinn thought. He found that ironic. Neither she nor her brother ever behaved like they considered it their school.

'Yes. As I told you, I gave him a job here

141

when he returned from Texas and...'

'And he dug up my father's grave and stole the jewelry?' Stuart asked.

'I'm not absolutely sure Barry did it,' Quinn said. 'He didn't show up for work today, so I had more reason to be suspicious.'

'What's this ridiculous thing you told my sister about a baby?' Stuart asked stepping forward.

'You can see for yourself,' Quinn replied, tired of his tone and attitude. He looked toward the highway. There was still no sign of a police patrol car. Why was that taking so long?

'You want us to go look at my father in his coffin since he was buried?'

'There's no other way,' Quinn said. 'I'm sorry, but...'

'We'll have to do it, Stuart,' Evelyn said.

'I'll go get my flashlight,' Quinn said and hurried to the garage.

When he stepped out, he saw the Kitchen twins arguing. Stuart was thrusting his arms about and Evelyn was standing in front of him with her hands on her hips.

'I got it,' Quinn called and they turned to him.

'I thought you said the police were coming,' Stuart said as he approached.

'That's what Jack Waller told me. He was calling the chief himself at home. You want to wait for them?'

'Yes, of course. It's a crime scene now,'

Stuart said. Quinn thought he meant the fact that there was a baby in the coffin, but he added, 'since a grave was dug up illegally.'

'I'm not hiding or running away from that,' Quinn said, 'but unless I'm missing something here, the real crime is an undocumented infant corpse in the coffin.'

'Of course. You're right,' Evelyn said. 'It's just that all this is quite disturbing for us. Please forgive us,' she said. 'You can imagine how traumatic. We just went through our father's funeral.'

Quinn felt himself nearly melt into his boots.

'Forgive us?' Stuart snapped. 'You're asking him to forgive us? He violated Father's grave.'

This guy can't be this thick, harping on the illegal disinterment rather than on what he said he had found in the coffin, Quinn thought. He looked back at the highway again. Where the hell were Siegman and Jack?

'Maybe we should wait for the police,' Evelyn said. 'Regardless of which illegal act we're discussing, my brother is right. It is a crime scene.'

'They should have been here by now,' Quinn said glancing at the highway again. He turned back to the Kitchen twins and then nodded. 'OK, why don't we wait inside? I'll try to reach Jack Waller again and see what's happening.'

Stuart looked at the funeral parlor.

'I think I'd rather wait in the car,' he said and before Evelyn could disagree, he started back toward the parking lot. She, however, did not follow.

'My brother is understandably very upset,' she said. 'Sometimes, it's best to just let him cool off alone. I'd rather wait in there anyway,' she added nodding at the funeral home entrance.

Quinn shot forward and opened the door for her. They entered and stood in the lobby for a moment.

'Would you like some cold water? We've got bottles in the kitchen.'

'Kitchen?' she said smiling. Now that he saw her up close and in the light, he was thrown back to his high school days. She didn't look much older than the teenage girl he had idolized. Perhaps it was his imagination, but she still had that angelic look in her eyes, that softness and calmness. Madonna eyes, he had though back then and still thought now.

'Yes. I know it seems incongruent.'

Incongruent? Did he actually use that word?

'But people hold wakes here and...'

'Of course. You're right. It's strange to think of a funeral home the way you would think of any home, but that's what it is, and a home is a home, even if this is a home for the dead,' she said.

144

He stood there staring at her like an idiot. She smiled.

'No, I don't need any water. Thank you, Randy.'

He indicated where she could sit and she went to it and sat. He admired how perfectly she lowered herself and how good her posture always was. He was always enamored of her every move, every gesture, no matter how small it was or how inconspicuous. She never knew, but he had memorized her the way an actor would memorize a character in a play. Were he an artist, he could have drawn and painted her from memory, even years later.

'I can imagine that you were upset with Stuart's decision to leave my father's grave be, but in his way of thinking that jewelry was gone anyway. It was as good as stolen. Only the first time it was stolen by a dead man.'

'Was your father always like that about his personal possessions?'

'No, but Stuart and my father didn't get along all that well. I think my father put that demand in his will just to annoy him.'

Quinn nodded. He appreciated her frankness. Actually, he was quite surprised by it.

She looked around and then gave him that soft smile.

'So, you've been here all this time, working here since high school?'

'No, not immediately. This cemetery is

only about twelve years old.'

She started to smile again, but stopped.

'You know. I always wondered about you.'

'Me? Why?'

'I know some of the other students made fun of the work you did. It was certainly a turn-off with many of the girls, but I admired the fact that none of that seemed to bother you. Did it?'

'Yes,' he confessed.

She nodded.

'It's understandable. You did a good job of not showing it, though.'

'I had no idea you gave me a second glance. I remember approaching you once and you being kind of cool; not impolite, just cool.'

'My life was complicated then as it is now,' she said. 'A belated apology. I meant no disrespect.'

'None taken.' He wanted to add that she could never do anything wrong in his eyes, but he checked the high school thoughts and looked out the door again. 'This is weird. They should have been here before you. Do you mind if I go into the office and call Jack Waller?'

'Please do,' she said. 'I'll be fine.'

He hurried in and went to the phone. When Jack's answering service picked up, he hung up and went out to the lobby again.

'No answer. He might be in a dead spot on the way here. Sure you don't want any water?'

'I'm fine,' she said. 'Are both your parents gone, too?'

'Yes.'

'You're not married?'

'No. Still living in my parents' house.'

'Me, too,' she said. 'We take different roads to the same place.'

'And what is that place?'

'I suspect, despite the way we present ourselves to other people, loneliness.'

He stared, unaware that his jaw had dropped. Never in a million years would he have expected Evelyn Kitchen to be a lonely woman, even less to admit it to him. She had beauty, intelligence and wealth. Why couldn't she have found someone with whom she could be happy? Were those rumors about her and her brother correct after all? And even if they were, he thought, being gay doesn't mean you have to be lonely.

'Maybe that's why I devote myself to my work,' he said, recovering.

'I suspect it is.'

'What have you done to deal with it?'

'Oh, I worked for my father. He was quite a demanding boss. We had to do a lot of traveling because of his various holdings and interests. You probably know he had many friends in high places. We always had a full calendar of social events, business meetings.'

'And you never got involved with anyone,

engaged, anything?'

'Dated but nothing substantial,' she said. 'Some of us just take longer to find the right person, if there is a right person. I guess you know that, being a bachelor.'

He looked out the window again.

'Your brother's all right waiting in his car all this time?'

'I'm sure he's on the mobile phone with someone. Like my father, he's always busy whether he has to be or not.'

Quinn nodded and looked at her. Even now, in the midst of all this horrendous madness, she was so cool, so calm. It was that suave self-confidence that energized her serene beauty, he thought.

'I'm sorry for this. Especially so soon after your father's death.'

'It's not your fault. Don't worry. As I said, my brother is a bit high-strung about it all, but once we get to the bottom of it all, he'll calm down. It's the way he's always been. My father used to say, Stuart is fire and I'm water. If it wasn't for me, he'd burn up.'

'I believe it.'

'I know Stuart always wanted to be just like him, to have that even temperament. It helped my father avoid making mistakes. Not that he never did. He just had a better success record than most.'

'Yeah, my father was the same way when it came to his temperament.'

'Was he?' She smiled. 'Someone's coming

now,' she said, nodding at the front. The headlights swiped across the windows before the vehicle turned into the parking lot.

Quinn opened the door.

'It's Jack,' he said. 'But where are the police?'

Evelyn came up behind him. He stepped back to let her out and then followed as Jack Waller emerged from his vehicle. Stuart stepped out of his car as well and the four of them met at the parking lot.

'Where's Lou and the posse?' Quinn asked.

'I thought we should check it all out first,' Jack said.

'Check it all out?'

'This is quite disturbing, Mr Waller,' Stuart Kitchen said. He nodded at Quinn as if he personified it all. 'My sister and I are beside ourselves. Our father's grave dug up after we gave you specific instructions not to do it.'

'I know. I'm just as upset about that as you are, Mr Kitchen, but Mr Quinn told you what he found, right?'

'He told us,' Evelyn said.

'Then let's all go look and take it from there.'

'I don't understand, Jack,' Quinn said as Waller walked ahead. He had his own flashlight in hand. 'Where's Lou Siegman?'

'Get your beam,' Jack replied instead of answering. Then he leaned in to speak sotto voce. 'We had better go through the motions first with them. Legal ramifications. Once they see what you saw, we have a better chance of avoiding legal unpleasantness.'

Quinn nodded even though he didn't agree. He went for his lantern that he had left in the lobby. As soon as he had it, the four of them headed into the cemetery. He looked at Evelyn. She was walking with her arms folded under her breasts and her head down and remaining a few feet behind everyone else. He suddenly felt terrible about what he was making her do. Maybe Scarlet had been right. He should have just covered it up. He certainly didn't want to be the one who gave Evelyn Kitchen nightmares for the rest of her life. He had already done that to Scarlet.

It seemed darker to him now, too, even though there were not that many clouds to block the moon or stifle the stars, darker and cooler. Winter already had its fingers in the wind. It wouldn't be that long before the ground froze. He glanced at Stuart to see if he would draw closer to Evelyn and perhaps comfort her at the sight of their father's corpse. He didn't. He continued to walk with his head high, his face a mask of indignation. It was as if she weren't there with him.

What a horse's ass, Quinn thought. They had labeled him correctly in high school: Hit and Run Kitchen.

They stopped at the edge of the grave. Quinn had closed the coffin so he had to get back into the grave to open the lid. He glanced at Evelyn. She couldn't see the apology in his face, but he thought she might be feeling it. He lowered himself as gracefully and slowly as he could and then stepped up to the coffin. Jack held his light above him. Quinn opened the lid and then lifted his own beam to throw more illumination on the contents of the coffin.

It was utter shock, the kind that could literally make your eyes bulge and your hair stand up.

There was no baby in the coffin.

Even though there was no infant lying on Matthew Kitchen's corpse, Jack Waller leaned over and asked.

'Where is it?'

'It was ... it was right there, on his stomach.'

'Jesus Christ,' Stuart Kitchen said. 'What did you do, dig up the grave, steal my father's jewelry and then make up this fantasy to throw us off?'

'Hell no,' Quinn snapped back at him. 'I'm telling you there was a dead baby here not more than an hour and a half ago.' He checked his watch. 'Two hours ago at the most.'

'So what do we call this then,' Stuart asked with a cold smile, 'infant resurrection? Is this a miracle? Are we going to bring thousands of religious nuts here to parade past my father's grave? What's this, a way to get publicity for your cemetery, Mr Waller?'

'Don't be stupid,' Jack said, but he looked

to Quinn for more of an explanation.

Quinn looked in the coffin again. He even looked on the sides of the corpse to see if there was any way for the baby to have slid off Kitchen's body. There was simply no room in there, but he didn't know what else to do.

'I can clearly see my father's jewelry is gone,' Stuart continued. 'Did you say you're calling the police?' he asked Jack.

'Yeah, sure. It's a robbery.'

'And the violation of a grave,' Stuart reminded him. Jack nodded.

'Listen,' Quinn said looking up at Evelyn. 'I'm not lying about this.' He hesitated but saw no other way but to reveal it. 'There's a witness to what I saw.'

'Huh?' Jack said. 'Get up out of there and start making sense, Randy,' he ordered.

Quinn crawled out of the grave, brushed himself off, and turned to Stuart and Evelyn.

'Scarlet Moore was here with me when I dug up the grave. She saw the baby, too.'

'Who's Scarlet Moore?' Stuart asked.

'She's a waitress over at the Centerville Diner,' Jack replied. He turned to Quinn. 'What the hell would she be doing out here? Is that your idea of a date?'

'No, she came looking for me when she didn't hear from me. She was with me the first time when I first looked at this grave and knew it had been dug up. She wanted to know what was done about it, and I had forgotten to call her. She arrived when I was out here with the backhoe. She stayed and saw what I saw. She'll testify to that.'

'What the hell kind of a cemetery is this?' Stuart demanded. 'He brings a date out here? What, are you screwing on tombstones?'

Quinn looked at Evelyn and felt himself blanch with anger.

'I just explained how she came to be here when I dug up the grave. I didn't exactly bring her. I don't bring women here. And I'd never defile a grave, especially one I had prepared.'

'You did defile this one,' Stuart shot back. 'You dug it up without legal permission.'

Quinn glanced at Evelyn, but she was looking down.

'Look,' he said, turning to Jack Waller, 'you know why we were here the first time, Jack. You can tell him I'm not lying. We stopped over to fax that paper work you needed and I noticed the backhoe had been used. I was suspicious and she followed me out to look at the site and knew I thought it had been dug up and the corpse probably robbed.'

'Corpse?' Stuart said. 'That's my father. Our father.'

Quinn looked quickly at Evelyn. She was still looking down.

'Sorry, I meant...'

'Let's just get the police into this quickly,' Stuart said. 'This is becoming a gruesome farce. I've already called my lawyer and will call him back. C'mon, Evelyn,' he said finally acknowledging that she was standing there, too.

She glanced at Quinn and turned to follow her brother who was marching away.

'Jesus, Randy. What the hell is going on here? There's no baby!'

'I told you the truth, Jack. I'll call Scarlet when we get back at the funeral parlor and she'll come over to corroborate everything I've said. I don't know what's going on here now, but I'm just as interested as you are in finding out.'

He looked back at the coffin. He had left the lid up.

'I'll close it.'

'Leave it. Siegman's only going to want to look for himself.'

Quinn lifted his light beam and held it so he could throw some of the illumination over the sides of the site. Then he stepped to his right and leaned over.

'There are footprints here.'

'Yeah. Yours, mine and the Kitchen twins. Don't tell me there are baby footprints, too, Randy, or I swear I'll have you committed.'

Quinn said nothing. He looked around a little more and then he started back with Jack.

'The minimum here is going to be a lawsuit, you know,' Jack said. 'Richard's going to be pretty hot about it, Randy. I really don't

154

think I'll be able to keep you on.'

'I'm not lying about any of it, and you know I wouldn't steal Matthew Kitchen's jewelry.'

'What I do and don't know will be worth shit,' Jack said.

Quinn nodded and followed him in silence. He noticed that Evelyn had gone back to the car with her brother who was on his cell phone. Because the car was awash in the parking lot lights, he could see that she sat like stone looking forward. He wanted to go to her and impress upon her that he was telling the truth, but he realized that almost anything he did or said at this moment would only make matters worse so he followed Jack into his office and stood by while he called Chief Siegman.

'Hey, Lou, sorry to disturb you at home, but we got big problems out here.'

Quinn lowered himself to a chair and listened as Jack summarized what he had done, what he had claimed and what just had happened.

'Yeah, I appreciate that. We'll be here.'

Jack hung up and looked at him.

'I don't know what you and Scarlet Moore got going here, Randy, but if you want, call her. Lou will be here shortly and have lots of questions for the both of you, I'm sure.'

'We don't have anything going here, Jack. I can't believe you're even thinking like this.'

'I'm not thinking. I'm dumbfounded,' he

said rising. 'Use the phone if you want and call her. I need to dig out that bottle of Scotch in my other office.'

He walked out. Quinn sat there for a moment, stunned. How could this be happening? He rose and went to the phone to call Scarlet. Her mother answered and sounded very pleased to hear him.

'I'll get her,' she said quickly. Of course, he understood. She was hoping her daughter would find someone substantial and get married again, get into her own home again, and let her live out her autumn years without all the old pressures and worries returning. She's certainly going to be surprised when she learns about this and what I've added to those worries, he thought.

'Hey,' Scarlet said. 'What's happening? I'm actually surprised that you called me so quickly. Randy?' she followed when he was silent.

'The Kitchens got here and then Jack arrived without the police. He wanted to see what was in the coffin first. We all went out there and I opened it again.'

'And?'

'There was no baby in the coffin, Scarlet.'

'No baby? What are you talking about?'

'It was gone.'

'I saw the baby, Randy. Are you making some kind of morbid joke or what?'

'I'm not kidding. The baby's gone. They all think I made it up or something to cover for

156

stealing the jewelry, which as you pointed out would make no sense.'

'Of course not. If you had done that, you could just as easily have refilled the grave and no one would have known the difference. But really, how can there be no baby, Randy?'

'Obviously, someone came along and took it out before I got back to it, I guess. I thought I saw different foot tracks, but with four of us walking around the site, it's hard to differentiate. I'll have to wait for daylight.'

'No baby. This is really a nightmare now.'

'Yes. Anyway, I'm sorry. I sent you home because I didn't want you involved, but I'm afraid I need you to come back to corroborate what I reported. If you don't want to return, it's all right, too,' he added. 'I could be getting you into more trouble. The implication that we both might be in on this was made.'

'That's ridiculous. Of course, I'll return,' she said. 'I'll just get dressed and get up there. Are the police still not there?'

'No, now they're on their way.'

'I'll be right there,' she said.

'Thanks,' he told her and hung up.

He was worried for himself and Scarlet and upset at how he had looked in front of Evelyn Kitchen, but lost in the middle of this were the questions who was that baby, and whose child had it been?

And where was it now?

TEN

Quinn wasn't at all surprised that Scarlet arrived before Lou Siegman. The Chief was sixty-three and hovering on the edge of retirement. Quinn's father had once told him that Lou Siegman had the perfect personality for the job.

'He moves slowly, thinks even slower, and reacts to events even slower than that. He's so laid back that it will take a medical examiner a week to confirm he's dead.

'But in a position that exposes you to a nearly continuous stream of complaints,' his father continued, 'a position that gives you the toilet bowl view of the community, and a position that locks you into an eternally low middle class life, you couldn't ask for a more perfect candidate. When he's gone, they'll realize what they've lost, especially if they appoint one of those hyper horse's ass military types to replace him.'

Jack came out of his inner office just after Scarlet walked into the funeral home. She had barely had time to greet Quinn.

'You come here to back up his wild story?' Jack asked.

'It's wild, but it's not a story. It's the truth. I saw the baby.'

'Why didn't you hang around, too?' Jack asked and then looked at Quinn. 'Lou's only going to ask her anyway.'

'I told her to leave. I didn't want her to be involved, Jack.'

Waller smirked and shook his head.

'Yeah, you kept her from being involved. Good job. I just got off the phone with Richard. He'll be here as soon as he can.' He looked at Scarlet and nodded at Quinn. 'There a job for him at the diner?'

'If you fire him, you're a fool,' Scarlet said.

'Yeah, right. I'm the fool.'

A patrol car pulled up the driveway, its bubble lights going.

'Here's Lou,' Jack said moving to the door.

'How could there not be a baby in the grave, Randy?' Scarlet asked in a loud whisper. 'I know what you think, but you didn't see anyone else here when we first looked or when the Kitchen twins were here, did you?'

'No, but I was inside a lot of the time and away from the cemetery sites. The Kitchens arrived before Jack and I were talking to them both,' he said, not elaborating on his private conversation with Evelyn Kitchen. 'I'm sorry I had to call you.'

'Don't keep apologizing. We're not lying about it, and I resent Waller's implications. I don't understand why he didn't call the police immediately after you had spoken to

159

him. What did he think you were, drunk?'

'He didn't want to believe it, I guess. Now he feels justified for holding back.'

'This is crazy.'

'I know.'

He nodded and they followed Jack out to meet Lou Siegman and his patrolman Ralph Bookman, who was unlucky enough to be on duty. Quinn could see Ralph looked pretty confused. He had heard it all third hand, and worse, from Lou, who had surely made it sound pretty incredible.

Evelyn and Stuart stepped out of their vehicle to join the group forming on the funeral home's front patio.

'I'm pressing charges against this man,' Stuart immediately declared pointing at Quinn. 'You're to arrest him for illegally digging up my father's grave.'

Lou had an unlit cigar in his mouth. He was chewing it softly. 'That so?' he muttered.

Siegman was an awkward six-feet five-inch man, awkward because he had a pronounced limp and poor posture. Many tall men and women slouched, perhaps because they towered so over most people. Lou Siegman never took pleasure in his height. He was too slow to be a good basketball player. Most of the girls he fancied in high school were a good foot or so shorter, and either he felt silly dancing with them or they did. He ended up marrying a woman five feet ten and they had two girls who at fourteen and six-

teen were already nearly six feet tall themselves. He'd love to change that Randy New-
man song about short people having no right
to live to *tall* people having no right.

Lou was also Abe Lincoln gaunt in his
appearance. The premature gray hairs that
invaded his dark-brown mat and his sunken
cheeks gave him a habitually melancholy
appearance. Right now, as hard as it would
be for anyone to believe, he just looked tired
and bored.

Ralph Bookman's stout, military demeanor
stood out in contrast. Ralph had been an
MP – a military policeman – in the service
and easily got the position when he returned
home. He wasn't ambitious, however, and
sat satisfied in his cushy job patrolling quiet
village streets at night and chasing teenage
wise-guys off the highways and corners. The
most dangerous thing he had done in the
four years he worked at the department was
drive off a black bear in South Fallsburg that
had wreaked havoc with Jimmy Wilson's gar-
bage cans.

Siegman put his hands on his hips and
turned to Scarlet.

'You work at the Centerville Diner, right?'

'Coffee and chocolate cream pie, Chief.'

Siegman smiled and nodded.

'That's me. OK, so what the hell is this all
about, Randy?'

'It's exactly what I told Jack and Jack told
you, Chief. I suspected someone had dug up

161

Matthew Kitchen's grave to steal the jewelry and then had filled it in again. I dug it up because I felt responsible.'

'Which you are,' Stuart interjected. Quinn glanced at him and turned back to Siegman.

'Scarlet was with me when I uncovered the coffin. I checked it to see if the jewelry was missing and discovered a baby was in there, dead, of course. When I went to show them,' he said nodding at the Kitchen twins, 'the baby was gone. Simple as that.'

'Simple?' Lou said. He came close to laughing aloud, but a glance at Stuart Kitchen wiped any smile off his face instantly.

'Those are the true facts, Chief,' Quinn said.

'Ralph, go get your flashlight,' Siegman told Bookman. 'We'd better take a look at this mess.'

'My light's enough,' Quinn said.

Bookman got one out of the patrol car anyway and they all started into the cemetery.

'Had one of these grave robberies when I was about ten,' Siegman said as they walked. 'Old man Landers ... you remember the Landers family, don't you, Randy?'

'Don't recall them, no, Chief.'

'Yeah, well, the old man got buried with his pocket watch, a real antique. His grandfather had it in the Civil War.'

'They dug him up for a watch?' Bookman asked. Siegman turned and nodded.

162

'Probably worth a few thousand today at least. Sloppy job. They didn't bother closing the coffin. It rained that night. What a mess.'

'Sounds like a Halloween prank,' Bookman said.

'You don't go to graveyards on Halloween, right, Randy?'

'That's when graveyards yawn.'

'Huh?' Bookman said.

Quinn paused and turned to him.

'Shakespeare.'

'Oh.'

Scarlet laughed.

'Didn't know you were a scholar, Randy,' Siegman said.

'Only when it comes to graves,' Quinn replied. He glanced back and saw the Kitchen twins were deliberately laying back a good six feet. Evelyn was looking up now, looking in his direction. Had she heard his reference to Shakespeare? He still felt it necessary to impress her.

They all stopped at Kitchen's open grave. Quinn shined his light down at the open coffin. No one spoke for a long moment.

'OK, so there's definitely no dead baby, but you say the jewelry's gone?' Lou asked.

'Ask them?' Quinn said nodding mostly at Stuart Kitchen.

'You can give us a description of it all?'

'Of course, but he's left out a pretty important detail, Chief.'

'And that is?'

'I specifically told them not to dig up my father's grave when Mr Waller called to tell me what Mr Quinn suspected. He did it anyway. Without permission.'

Lou nodded. 'Yep, that's illegal. You should have known that better than anyone, Randy,' he told Quinn.

'I had my reasons to check.'

'Well, you'll tell us all about them at the station. Ralph, you better get the tape. This is a crime scene now,' Siegman said.

'Right, Chief.'

'You find anything unusual around the grave either the first time or second?' Siegman asked Quinn.

'Didn't really look that much the first time, Chief. Saw it had been tampered with and brought out the backhoe.'

'OK. I'll get on the horn, get some forensics out here in the morning.' He looked up. 'No rain in sight tonight. I guess we can leave the coffin as it is.'

'I'd like it closed,' Stuart said. 'You've got animals. Other than human ones,' he added.

'Yeah, of course we'll close it. There's no reason for you to be out here any longer, Mr Kitchen. You should take your sister home. There's plenty of time in the morning for you to follow up the way you want.'

'Oh, I'll follow up,' Stuart said. 'Let's go, Evelyn,' he said nudging her. She turned and started back with him.

'Wrong family to upset, Randy,' Lou said.

He looked at Scarlet. 'You always bring someone to the cemetery?'

'We were heading somewhere else, Chief. I stopped to fax some document to Jack. He had left it behind and needed it for a meeting. I noticed the garage had been tampered with and saw the backhoe had been used.'

'And thought of this?'

'Exactly.'

'How come? You don't have to wait until we're at the station. You can tell me what got you so hot about it now.'

'I hired Barry Palmer for part-time.' He looked at Jack. 'I screwed up and mentioned the jewelry that was down there. Barry didn't show up for work today, but even before that, when I saw the backhoe had been used, I suspected him, suspected the grave had been dug.'

'Palmer? Just recently returned home, didn't he?'

'Yes. We were buddies in high school. I met him at Stacks and offered him a job here.'

'OK.' He turned to Scarlet. 'You have anything to add?'

She looked at Randy and then turned back to Siegman.

'Just that I came close to throwing up a few times. There was definitely a baby down there. I saw him. It wasn't an aborted fetus, either. I can tell you that. The umbilical was cut and tied.'

Siegman nodded.

Ralph returned with the tape.

'What the hell am I going to tie this to?' he asked.

'I got some stakes in the garage you can use,' Quinn told him.

'It's too dark to do much else here,' Lou told Jack. 'Let's have everyone at the station about eight. We'll call the Kitchens after I review it all again. Sorry, I can't avoid it, Randy.'

'That's OK. I'm not running from what I did, Chief.'

'Right. Palmer's staying with his aunt Lily at the old house, I imagine.'

'Yes.'

'She's quite a woman. You know her, Jack?'

'No. Maybe she's not in my social circle,' Jack said dryly.

Lou laughed.

'Look,' Quinn said. 'I'm not saying he's the one who robbed the jewelry for sure. Jack will tell you the Kitchens' had control of this coffin up until the time it was lowered into the grave.'

'What's that mean?' Lou asked, taking the cigar out of his mouth.

Quinn shrugged.

'I don't know absolutely that there was jewelry down there and neither does Jack.'

'Jack?' Lou asked.

'Well, they did insist on their locking the coffin closed before it was returned with Mr Kitchen to the funeral home.'

166

'That so?' Lou thought a moment and looked at Scarlet. 'I suppose you'll suggest that they put a baby in there, instead of the jewelry, huh?'

'I don't have to say it. You did,' Scarlet replied.

They heard someone shout up to them and turned.

'It's Richard,' Jack said. 'My partner.'

'Forensics isn't going to get anything out of footprints here,' Quinn complained, 'with everyone traipsing about like this.'

'That's true. We've seen what we had to see. Appreciate your helping Ralph set up the tape.'

'What's going on?' Richard Valentine demanded. The short run had him gasping. 'Where's this dead baby he claims to have seen? Did you find it?'

'No. Jack can fill you in,' Siegman said. 'We're all meeting at the police station eight o'clock tomorrow morning.'

'There's no baby!'

'There's no baby,' Lou repeated.

'What about the Kitchens?' Richard asked looking back toward the parking lot. 'Neither of them would even say hello.'

'They'll be down at the station some time tomorrow, I'm sure, but probably with their attorney. Might be a good idea for the two of you to have one primed and ready, too,' Siegman muttered and looked at Quinn. 'Ready?'

'Yeah, sure. I'll get you the spikes,' he told Bookman and they started away.

'No need for you to hang around any longer, Scarlet,' Quinn told her as they walked back to the funeral home and garage. 'I'll help him tie off the grave site and then head home myself.'

'I can go with you,' she said.

'I'm not going to be worth a dime to myself, much less you tonight, Scarlet. I'm just going to have a drink and go to sleep. Maybe that'll clear my head.'

Her body sagged with disappointment and she remained silent until they reached the front of the garage.

'I guess I'll see you in the morning then,' she said.

'Yeah, I guess. Thanks for coming.'

She shook her head and grimaced as if he had said the dumbest thing and walked off to her car. He looked after her a moment and then went in to get the spikes for Bookman. When they started back toward the grave, he saw Richard and Jack were still there talking.

'I'm gonna have to ask you to step away,' Bookman told them.

They watched as he and Quinn tied a square around the open grave. When they were finished, Bookman hurried to catch up with Chief Siegman.

'You could have said you found the grave dug up,' Richard told Quinn as they all started back to their cars. 'That way we'd have no legal troubles at all. Maybe he could still say that, huh, Jack?'

'I don't think so, Richard. We called Stuart Kitchen to ask for permission, don't forget.'

'Why didn't you think how this would play out for us?' Richard asked Quinn.

'I did. I thought if I dug it up, found the jewelry still there, I'd fill it in and forget it. No harm done. It was when we saw the dead baby that things went awry.'

'Awry? I don't get it. Why isn't the dead baby there now? Can you explain that?'

Quinn stopped.

'Someone who knew I had dug up the grave and found it arranged for it to be removed while I was distracted. Simple as that,' Quinn said and walked faster.

'Simple?' Richard shouted after him. 'You'd better change your story. You're what's sounding simple here!'

Quinn didn't look back. He locked the garage and headed for his truck. Minutes later he was on his way home. He was feeling guilty about sending Scarlet away so abruptly. Besides the comfort she was hoping to give him, there was no question she was hoping he would do the same for her. It was, after all, a thriving, pulsating nightmare eager to sweep in the moment either of them fell asleep.

The truth, however, as weird as it might sound to anyone else, was that he wanted to be alone to think about Evelyn Kitchen. He was like some teenager who wanted to go home and write her name a thousand times. Despite the weirdness of the baby not being in the coffin, the emotion he felt the most during the whole episode was sympathy for Evelyn Kitchen. He should be thinking about himself. He was in trouble, but beside the wonder of being with her alone in the lobby of the funeral home and having the longest conversation with her that he had ever had, the image of her walking with her head down toward her father's grave haunted him, as well as the look she gave him when they all looked into the coffin and saw no baby.

It made him sick to think she was heading home with the suspicion now that he had stolen the jewelry, that this whole thing had been some sort of ridiculous attempt of his at a cover-up. But what was the truth? Without the dead baby, how could any of this be explained?

When he got home, he flopped in his father's old heavy cushioned easy chair and nearly fell asleep, but it suddenly occurred to him that he had nothing to eat since lunch. It was as if that part of his body suddenly woke up and shouted, 'Hey, what gives?'

Despite the hour, he made himself an omelet, but instead of coffee, he had some chamomile tea. All the work and tension finally settled like a lump of clay in his body and he almost fell asleep eating. His fear of ruminating about the events keeping him awake all night proved to be a paper tiger. When he finally lay down, he practically passed out and didn't wake up until the phone rang. It was already close to eight. He imagined Jack was nervous about him not showing up.

'Yeah?' he said, scrubbing his cheek with his left palm to bring some blood into his face.

'You're a lucky son of a bitch, Randy,' Jack said.

'Not exactly how I feel. What's up?'

'Stuart Kitchen's dropping any charges. Lou called first thing this morning. He only wants the grave refilled immediately.'

'But it's a crime scene.'

'Not if Kitchen's not pressing charges against you or us and doesn't care about missing jewelry.'

'But...'

'There was no baby in the coffin, Randy. Remember? It's over. Get your ass over here and fill in the site, and then thank your lucky stars. Richard has no interest in firing you any more.'

'That grave was...'

'Randy, get over it. There's nothing more to do or nothing more you can do anyway. Just do me a favor, will you. Tell Scarlet to keep this whole thing to herself. There'll be no story now and no bad publicity for us.

Can you do that immediately, please? We have some important business on the front burner and don't need the bad publicity right now.'

He was silent.

'Randy?'

'OK, Jack. I'll speak to her.'

'Do it now before she gets a chance to spread this crap around. It wouldn't do her any good either to get them any angrier.'

'Why?' His full mental capacity slipped out from under the fog of a deep sleep. 'They still believe we took the jewelry?'

'It doesn't matter what they believe. It's over, dead and buried as soon as you get over here and start the backhoe. Get moving. Why are you so sleepy anyway? You were supposed to be here in twenty minutes, as it was.'

'I know. Sorry,' he said. 'I'll call Scarlet and I'll get it together.'

'Good,' Jack said and hung up.

Quinn sat there staring down at the floor. A number of things burrowed into his heart at the moment, despite Jack's declaration of good news. Barry got off with the jewelry for sure. Evelyn Kitchen was now probably convinced that he was a ghoulish thief. And that baby was gone and forgotten. Jack could put it all to bed and pretend none of it happened, but how could he?

He took a deep breath and then called Scarlet. Her mother answered and whether it was his imagination or not, she sounded annoyed with him. It took a good minute for Scarlet to come to the phone.

'Just got my daughter off to school,' she said. 'If you had let me go home with you, you would have had only to roll over in bed.'

'I know. I'm sorry. Listen, Jack just called.'

'I'll be there on time.'

'No, no one has to be there. Kitchen's dropped all charges.'

'I don't understand.'

'Right now, since it's only you and me talking about some missing dead baby corpse, the only illegal acts were my digging up the grave without permission and the theft of the missing jewelry. Stuart Kitchen apparently does not care about the jewelry and thought twice about raising a ruckus over the violated grave. I've got to get up there immediately and fill it in.'

'They'll just forget about what we saw?'

'You saw the chief last night. Did he look ambitious to you?'

'This makes me feel sick to my stomach, Randy.'

'Doesn't help my digestion much either, but what can we do about it? Jack asked me to ask you to keep it all to yourself so there'll be no bad publicity for the funeral home. I don't imagine you've spoken to anyone about it.'

'Just my mother, but she won't talk about it. She didn't even want to hear the story.'

'She sounded a bit cold this morning. I guess she thinks I'm a bad influence now.'

'She'll get over it.'

'Yeah, but will we?'

'I'll do what you want, Randy. If you say forget it, it's forgotten.'

'I didn't say that. I just said don't talk about it.'

'Not hard to do,' Scarlet said. 'Let me ask you this question.'

'Go on.'

'If Stuart Kitchen doesn't care about the stolen jewelry, why did he make a big deal of being in control of the coffin?'

He was silent.

'Well?'

'I don't know.'

'But it's something to think about even if no one else wants to.'

'Like I can stop from doing that,' he said. 'I'll call you,' he promised.

'Good,' she said and hung up.

He made some coffee, stuck a piece of bread into the toaster, took a shower and gobbled it all on his way out to the truck, leaving the empty mug on the back seat.

He had dug this grave twice, he thought as he headed for the cemetery, and he would fill it for the second time, but deep down he had the nagging belief that it wouldn't be the last time.

In fact, he was convinced of it.

ELEVEN

The dreary overcast sky encouraged the depression Randy felt. He had little appetite for any more breakfast. By the time he reached the cemetery, he plodded about the garage like someone with a bad hangover. The frustration he was feeling gnawed at his insides. He felt like he had swallowed a live rat. He couldn't get over the sense of his being violated, but there was nothing he could do about it.

The sound of the backhoe's engine rattled him out of his musings. He cursed under his breath and started into the graveyard. When he reached the open grave, he paused and shut off the engine. Then he dismounted and took down the police ribbon he and Patrolman Bookman had tied around the site. He folded it all neatly and put it with the four stakes, but rather than go right at replacing the dirt and covering the coffin, he studied the ground and then he lowered himself into the grave again.

This was the first time he was looking at it all in daylight, which, despite the heavy cloud cover, was still bright enough to permit a closer look around the coffin. Yesterday, by the time he had decided to defy Jack and Richard, it was already too dark for such an examination. He knew his own boot imprints so he was able to differentiate them from the smaller ones he saw around the coffin. Since this area had all been covered in dirt, there was no doubt someone else had been in this grave and around this coffin after he had uncovered it. He didn't know Barry's foot size precisely, but the footprints looked very much like they could be his.

He probably wore gloves so forensics wouldn't have gotten any fingerprints off the coffin, Quinn thought. He boosted himself out of the grave and studied the ground to the right. It was, despite the grass, easy to locate those same footprints here and there. They trailed off through the cemetery toward the west end. He walked in that direction and found them again at the beginning of the wooded area.

Because of the fallen leaves, it was a little more difficult to track, but years of living on the edge of the woods, playing in them as a young boy, taught him how to look for signs of travelers, whether they were deer, rabbits, foxes or people. The woods on this side of the Sandburg Cemetery weren't deep. After about a third of an acre, they ended at the side of Church Road, a road that led back into Sandburg proper. He saw the footprints in the side of the small bank that ran down to the ditch and then found them again where a vehicle had surely been parked. The whole exploration from the edge of Matthew Kitchen's grave to this spot had taken less than fifteen minutes. He could easily have shown this to the police today if Stuart Kitchen hadn't dropped the charges. For a few moments he stood there looking down the road as if he could somehow still see the vehicle pulling away. He felt certain that vehicle was Barry Palmer's truck.

The short examination only fanned the flames of anger and frustration burning inside him. He marched back through the woods and the cemetery and stared down at the coffin. If he called the police and told Siegman he had proof someone else had been in the grave, Siegman would say, 'So? Kitchen doesn't want to pursue any robbery or anything else.' What could he do about that?

After a few more moments, he shook his head and muttered, 'I'm sorry,' to the dead Matthew Kitchen. He mounted the backhoe and began to fill in the grave.

On his way back to the garage, he saw Jack Waller waving to him. He pulled closer and shut the engine.

'What's up?'

'Ira Elmore keeled over this morning while he was raking the front lawn. His son Gerald just called. You know their family site. We took care of his wife two years ago. He was ninety-four and not sick a day in his life, according to Gerald. Only way that's better to go than Ira's way is to be shot in bed with someone else's beautiful wife.'

'OK. I'll pencil it in for Friday?'

'Yeah, that's right. Oh. Richard thought we should do something about the bushes on the east end.'

'Surprised he noticed.'

'We'll have some government types looking us over in a few weeks. We're looking good for the Morton property. You'll have a lot to do soon.'

'Suits me,' Quinn said. Waller started to turn. 'Jack?'

'Yeah.'

'I know you don't care, but I found footprints from the floor of the grave and tracked them through the cemetery and woods to Church Road. Had to have been made after I uncovered the coffin last night.'

'You're right,' Waller said. 'I don't care.'

Quinn watched him walk off and then he started the backhoe and drove it to the garage. With his rage turning his face crimson, he almost drove the backhoe right through the building. He kept himself busy the remainder of the morning as a way of calming himself. Because he didn't take time to prepare his lunch, he decided to go to Kayfield's in the village and have something to eat.

The small restaurant at the center of the

hamlet was one of the few businesses that had managed to hang on during the economic downturn that hit the resort area once the summer clientele had begun to go elsewhere. All the locals had a variety of theories about it, from blaming cabana clubs on Long Island to the growth of jet travel and the resistance of teenagers to long family holidays. Without any real second industry to take the place of resorts, the businesses totally dependant upon vacation goers began to suffer financial heart failure. Villages and hamlets that were once booming little summer extensions of New York neighborhoods began to look like ghost towns or facades for Hollywood sets after the movie had been shot. Any significant pedestrian traffic basically disappeared. Store windows were boarded and, without loving care and attention, the facades of buildings began to fade. It was as though there were a perpetual gray sky over every Main Street in every hamlet and village.

Kayfield's had survived but had changed owners. Old timers and locals had a built-in adversity to new owners of businesses they frequented. In these small, somewhat rural communities, relationships took time to build and once they were built, they became stuck in cement. Getting used to someone new was a long, battleship-size turn. There was always distrust, but somehow, there was also some willingness or perhaps just curiosity that gave the new owner a fighting chance in the end. It was working for the new owners of Kayfield's, Bob Feld, a forty-year-old man and his wife, Sarah, who looked a bit older. She worked the counter and he did the cooking. They had no children, and from what the clientele could decipher, that was a result of choice and not something medical.

Quinn had been there only three times since the new owners took title. He liked them and thought Bob did a fair job with short order cooking. The three times he was there, he had the ham and cheese melt on a toasted bun with their home-made coleslaw and potato salad. The fifty person capacity restaurant had a little more than twenty having lunch when he entered. You could take a table, but you had to pick up your order at the counter. This was a close to the breast run business, no waiters or waitresses. A sign prominent on the counter read, *Please bring your dishes and glasses back to the counter when finished.* Whenever she had the chance, Sarah ran around the counter to wipe off a table. Whether it was because she and Bob worked so hard, the long hours, or just not wanting to look like a slob, most of their regular customers took care not to mess up their tables and give Sarah more work.

Since there was one seat left at the counter, Quinn slid on to it and ordered what was now his usual.

'You're a man who, when he finds something good, sticks with it,' Sarah said, smiling. She had what Quinn called *a comfort face,* a face with warm, gentle eyes, a soft mouth, and thin, shallow lines. There were no hard wrinkles resulting from frequent smirks or angry expressions. Her complexion was rosy, her voice almost melodic.

She would have made some child a wonderful mother, he thought, and wondered what the real reason for their being childless was. But that wasn't his business. He always believed everyone was entitled to his or her privacy despite how quickly and deeply everyone's personal life was examined in this small community.

'It does the job for me,' Quinn said and she ordered his ham and cheese sandwich platter. Bob waved and added it to his list. Sarah served him a cup of coffee.

Quinn had his back to most of the customers, all of which he knew and knew him, some since he was a little boy. He was too deeply lost in his own thoughts to hear any specific chatter, but when Paul Muffin, one of the township policemen who covered Sandburg in his beat stepped in, the chatter stopped and Quinn, noticing the silence, turned to the door.

Muffin was a career law enforcement agent possibly only two years from retiring and probably becoming a part-time store or school security guard. He was five foot ten and despite his ageing paunch, looked built out of granite. Every line in his face was etched like the lines in a nearly closed palm. He fixed his gray-blue eyes on Quinn and jerked his head slightly to indicate Randy should step out with him. Quinn slipped off the stool as nonchalantly as he could, realizing all eyes were on him. Something like this swept every ordinary topic off the table and gave the locals something exciting to consider.

'What's up, Paul?'

Muffin leaned against his patrol car.

'Chief wanted me to find you. Jack thought you might be over here for lunch.'

'You found me,' Quinn said. Had Stuart Kitchen had second thoughts and decided to go forward with pressing charges against him?

'We located Barry Palmer.'

'Did you? Great, but I thought there was no longer a reason for you guys to look.'

'Didn't look. Coupla city fellas out with bows and arrows for early big game season spotted his truck overturned in the gully below Slauson's hairpin turn in Glen Wild.'

'And Barry?'

'Gone.'

'Gone?'

'Well, not gone like that. Dead. Lou called in state forensics. Everyone's still over there. Point the chief wanted me to make to you was this might be the reason he didn't show at work and not something else, whatever that means. He said you would understand.'

Dead, he thought, and for a moment could think only of Barry's youthful smile in high school.

They both turned to the front door of the restaurant when Sarah stepped out.

'Just want you to know your sandwich platter is ready, Randy,' she said.

'Thanks, Sarah. I'll be right there.' He turned back to Muffin. 'He didn't say anything was found on his body, anything else?'

'That's all I know, all I was supposed to tell you.' He nodded at the restaurant. 'How's the food here these days?'

'Good,' Quinn said. He stood there thinking a moment. Muffin's information didn't clear his mind, even if that was the chief's intent. 'Thanks.'

Even before he re-entered the restaurant, he could feel all eyes were on him, everyone looking for a hint as to why Bob Muffin called him outside. He avoided looking at any of them and went right to his sandwich. Nevertheless, Sid Rosen was at his side. The retired retail dairy owner was the titular mayor of the diminishing hamlet.

'Anything serious?' he asked.

Quinn paused, wiped his mouth and nodded.

'Barry Palmer was found dead. Truck accident. He had just started some part-time work for me.'

'Oh jeez, I heard he had come back.' Sid turned to the anxiously waiting crowd. 'Lily Palmer's nephew was killed in a truck accident,' he announced.

'Where?' someone shouted.

'Where?' Sid asked Quinn.

'Slauson's turn,' he said and that started a new round of talk about that turn and others like it in the area, which recommended one tragic automobile memory after another. Quinn practically gobbled his food to speed his retreat from what was becoming a buffet of morbidity. He paid his bill and hurried out.

After he got into his truck, he sat staring ahead for a moment and then made an impulsive decision and headed out toward the scene of the accident. There were three township patrol cars, an ambulance, the medical examiner's car, a state highway patrol car, and the Carnesi brothers' tow truck, lined up near what was clearly Palmer's truck's departure point. The low wooden border was smashed. One of Siegman's newer officers was keeping traffic moving, not that there was much. He beckoned at Quinn, but Quinn shook his head and pulled to the side.

'I've got to keep this road open here,' the officer whom he didn't recognize said.

'Anyone can get by. Siegman called me,' he added, which was an exaggeration, but one the young officer quickly accepted.

'Figured you might show up,' Lou said, turning when Quinn approached him and the state highway patrolman. The two hunters were off to the side watching the action. Siegman glanced at the patrolman and then stepped off to the right. 'Let's talk about this ourselves. I want to keep my promise to Stuart Kitchen and Jack,' he began. 'There's nothing here to bring that mess into this. I wanted to cut you off at the pass. Don't start some new theories on me.'

'You were down there?' Quinn asked gazing over the edge. Barry's truck was on its roof, the windows smashed.

'Not exactly. I'm past having to climb down slopes like this one and then struggling to climb back up.'

'Well, how...'

'Bookman's down there. He knew what to look for. If he saw anything, he'd know. He signaled there was nothing, no expensive jewelry and especially no baby's body.'

'I'd like to go down there,' Quinn said.

'State medical examiner is on it.'

'I won't get in his way. Look,' he added when Siegman didn't respond, 'before I filled in Matthew Kitchen's grave this morning, I found footprints around the coffin that weren't mine. I followed them into the woods on the east end. Someone was in that grave after I uncovered it. Can't prove it now since I filled in the grave, of course, but I saw the prints around the coffin and they looked like Barry's.'

'Why continue this? You're off the hook, Randy.'

'We saw that dead baby.'

'I'm telling you. There wasn't a baby in that truck, if that's what you're hoping to find.'

'Like to look before Steve Carnesi hooks on to it and drags it back up here.'

'You get hurt going up and down, I'm on the hook.'

'C'mon, Lou. I could run up and down this slope all day and you know it.'

He scratched his head.

'You know it's guys like you that make guys like me work harder, don't you? Go on, if that's what it takes to shut you up.'

'Thanks.'

Without any hesitation, Quinn stepped over the road guard and began a careful descent down the rocky slope. Bookman and the two paramedics looked up and watched him make his way. He did nearly slip once, but caught himself in time and then was able to just step off a large boulder and approach the truck. The medical examiner was inside the smashed cab, working on Barry's body. Barry's arms dangled below the seat, his head lacerated and smashed against the dashboard. The windshield was shattered, but not completely gone. Quinn couldn't get a good view of his face, but wasn't sorry about it.

'You check inside, under the seat, the glove compartment, behind the seat?' Quinn asked.

Bookman squinted.

'For a baby?' he whispered, obviously ridiculing the idea.

'No, for any jewelry.'

'Yeah, Lou told me to check for that. Nothing valuable in that truck. There's a pint of brandy or what was a pint. It's smashed to bits. He wasn't wearing his seat belt. Dr Woods says it might have made a difference, even in a fall like this. Says he's seen people survive worse.'

'You looked all around here?' Randy asked gazing at the immediate vicinity. 'Things can get thrown from the back of the truck when it takes a tumble like this?'

'Yeah, I looked,' Bookman said, but not with the confidence and authority Quinn anticipated. He shook his head and walked a circle, checking the slope and the area around the truck himself. He saw nothing and returned to watch the medical examiner working for a few moments.

'Told you there was nothing,' Bookman said. 'He didn't even hit the brakes up there. No tire marks. Almost looks like a suicide.'

Quinn thought a moment and then shook his head.

'No. He was depressed, but I don't think it was that bad.'

'You never know,' Bookman said. 'Remember that hair stylist all the women loved, the one in Monticello? He wasn't gay. No bad relationships and no financial troubles. Still can't figure that one out.'

'Can you do me a favor?'

'What?'

'Let me look at the bottom of Barry's boots.'

'Huh?'

'That's all I want.'

One of Barry's legs was twisted awkwardly, this foot facing the passenger's side.

'I just want to look at it,' Quinn emphasized.

Bookman looked up at Siegman.

'It's nothing. He won't get upset,' Quinn said.

Bookman shook his head, hesitated and then opened the passenger side door a little more. Dr Woods turned.

'If it's all right with you, Doc, he wants to look at the bottom of Palmer's boot.'

The medical examiner stared a moment and then quickly nodded and returned to his examination of the corpse.

Bookman stepped back and Quinn approached the truck. He leaned in and touched the dirt on the boot sole. Then he brought it to his lips to taste it.

'What the hell are you doing?'

'Confirming something,' Quinn said. 'I know my ground.'

The medical examiner backed out of the

truck cab.

'I've done all I can here. We'll do the rest back at the lab,' he told Bookman. He looked up at the road. 'I don't get paid enough for this. You can signal the paramedics,' he told Bookman.

'There's an easy way up just down the way to the right,' Quinn said. 'C'mon, I'll show you.'

'Oh yeah? Thanks.'

Quinn led him away from the truck.

'Any early thoughts?' he asked.

'Well, he's been dead about fourteen hours. Don't know how much of a role the alcohol played yet, of course, but he has quite a few traumas over his skull and a broken neck among an assortment of delectable injuries,' Woods added. 'Without a seat belt holding him in, he must have bounced around like a ping pong ball. Friend of yours?'

'Yeah. I just gave him a part-time job, too.'

'Oh. Heavy manual labor.'

'No, not really. Raking, lawnmower stuff. Why?'

'I noticed some recent calluses on his palms. Thought it might be result of clinging desperately to the steering wheel. Body will do amazing things when it's facing expiration.'

'You make it sound like a parking meter, Doc. Up here,' he added showing a smooth ascent.

'Well, I supposed we all have a clock running. Only difference is, the ticket you get when this clock runs out is pretty much a permanent fine,' Woods said and they began to climb.

Quinn made his way back over to Lou Siegman.

'Well? Worth the effort?' the chief asked.

'Might be, Chief. Save the dirt on the bottom of Barry's boots.'

'Why?'

'Comes from the bottom of Matthew Kitchen's grave.'

'How do you know that?'

'I know my dirt. It won't be hard for forensics to confirm it.'

'No one's pursuing that, Randy. We're not going to spend the county money on some possible graveyard robbery the family no longer cares to pursue. I repeat, why did you bother checking it out? You didn't find any jewelry or a baby down there, did you?'

'Just call it insurance, Chief. You won't be sorry if you keep that soil. Some day the truth will come out here,' Quinn said and started for his truck.

'I'm not the one in danger of being sorry here, Randy,' Siegman called to him. 'If you keep pushing on this,' he muttered to himself.

Quinn looked back and nodded. He stood a moment and watched the paramedics get Barry's body up the slope and to the ambulance. Immediately after, the Carnesi brothers began the process of dragging the truck out of the gulch.

'Take care, Chief,' Quinn called.

Then he turned and headed back to the cemetery, a place where all things were supposed to end.

Not begin.

TWELVE

Late that afternoon, Jack Waller came to the
garage to find Quinn, who was servicing
some of their machinery and so deeply in
thought he didn't hear him enter and had no
idea how long he had been standing there
watching him talk to himself.

'Hey, Randy.'

He looked up.

'Why didn't you tell me about your friend,
the guy you had work here and suspected
robbed Kitchen's grave?' he asked. 'Lou
Siegman says he informed you as soon as he
could and you were at the scene of the accident looking at the guy's body and the
truck.'

'You made it clear before that you weren't
interested in any of this, Jack.'

'Yeah, well, you're going to love the irony.'

'What irony?'

'His aunt called. Wants to pay for his burial
here.'

'Huh? Why wouldn't she bury him with his
parents?'

'She claims they didn't leave a place for
anyone else. They're at the cemetery in Rock

192

Hill. He wouldn't be anywhere near them, she says. Her exact words were "I'd like Spike's boy to take care of him". Forgot that was your father's nickname. Anyway, one way or another, you got him back here,' Jack said in his characteristically sardonic manner. 'She'd like you to give her a call. Don't forget those bushes,' he added.

Quinn just stared at him until he walked off.

It was more annoying than ironic that he would have to prepare Barry Palmer's grave. He could see himself digging that dirt with a vengeance.

Ordinarily, he would have called Lily Palmer on his own to commiserate with her, but his anger toward Barry hadn't subsided with Barry's death or this news. It lingered inside him like an echo that just wouldn't die. Now, he felt a little guilty about it. Why take it out on the old lady, especially someone whom his father liked and who had liked him?

When he completed his work and called it a day, he went one better than a phone call. He decided to pay Lily a visit and console her in person. His father's fondness for her trumped all other considerations and feelings he had at the moment. Maybe he really was obsessing about all this. He knew he hadn't treated Scarlet as well as he should have.

Like him, Lily Palmer still lived in her

father's house. It wasn't really something uncommon for people in her generation to hold on to family property. Today, of course, people bought and lived in their houses as an investment first and a home second. On the whole, children didn't go through school, find careers and jobs and after marriage inherit and live in their parents' homes. They had their own and for the most part, especially here during his history, moved away, just as Barry had done.

The Palmer's homestead had actually begun with Lily Palmer's grandfather. He had bought property just outside of Centerville and built his house serving as his own general contractor. The house had been expanded considerably by the time Barry and his parents joined his aunt Lily to live in it. Now it was a sprawling eclectic Queen Anne with an attached two-car garage, and a small workshop that had once been a makeshift barn for old man Palmer's half dozen milk cows. He recalled that Barry had wanted to take it over and turn it into his own apartment when he was a teenager, but his father refused to let him, even if he used only his own money and did all the work himself.

Probably his father knew there was something untrustworthy in his son, Quinn thought, something I had missed then and certainly missed now.

When he drove up, he wasn't surprised to see that no one was there visiting Lily Palmer. He was sure most of her friends were long gone, and the news of Barry's death was just settling in the community. People might have called her, but there was no one sitting with her to share the grief.

Quinn thought there was always something stoical about many of the people who lived in the area anyway. Some covered their grief with religious wrappings and talked about the dearly departed going off to a better place, but most seemed embarrassed by any show of emotion, even happy emotions. Perhaps Barry had been gone too long for most to really remember him enough to feel anything more than they might feel hearing about a death on the television news. They'd shake their heads, mumble something that helped them justify immediately forgetting about it and that was that. From what he remembered about her, Barry's Aunt Lily struck Quinn to be like that. He recalled his father calling her a 'pioneer woman.'

She opened the door quickly and smiled at him as if he were making just another visit. There was nothing in her demeanor, her dress, her hair, anything about her that suggested she had been crying, mourning, and wringing her hands after such shocking news about her nephew. She looked perfectly put together and ready to attend church on Sunday.

Quinn knew from his own experiences at the Palmer's home that Lily had played a major role in Barry's upbringing. With no husband or children of her own, she surely must have seen him as her surrogate child, he thought. Barry's parents were certainly willing to abdicate as much of their responsibility as they could.

'Randy,' she said and then stopped smiling and shook her head as if she had just remembered what would bring him to her home. 'What a horrible thing.'

'Yes. I came to see how you were,' he said. 'Jack Waller told me you had called him.'

For now he thought it better that she did not know he had visited the scene of the accident while Barry's body was still in the truck. He didn't want her even to get an inkling of what he suspected.

'Come in,' she said stepping back.

The air was rich with the aroma of some sort of chicken dish. He remembered now that she was the one who did most of their cooking. Barry's mother, who died a year or so before his father had died was something of a barfly, working in the Kentucky Club in Centerville as a bar waitress and keeping late hours if not there then at other bars after work. His father had been a hard-working truck driver for a wholesale plumbing outlet. During their teenage years, Quinn felt a special kinship to Barry because of their both being only children.

As soon as he stepped in, he looked around. Although the house reeked of time,

196

looked worn and tired, it was still quite well kept. He wondered how she could manage it. Everything in the living room on his left looked neat, not even an opened newspaper lying on the sofa or an empty glass on a table. Memories came rushing back as though all the intervening years that had dammed them up had rotted and were easily washed away. It took only a few seconds in the house.

'I haven't been here for some time,' he said nodding at the brass teardrop chandelier above him and at the living room, 'but it looks unchanged, Miss Palmer.'

'I didn't give anything away and I haven't bought all that much since you were here last. Everything is an antique like me,' she said. 'Come in. Have a seat. Can I get you something cool to drink? I have some fresh lemonade.'

'Oh, don't bother.'

'No, no, it's times like this when you want to be bothered,' she said. 'Go on. Sit. I'll bring us each a glass,' she insisted and went to the kitchen.

He entered the living room slowly, gazing at the artifacts he vaguely recalled, like the Chinese vase and figurines Barry's father brought back from his stint in the army. He remembered the oil painting that hung over the fieldstone fireplace, too, a print of Andrew Wyeth's Christina's World. He and Barry used to stand in front of it and make up possible stories about the girl and why she looked so thoughtful. Barry's ideas were invariably raunchier than his.

'So when did you hear?' Lily asked when she returned with the glasses of lemonade.

He sat on the sofa and took one from her.

'Thank you. About twelve thirty, I think.'

'Explains why he never came home last night,' she said sitting across from him. She smoothed out the skirt of her one-piece light-yellow dress and crossed her legs.

She's no thinner than she was twenty years ago, Quinn thought. Age has yet to take a bite out of her. Her soft, ash gray hair was pulled back gently and pinned. She wasn't a bad looking woman, stately in some ways, with a nose that was a little sharp perhaps and a thin tight mouth. Her lips still that tinted orange that matched her fair skin. There were some light freckles dotting the crests of her narrow cheeks, but no age spots blotched any part of her face.

'When did you say you last saw him exactly?' he asked and sipped his lemonade.

'Oh, like I told you when you called me, Randy, late in the afternoon that day you said he was working for you. I told you that he didn't stay for dinner and he knew I had prepared something for us, but that was like him when he was younger, too.'

'You had no idea where he went? I thought he was pretty tired.'

'He didn't say and I wasn't going to ask.

198

He was just very nervous and excited. When Barry grew older he was like that more and more, you know, keeping to himself. Even as a child when something was bothering him, you had to pry it out of him with a crowbar, and believe me, there were plenty of occasions when I threatened to take one to him literally. I was the only one who could get that boy to admit to doing something mischievous and clean up after himself.'

Quinn smiled. Despite her dainty, ladylike manner, he believed Lily Palmer still had the grit to chase off a stray dog or even bully a bear into fleeing from her refuse pails.

'What did the police tell you?' he asked wanting to see if there was anything more to know. He drank some more. It was damn good lemonade, perfectly sweetened so the tartness remained in good proportion, just the way he remembered it here.

'Not much. He went off the road at Slauson's turn and the truck toppled. I asked them if he was drunk and they said they didn't know much more yet, but I got the feeling they did. The officer who came by brought me his things,' she said nodding at something to the rear and right of Quinn. He turned to look and saw the clothes and what looked like Barry's wallet and cell phone.

'Oh. Mind if I look?'

'Of course not. There's not much there to look at, however. I went through his pockets. Nothing except a slip of paper with a phone number. Don't know whose it is,' she said.

He rose and went to the table.

'You're sure he didn't come home after some time at night?' he asked as he looked at Barry's wallet and then plucked the piece of paper off the table.

'If he did, he was quieter than air coming and going and remade his bed as well as I did,' she said. 'That boy could sleep on sheets with blankets months old. "You're a born hobo," I'd tell him and he'd smile and nod as if I was telling him something good about himself.'

Quinn smiled.

'Yeah, that was him,' he said. Then he gazed at the phone number. It was a local number. A thought came to him and he turned to Lily again. 'Mind if I check his cell phone. I thought he might have called me that night.'

She shrugged.

'Cell phones. Never had one, never will,' she said.

He flipped it opened and turned it on to find there was still battery life. Then he scrolled to recent calls and saw the same number that was on the piece of paper. Barry had called it once and whoever it was had called him too, all happening last night. He turned it off and closed it, but he kept the piece of paper in his hand. Then he returned to the sofa.

'Poor Barry,' Lily said, finally showing

some emotion. She dabbed at her eyes with a frilly linen handkerchief. 'Despite his faults, he was always a polite little boy. He didn't do too well in school, but he wasn't in trouble like some. I remember that you were a good friend and a good influence on him, I'm sure.'

She paused and took a deep breath.

'When he returned, however, he was quite different. I could count on the fingers of one hand how many times he smiled.'

'He was pretty unhappy down in Texas, I guess. We went out together the night before he came to work for me and told me about his uncle losing his business and the trouble with his wife.'

'Uncle losing his business?' she asked.

'Yeah, some tax problem.'

'Oh. Charlie, my sister-in-law's brother, but that was ... let me see ... at least three, maybe four years ago.'

'Really? But I thought Barry was working for him up until recently.'

'Not Charlie. Charlie died last year. Emphysema. He was a heavy smoker. Nearly set this house on fire once, falling asleep with a cigarette in his hand.'

'I don't understand. What was Barry doing recently in Texas then?'

'Texas? Oh, he left Texas year after he got married. He and Chi Chi or something ... a Mexican girl he met down there ... were living in Arizona. You know the story about that disaster?'

'I'm not sure now. Tell me,' Quinn said.

'She was fooling around and got pregnant. It wasn't until her ninth month that Barry decided to return here. I thought he had told you all about that.'

'Not in that sort of detail. He was with her into her ninth month?'

'That's what he told me.'

'Well, what happened?'

'He left her and came back. I guess he would have been better off if he had stayed and been father to some other man's child.'

'He did say his wife was pregnant with another man's child, but he didn't say she was in her ninth month when he left her,' Randy said really talking to himself more than to Lily Palmer.

'Don't know why he stayed with her that long once he found out what she had done,' Lily said. She looked at her watch. 'You're welcome to stay to dinner, Randy.'

'No, I got things to do, thank you. As I said, Jack Waller told me you had called and...'

'Well, I just thought it would be nice if Barry was in your hands now. You know what I mean.'

'I have to tell you, Miss Palmer, it's considerably more expensive in Sandburg Cemetery. The whole package, even a streamlined one, will be twice if not three times the cost as it would almost anywhere else in the area.'

'Oh, the money's not important now. I have more than I need, but thanks for caring,' she said.

He nodded and rose.

'You don't remember what his wife's name was really, do you? We should probably let her know anyway, don't you think?'

'You think so? Even after what happened?'

'Maybe they were still technically married.'

'Well, maybe, I suppose. I have a card from them. Just a moment,' she said and went out to the kitchen again.

He returned to the table behind him and looked at the cell phone again. Perhaps he should go through all the numbers, he thought. Lily returned.

'I wasn't off that much. Her name's Chiquita. Here's the envelope with their address on it.'

She showed him a birthday card. He nodded and looked at the envelope. It had come from a street in Surprise, Arizona. Lily hadn't gotten that wrong.

'Would you mind if I borrowed Barry's cell phone for a while? His wife's number might be on it or numbers that would lead me to her faster. Lots of people don't have land lines any more, just cell phones.'

'Oh, I have no use for it. Keep it. Here's the charger,' she said.

He took them. Another thought came to him.

'Barry slept in his old room, I bet,' he said.

'Oh yes. Nothing was changed there either.'

'I spent a lot of time in there. Mind if I look at it for old time's sake?'

'No, no, of course,' she said. 'You know where it is. I have to check something in the stove.'

'Thank you.'

He climbed the stairs and went to the first room on the right. Barry's aunt was right, he thought. Nothing looked any different. He could close his eyes for a few moments and then open them and see himself and Barry back in high school, coming back to this room to talk.

He walked into it, glanced at everything and then went directly to the dresser drawers. He checked every one before looking in the closet, even checking the pockets of garments, old pants and old jackets. Finding nothing, he looked under the bed, under the mattress and pillows.

Of course, he could have easily hidden jewelry anywhere on this property. He left the room and found Lily was waiting at the bottom of the stairway.

'Bring back old memories?' she asked.

'And how.'

'That's probably why I keep everything the way it was. I like living in the past these days, if you know what I mean.'

'More and more, I do, Miss Palmer. Thanks for the lemonade. I promise I'll make sure Jack does a top job for you taking care of Barry.'

'Poor soul. I always felt sorry for that boy. Thank you, Randy. See,' she said, 'the longer you live, the more trouble you'll see.'

He nodded.

'But it's better than the alternative,' she added and he smiled.

She followed him to the door and thanked him again for stopping by. The sound of the door closing behind him reminded him of closing the lid of a coffin. She was just as alone in there as some departed soul. Maybe she kept company with ghosts he thought as he went to his truck.

He had no trouble figuring out why Barry would have lied about his past. He was probably down on his luck for much longer than he had made out and covered up for it by saying his uncle had just gone out of business, but there was something more about his wife that intrigued him, his wife and that baby. If he had told his aunt Lily the truth, Quinn couldn't help but wonder why he would have stayed with his wife that long? Was it simply the shame of revealing his wife had strayed on him?

He had come here still burning with anger toward Barry, but he was leaving feeling more sorry for him than anything else. People don't always lie to get away with something they had done wrong, he thought. Sometimes they lie to keep their dignity, or whatever of it was left.

When he arrived home, he saw he had a message on his answering machine. It was on a counter in his kitchen. Usually, he didn't check first thing, but he did so this time. It was Scarlet.

'I just heard about Barry Palmer. How weird. What do you know about it? Was there anything found on him? You know what I mean. Every time I see someone with a baby, I see what we saw in Kitchen's coffin,' she added.

He nodded as if she were standing there and then sat to think for a moment. Except for him and for Scarlet, this would all go away very soon. Surely neither Jack nor his partner Valentine wouldn't bring it up again. He felt confident of that, and Lou Siegman would file it all away in some storage cabinet the way some people buried unpleasant or annoying memories.

I'm not a trained detective, he thought, and I have no personal interest in the matter beyond my own unspoken promise I make to anyone I bury, but, as corny as some might see it, there is also an obligation to that dead baby. The others could ignore it because they hadn't seen it. Scarlet was right. It wouldn't fade away easily. Maybe it never would.

By telling Lily Palmer he felt they should call Barry's wife to tell her the news, he had gotten her to find Barry's wife's name and their address. He had to follow through on that first, he thought, and turned on Barry's cell. There were at least three dozen numbers with the Arizona area code. Information service might be faster, he thought and called the long distance operator, which turned out to be some automated voice. He smiled to himself remembering how his father had lived long enough to experience some of this and how he would just hang up, swearing he would never talk to a machine and pretend it was human.

Nevertheless, he gave the computerized voice Barry's name and address and the automated voice brought back a number instantly with the added codicil that for fifty cents it would be instantly called. He opted for that and waited as it rang. A woman answered and he knew she was a Latino as soon as she did.

'Chiquita Palmer?' he asked.

The voice rattled off something in Spanish and then there was a moment of silence.

'Hello?'

'Hello, who is this please?' a male, also with a Latino accent, asked in decent English.

'My name is Randy Quinn. I'm calling for Chiquita Palmer, Barry Palmer's wife. There has been a bad accident here involving Barry. I'm in New York, upstate.'

'What accident?'

'Well, is Chiquita there? I'm afraid I have

some bad news to give her.'

'Who is this?'

'I'm one of Barry's old friends from high school.'

'He was in an accident?'

'Yes.'

'And he died, I hope.'

'You hope? Who are you?'

'I'm Chiquita's brother, Gabriel. My sister is not here no more. She's dead, too. You want to know why?'

Randy was silent. He could feel the rage flowing through the telephone lines. He didn't have to say yes. Chiquita's brother was eager to tell him.

'He took her on the road in her ninth month. Somewhere in Kansas late at night, she gave birth, but she hemorrhaged and she died. It was in his truck. He made her give birth in the back of his truck. You bring us the only good news we've had this week,' he added.

Randy quietly digested the information and then had another quick thought.

'What about the baby?' he asked.

'The baby died, too. You hear that crying behind me? That's my mother. Some of her tears are tears of joy now. *Gracias*,' he said and hung up before Randy could ask another question.

He held the receiver away from his ear as if he thought something painful might come flowing through it. Then he slowly returned it to the phone cradle. Bizarre, nightmarish scenarios began to flow through his mind. It was like being tied to the seat in a movie theater showing gruesome horror films. The suspicions seemed to form in the base of his stomach first and then come up like rotten acid into his throat. He stood up quickly, glanced at the phone and stepped away.

No, this is too weird, he thought. Never, during all the time he had worked in cemeteries did he suffer from any macabre visions or grisly dreams. Somehow, it was always just work. Maybe he had been born with a love of the earth or maybe he did feel more like an artist than a laborer, but graves just weren't the beds of loathsome, gross or hideous thoughts. He didn't envision worms and cadavers. He saw only the beauty of a final resting place.

But this was very different. To sustain such a suspicion, he would have to accept that someone he had thought he had known reasonably well would be so twisted and crazed he could carry a dead infant with him and then deposit it in someone else's coffin. Maybe he had begun to feel guilty and saw this burial in a rich man's coffin and grave as redeeming. If Quinn were to follow this train of thought, he would have to believe that Barry was so angered about his wife having another man's child that he literally kid-napped her to go on this cross-country journey just when she could go into labor, and when she had, he saw her suffering as justice and let her die in the back of his truck, perhaps not anticipating the baby would die as well.

'Never underestimate the grip revenge can have on someone,' his father once told him. 'A person's real spine isn't part of his skeleton. The real spine is ego. Strike that and you've unleashed the caveman inside.

'And don't listen to that old chant, sticks and stones can break my bones, but words can never harm me. Words are often sharper than knives, especially when they're spoken in front of an audience. Nothing more makes it better than the feeling of getting even, getting even with someone, even getting even with God.

'It's just the way we're built. It's why my father used to say, turn the other cheek and they'll slap that one, too. Cover up and slap back.'

Quinn could hear the words clearly. Maybe he was getting cabin fever, but he'd swear his father was standing right there.

He checked the time and then shot out of the house and got into his truck.

It wasn't until he pulled into the parking space in front of the town police department that he remembered he hadn't called Scarlet back. Maybe he'd stop at the diner. It was too late to make himself any dinner, and it would be better to see her than speak on the phone.

Only, he wasn't going to tell her any of this.

He cared for her too much, and besides, he was already responsible for too many of her bad dreams as it was. Why add a nightmarish horror scenario like this?

THIRTEEN

'What's really driving you like this, Randy?'
Lou Siegman asked.

'Don't you even wonder why we would lie
about seeing a dead baby in the coffin,
Chief?'

Siegman sat back and looked up at the ceiling, squinting as if he was hoping for some
response to be printed up there.

If you get to the point where you'd rather
look for the easy way out of doing your job,
Quinn thought, then isn't that time to leave
it? Dare he say it? It was on the tip of his
tongue and he was angry enough to do so,
but waited a moment more.

'Let's say your horror movie theory is right
and he did carry a dead baby back with him,
and he did bury it in Kitchen's coffin. How
would he know to return to take it out again
just before you got there to show the Kitchens, Randy? And even if we could prove he
did all that, he's dead now. What am I supposed to do, serve him a subpoena in hell?'

The chief held his palms out and turned
up.

'You know we didn't find any jewelry on

him or in his truck. In fact, he had less than one hundred dollars on him so you can't even say he was able to fence it quickly.'

'I'm not interested in the jewelry right now.'

Siegman leaned forward.

'Oh boy. Try to get this through your thick skull. It's over. No one has called about a missing baby. It's not important whether I believe you and Scarlet about this. If you reported a murder, and we investigated and couldn't find a dead body anywhere, in a coffin, in a house, on a street, whatever, and no evidence of violence like blood and no one reported missing or hurt, we'd behave the same way. What else could we do?'

He sat back again and shrugged.

'I wish I could have somehow corrected all the wrongs I've seen over the years, but some were just impossible to change and not worth the effort anyway. We live with it. Life's imperfect.'

As if he hadn't heard a word, Quinn countered.

'It could have all been just coincidence. Maybe he returned because he had second thoughts and saw I had dug up the grave so he got the baby out.'

Siegman shook his head.

'Second thoughts? Why would he suddenly have second thoughts? You mean, a surge of conscience?'

'I did call his aunt to try to reach him. He

knew I was looking for him. Maybe he thought I realized he had dug up the grave, and, as I said, returned and saw that I had. It's one thing to be accused of digging up a grave to look for jewelry, but it's a helluva lot more to explain a dead baby.'

'But if he saw you had, he'd know you saw the dead baby already.'

'Exactly, but you weren't there yet. It took quite a while because of the complications with Stuart Kitchen, so he made his move and the result was exactly what we have ... disbelief and who knows what the hell else?'

'What the hell else? What are you saying?'

'I heard Stuart Kitchen infer that I might have taken his father's jewelry and gone through all this to cover up for it, as ridiculous as that would be because no one could know what was or was not in a coffin six feet down.'

'Nobody has formally accused you of anything.'

'They didn't have to do it formally, but it still hangs out there.'

'I doubt that he'd spread such a story, Randy. That would bring attention to the whole thing and he clearly wants to get it off the front page. Otherwise I'd be filing the paperwork on you for illegally digging up a grave.'

'I'm not here to talk about Stuart Kitchen. I came here to tell you about Barry Palmer. Did you do what I asked and have the dirt on the bottom of his boot saved?'

Lou sighed deeply.

'You didn't, did you?'

'I did, damn it, just in case you came around making a stink or something.'

'That's good, Chief.'

'Good? It's good? OK,' he said. 'Let's say you're right about everything. You can show the dirt matches the soil around Kitchen's coffin and more. Now what do I do? You want me to go over to the morgue and question him?'

'Of course, not, but...'

'But but. There's no but. Go home, will ya, Randy.' Siegman looked at his watch. 'I'm missing House reruns and the rate I'm going, I'll need all the medical information I can get.'

Quinn leaned over Siegman's desk.

'I'm no cop, Chief. I'm no priest. I'm just a glorified day laborer. Never went to college, don't read as much as I should and don't go to church since my parents passed, but I don't distinguish between what we owe the dead and what we owe the living,' he said, rose and started out.

'All right,' Siegman called after him. 'I'll see what I can find out about Barry Palmer's wife's death and whatever if that will shut you up.'

Quinn turned back.

'Thanks. That's all I came to ask you to do,' he said and left, but he didn't feel as if

215

he had won any victory. He felt a lot like Sisyphus in the Greek myth, cursed to forever push a boulder out of a hole, his own grave essentially, only to have it roll back every time he reached the top.

He went directly to the Centerville diner. At first he thought Scarlet was off, but then she stepped out of the kitchen, saw him and waved. The diner was crowded. He had only a stool at the counter available.

'What makes tonight so special?' he asked her as she came by with three dishes for a couple and a child at a booth.

'I don't know. But I'm glad I'm busy. Can't think too much that way,' she said and continued on. He looked at the menu and ordered the turkey roast dinner with a bottle of beer.

For a while he watched her work, admiring how quickly she moved and satisfied her customers. You can tell a great deal about someone from the way he or she worked, he thought. They didn't have to be in love with the labor like he was, but it meant something if he or she didn't wholly resent it, fight it and telegraph that to customers or clients. Since work was so much a part of life, it would mean he or she hated so much of their lives, and in Quinn's experience, when someone hated themselves that much, they made life unpleasant for everyone around them, even those whom they loved. He suspected that might have been true in Barry's case.

Scarlet wasn't a flaming beauty, but she had her feet solidly on the ground, he thought. Why wasn't that enough to put her on a pedestal as high as the one upon which he had placed Evelyn Kitchen? Who could he blame for that failure of judgment beside himself?

Scarlet didn't have another spare moment until he was nearly finished with his own dinner and had just ordered a cup of coffee.

'I called and left you a message,' she said.

'Yeah, I got it and decided to stop by instead of trying to reach you on the phone.'

'So what do you make of this thing about Barry?' she asked, sliding on to the empty stool beside him. 'Was he running away? Was he drunk?'

'Don't know yet. The investigation is still ongoing. There was whiskey in the truck cab and no sign that he tried to stop. No tire tracks.'

'Well, have you heard anything at all? Did they find anything in his truck or on him?'

'There was no jewelry and he didn't have very much money on him. And no baby's body anywhere in the vicinity of the accident, but the investigation isn't complete yet. They're still doing the forensics.'

'How do you know?'

'I was there,' he said.

'There? Where? The accident?'

He nodded.

'How come? I mean, how did you find out about it so quickly?'

'Siegman sent Bookman to find me to tell me. I think he just wanted to drive home that there was no jewelry on him or any baby corpse in the truck. Of course, he could have dumped it anywhere along the way to feed wild animals.'

'Ugh,' she said. She looked down for a moment and then shook her head. 'I guess we should try to forget it.'

He sipped his coffee. Maybe he was just being too considerate, but it bothered him that he was withholding what he knew could be part of the answer, the facts that he had learned about Barry and the treatment of his wife. It seemed unfair to hold out on Scarlet. She had invested herself in this almost as much as he had now.

'I'm looking into some possible explanation for all this,' he muttered. 'I have some ideas.'

'What?'

'Let me see if there's any validity to anything before I add to your nightmares.'

'Thanks for that,' She said. He nodded, happy she accepted his excuse. 'My mother's not feeling well so I got to go right home,' she said. 'Not that you asked me to do otherwise.'

'You didn't give me a chance,' he replied smiling.

'Woman's intuition. You look like you want

to hold on to your space tonight.'

'Well, if she gets better, just come on over,' he said, 'and invade some of that space.' She laughed.

'Wouldn't you be surprised?'

Before he could respond, she was off and running again to take another order and finish up what she had. The truth was he did want his own space tonight. It was difficult being with her and not telling her everything anyway. He couldn't imagine he would be anything like good company, and, in the end, she'd pry it out of him and he'd be even sorrier about it than she would be.

She had another break and followed him out to his truck when he was ready to leave.

'You gonna be all right?' she asked.

'Me? You're the one we have to worry about.'

She smiled, kissed him, gave his arm a gentle squeeze and headed back into the diner to finish her work. He stood there watching her for a moment through the diner's windows. She's really a jewel, he thought. If he could put all this aside, maybe he could settle down with her and begin to have a real life. The sadness these thoughts laid on him made him feel twice his age.

He got into his truck and drove home, mumbling to himself.

He did try to forget it all by following her formula: work, work, work. He went after the bushes the next day and then began the preparations for the Elmore funeral. That grave would be dug before Barry's. There was also still a lot of raking up to do and some grass trimming. He was well into it when Jack came out to have him walk the new parcel of land with him. There was a great deal of clearing to be done.

'So this is really a done deal?' he asked.

'Long as nothing scandalous interferes,' Jack said pointedly. Quinn felt certain Jack knew about his conversation with Siegman. 'If we can only put our troubles to rest as easily as we put those who die to rest,' he added. He didn't have to say much more. Quinn got the point.

Late in the afternoon, only minutes before he was getting started to clean up to prepare to leave, his cell phone vibrated on his hip.

'This is Randy,' he said.

'You can close the book on Barry Palmer,' he heard Lou Siegman say. 'The police report includes both the wife and the baby.'

'Yes, I knew they were both dead, Chief. What we wanted to know was...'

'He didn't drive here with a baby corpse, Randy. His wife and baby were sent back together and yes, somewhere in Arizona you might find a mother and a baby in the same coffin. There was a police investigation of the incident and no charges were levied against Palmer, except the charge of stupidity. Now what? You gonna leave me alone so I can trickle down to retirement or what?'

'I saw a baby in the coffin,' he repeated in a tired, defeated voice. 'We both did.'

'You know what, Randy. You're digging your own grave now. Give it up,' Siegman said and concluded the call.

Quinn flipped his phone closed and looked out across the cemetery toward Matthew Kitchen's grave. The afternoon was waning, the fall night pressing down on the sun like a bully pushing a smaller kid's head underwater, but he knew where Kitchen's site was located and didn't need much light to visualize it. It seemed to be haunting him now, but maybe that was all in his overworked imagination. Maybe Siegman was right. Maybe I'm digging my own grave, he thought, but he asked himself who was better to do it?

It's what I do for a living, he thought, the irony of digging his own grave not lost on him.

He recalled his father telling him about the Rileys, a childless couple who bought cemetery plots and actually set up their tombstones with everything engraved except for the date of their deaths. They had no confidence in any relative or friend doing it for them properly. His father said he had seen them from time to time visiting their own site.

'It was as if a part of them was already down there, Randy,' he said. 'Maybe they thought they had to cry for themselves as well. That, my boy, is what I call being alone.'

What about me, he thought? I'm not close with any of our relatives and I'm still un-attached. Who would look after me? Maybe I should do what the Rileys did, but he thought his father was right. That was the ultimate act of a lonely person. He wasn't ready to give up on himself just yet.

After he put everything away, he went into the funeral home to get some water and then just sat a while in the chapel. Jack was gone for the day. There was a stillness and a peacefulness in here that he thought really was special. He could go into other empty rooms, but not feel what he felt here. Too many tears had been shed in this room. Too much grief stained the walls for it to be just another empty room. It echoed with whys and goodbyes. No church sanctified it, but it was a sacred place because of what hap-pened in it periodically. The icons could be changed or completely eliminated as it had been for a few truly non-denominational funerals, but it still held on to its sacred ambience.

Whoever that baby was that he and Scarlet had seen mattered even more because he had never had a funeral. Even some primi-tive ceremony would have been better than simply being discarded like spoiled fruit. He wasn't going so far to think like some strict Catholics that if he hadn't been baptized, he couldn't get into heaven. He didn't know all that much about babies, but Scarlet was pretty certain that he was too big and developed to be some aborted fetus, and she had pointed out the umbilical cord had been cut. He was now convinced that someone had gone through a birthing and the baby either died or...

He sighed, stood up and then walked out to the lobby. As he started to turn off lights, he paused and then dug Barry's cell phone out of his pants pocket. He flipped it on and located the recent calls. Yes, no jewelry had been found on him or in the truck, but what if Siegman was wrong and Barry had fenced it that quickly? The money could be tucked away somewhere on the Palmer property. It didn't matter that he found nothing in his room. Barry knew where to hide things in the old barn for sure.

This number could be related to all that, he thought, as he looked at it. It was a lead, wasn't it? With or without Lou Siegman's blessing, he could at least tie up this part of the theory. And if he did find the jewelry, that might open up the investigation concerning the dead baby whether Stuart Kitchen liked it or not. Jack's words were resonating, however. 'If we could only put our troubles to rest...'

He sat, stared at the number and then hit the redial. It rang nearly four times. He thought no one would answer and then he heard her voice.

It wasn't only his recent conversation with her that enabled him to recognize her voice. Along with every part of her face, her hair, the way she sauntered through the school, even the scent of her perfume when he was close enough to smell it, had all remained in his memory as vividly as any of his remembrances. She was always there, the dream girl, someone to idolize and against whom to measure any beautiful girl he had seen or had spoken to ever since. Even poor Scarlet was bathed in her shadow, and when he made love to her, at times he would imagine Evelyn Kitchen in his arms, her lips pressed to his, her breath in his mouth.

'Hello?' she said again. 'Who is this?'

He couldn't speak. He flipped the phone closed. Why would Barry have called the Kitchens? If he had the jewelry, he wouldn't call them to sell it back to them? What he might do, Quinn thought, was blackmail them after he had seen the baby in the coffin.

It was Scarlet who had put the idea into his head that all this had originated with the Kitchens. He didn't think of that as quickly as she had simply because he couldn't get himself to think of anything this gruesome involving Evelyn. Of course, Stuart was credible as the engineer of anything ugly or evil. That was possible, very possible.

He left the funeral home and got into his truck, but again he just sat there for a while thinking. What he should do is bring the cell phone over to Siegman and lay out another theory about the baby. Of course, without any infant's body, he would be back where he had started and then worse of all, Stuart Kitchen, further enraged, would return to pressing charges against him and suing the cemetery. What would he have gained and what would he really have proven? Jack and Richard would surely fire him then to boot.

'Barry made a call to the Kitchens?' He could just hear Lou Siegman ask and add, 'So what? It doesn't prove anything in and of itself. I'm going to have to get a court order to keep you away from me.'

He started his engine and drove out slowly. He changed direction and made the turns without any purpose other than to look at her house. As he drove, he asked himself what he was doing. Get hold of yourself. Put an end to this. Twice, he slowed down to turn around, but kept going instead.

Of course he had seen the Kitchens' beautiful house before, but he had never been in it. There were occasions during that high school period when he had such a deep, unrelenting crush on her that he would find any excuse to drive past the property and sometimes stop across the road to gaze at what was, for this area of upstate New York, a fairyland mansion.

It was, in fact, a replica of a traditional Georgian style mansion. It had a central pavilion with pediment and bold pilasters as well as Palladian windows that crowned it. The large cupola above it gave the house a stately look. There were scroll decorated dormers and bold cornices. The house had an east and west wing connected by smaller segments called hyphens. There was a large courtyard entrance.

The Kitchens' magnificent home had been built on what Quinn knew was an almost one hundred and twenty acre property with nearly an acre and a half's length fieldstone front wall boarder and a scrolled hammered brown iron gate. The house was high enough on the crest of the property to be completely visible from the road. Matthew Kitchen was not one to hide his wealth and accomplishments.

Quinn knew the Kitchens had riding horses. Off to the right was the stable and a circular riding track for practicing. Twice when he had come up here, he had seen both Evelyn and Stuart riding toward the rear of their property. From what he could see, she rode with much more confidence and agility than her brother, who looked like he was hanging on for dear life.

The Kitchens had permanent staff for the house and the maintenance of the grounds. He had heard estimates of six to ten, including two maids, a cook and a house manager. The tiled driveway curved a little to the right on approach and then curved a little to the left on return. The area in front of the house for parking was cobblestone. When he slowed down to pull over about a thousand feet or so from the main gate, he counted at least three dozen Pickwick driveway lanterns along the driveway, all now lit and flickering like torches.

Just to the left of the house was a small man-made pond with stone benches around it, and scattered throughout the front of the property were fountains and statuary. The front of the house was awash in light and there were lights near the fountains and benches as well. When someone came to visit or make a delivery, they would have to pull up to the box in front of the gate and push the button to ring the phone inside the house. He saw there was a video surveillance system as well. After announcing themselves, someone from within pressed a buzzer and the gate was opened. No one could enter without feeling as if they were about to access royal property. An invitation to a Matthew Kitchen party was akin to being invited to the governor's mansion as far as people in this community were concerned.

'What the hell am I doing here?' he muttered to himself and then, just before he was about to drive away, saw a car coming down the driveway. He recognized their Mercedes sedan when it passed through the gate. There was enough light for him to see that Stuart Kitchen was driving. He turned to the right and disappeared around a turn.

Along with most of the other guys in his class, Quinn had always had an almost organic distaste for Stuart Kitchen. He wasn't ugly or deformed, but somehow the mere sight of him or his close presence filled him with disgust, even before all this had occurred. No matter what the other students said about the Kitchens, however, he could not tar Evelyn with the same brush and especially couldn't do it now. He was confident that she knew nothing about whatever had gone on.

Impulsively, he put his car in drive and approached the access box in front of the gate. He thought a moment and then he pressed the button.

A woman responded, but it wasn't Evelyn. It had to be the Kitchens' house manager, Alice Chapman. He had helped his father dig her sister's grave more than fifteen years ago. He remembered that she was a tall, thin woman, probably now in her early sixties. He knew she had been with the Kitchen family for more than thirty years and was as loyal as a mother. As crazy as it would sound to anyone, Quinn had collected trivia about the Kitchen family ever since he had first set eyes on Evelyn.

'Yes?'

'I'd like to see Evelyn Kitchen, please.'

'Who is this?'

'Randy Quinn.'

'Did you have an appointment?' she asked. He nearly laughed aloud. Appointment? What was she, a dentist? The most any other servant would ask would be "is she expecting you?"

'No.'

'One moment please.'

It was longer than one moment. It was practically a full minute, but Evelyn herself came on the intercom.

'This is Evelyn,' she said. 'What can I do for you, Randy? Why do you want to see me?'

'I have some things to tell you about this whole mess,' he said.

'Oh, well, my brother isn't home. He had an appointment and...'

'I'd rather speak with only you anyway.'

She was silent a moment.

'He dropped all charges,' she said. 'You don't have to be concerned any further.'

'It hasn't anything to do with me, Evelyn. I won't take up much time,' he added. 'But there are things I feel you should know.'

Again, there was a long pause. He worried she had simply hung up, but then she came on.

'OK,' she said and he heard the gate buzz. It started to open.

He took a deep breath and then started through the gate, but he was trembling like a young school boy about to have his first experience with a girl.

He drove slowly up to the house and parked. There was a ten step marble staircase approach to the front door which opened before he reached it. Alice Chapman was standing there. She didn't look much different from the way she looked at the cemetery nearly fifteen years ago. Some women are old before their time, he thought, but don't seem to age beyond it. If she recognized him, she didn't show it.

'Right this way,' she said stepping back, her voice crisp and overly formal, he thought.

People who had been invited to the Kitchen home did speak of the inside of it as if it were truly a castle. Whenever he heard anyone mention being inside, he would listen carefully to his or her descriptions of the furnishings, the decorations, curtains, paintings and statuary as well as the expensive European tiled floors and Persian area rugs. He knew quite a bit about building materials, lights and fixtures. The chandelier above his head in the wide entryway was surely imported and easily cost ten or more thousand.

Despite all there was to look at, his attention was drawn immediately to Evelyn Kitchen as she descended the circular stairway. She was wearing a long, flowing red velvet robe. Her hair was down around her shoulders. For a moment the sight of her took away his breath. She did look like she was floating.

'Let's go into the drawing room,' she said.

He nodded, glanced at Alice Chapman, who looked almost angry, and then he followed Evelyn. He thought the room resembled a room in some museum. There was little to suggest it was ever used. Red was the dominant color, from the area rug to the red striped Damask sofas to the crimson curtains. Evelyn nodded at a chair and took the sofa. She glanced around as if she had never been in the room before either.

'My father liked to identify his rooms with colors,' she said. 'That chair is an original Chippendale. His background was English and he went about tracking down their various homes in London. It was his hobby, I guess. Maybe it was more. It was an obsession. So?' she said. 'What have you come to tell me, Randy? What's become so important?'

Her little introduction had mesmerized him and for a moment, he had almost forgotten why he had come.

'I really felt very bad about all the things that were said around your father's grave that night,' he began. 'I think you were almost as uncomfortable about it as I was.'

'I was, but I told you my brother can be very high-strung. I appreciate your coming to tell me how you feel,' she added, but made it sound as if that was the sentence before good night. He thought she was about to stand up.

'That's not why I came,' he said quickly.

'Oh?'

'I don't want to belabor it, but I did see a dead baby in your father's coffin.'

She nodded and then shrugged.

'You told the police, Randy. What more can you do about it?'

'I was hoping you'd be more upset.'

'I was very upset, but we looked inside the coffin and there was no baby there, Randy. I certainly can't do anything more and frankly, I'm glad there was no baby in there. If it's any consolation, I do not believe you took anything from my father's coffin. So, if this is about your need to defend yourself, don't worry about it.'

Her reaction and her demeanor were disappointing him. He was hoping to find her far more interested.

'Then you have no idea how a baby would have gotten into the coffin?'

'Of course not,' she said. What softness had been in her face quickly dissipated. 'How could you ask me such a question?'

'I'm sorry,' he said quickly. 'It's just that logically ... if the baby was placed in the coffin, it would most likely have happened between here and the funeral home. Your father's casket was brought here and your brother said he would seal it here. I'm assuming when it was lowered into the grave, it was sealed. Right?'

'I think you had better go now,' Evelyn said

rising. 'I'm glad my brother isn't here. If he were...'

'Look, I'm sorry to say these things. You know I felt guilty about mentioning the jewelry to Barry Palmer, who had just begun working for me.'

'Yes, I do, but you've said enough about it, Randy. I don't think I want to talk about the jewelry or Mr Palmer or...'

'Did you know he was killed in a truck accident?'

'Who? Barry Palmer?'

'Yes.'

She lowered herself back to the sofa.

'No, I hadn't heard.' He didn't think she was lying. 'When did this happen?'

'Some time during the night we were all at the cemetery.'

'I see. Well, I imagine that if the police had found anything, they would have phoned,' she added. 'My brother certainly would have mentioned it.'

'No, there was nothing in the truck or around it. I went to the scene of the accident and looked for myself.'

'Oh, so that ended any investigation of him, I'm sure.'

'Any official one, anyway. Not that there ever was any vigorous investigation. However, I went to visit his only living relative here, his aunt Lily, after I had learned of Barry's death. Do you know her?'

'No. I mean, I knew of the Palmer family,

but my brother and I never had anything much to do with Barry when we were in school.'

'The police had given her Barry's things. One of the items was this cell phone,' he said, drawing it out of his coat pocket. 'It wasn't damaged in the accident.'

She simply stared.

'I was looking through his recent calls because I knew he had been married and thought we should contact his ex-wife.'

He turned on the phone.

'He actually never got a divorce,' he continued, 'and according to his wife's brother, he was taking her with him across country. She was pregnant. He had told me he had left her as soon as he had found out she was pregnant with another man's child, but he apparently lied to me about that. He never left her. Maybe he was ashamed. He took her on a trip when she was in the final days of her pregnancy and she gave birth on the road.'

He paused as if that should have impressed her as much as it had him when he first heard it.

'And?' she asked without any note of excitement or interest.

'She gave birth in his truck.'

'Really?'

'She died and so did the baby.'

'How tragic.'

'At first I thought maybe he had brought

the dead baby with him and put it in your father's coffin.'

'Oh, my god. Is that what happened?'

'No. Thanks to me, the police finally checked it out and both the baby and mother's bodies were sent back to Arizona. Or at least that was what we were told.'

She shook her head.

'I'm sorry. You thought you had it all solved. I understand. This has been a horrible roller coaster ride for you. As you might imagine it has for us too, so...'

'However,' he said, standing, 'I called the most recent phone number on Barry's cell phone thinking it might belong to the person he had gone to in order to fence the jewelry he had taken from your father's body.'

He held it out open so she could read the little screen.

'And?' she asked gazing at it.

'You answered,' he said.

FOURTEEN

Evelyn continued to stare at the phone for another long moment and then looked up at him.

'That was you who called then? But you didn't speak. Why not?'

'I didn't know what to say. You can imagine how surprised I was to hear your voice.'

She nodded. Of course, with the little contact he had with her all these years, it wasn't easy to read her face, but he saw nothing in it to indicate anything more than surprise.

'I have no idea why he'd call here, Randy.' She thought a moment. 'Let me see that again.'

He handed her the phone. She nodded to herself.

'Would you mind if I kept this to show Stuart? He's not very fond of you at the moment and wouldn't believe me if I told him what you said or showed me. He'd question whether or not this was really Barry Palmer's phone. I'll ask him about it later tonight,' she said standing. 'I'm sure there is some sort of logical explanation and believe me, it would be better if I do the asking. He's

236

been high-strung ever since this started, and you know, undeservedly of course, he's placed most of the blame with you.'

'Yeah. I'm sure I fell off his guest list. The thing of it is, Evelyn, if Barry had, as I firmly believe, dug up your father's grave and open-ed the coffin, he would have seen the dead baby, too. I mean, now that I know it wasn't his wife's dead baby.'

'And you think he called here for ... what?'

'Maybe to blackmail you or your brother or both of you,' Quinn said.

'What? Blackmail us? I can't believe you're sitting there telling me you think we put a dead baby in my father's coffin, Randy. I don't even want to ask you how you think that baby came about. Can we end this? I said I would ask Stuart about it and show him the phone.'

'At this point I don't know what to think. I did want to come to you first and show you the phone. I don't want you to think I believe anything bad about you, Evelyn.'

'Thank you for that. Leave me your phone number. I have a pad and pen out in the entry way. I'll try to get some answers for you and get back to you tomorrow.'

'I don't mean to cause any more trouble for you,' he said. 'I can appreciate what you are going through, but...'

'I'm not sure you do or you wouldn't come here asking these questions, Randy. But I do understand what you've gone through so I promise to see about this,' she said holding up the phone.

She walked him out to the entry way and handed him the pen and pad. He wrote both his home phone and cell phone numbers. She took it and opened the front door for him.

'Look, it means a lot to me that you believe me, Evelyn, and don't have any thought of my having taken your father's jewelry, of course.'

'I don't believe that for a moment,' she said. Her hard expression softened into almost a smile. 'Anyone who is going through all this trouble to do what he thinks is right couldn't possibly be a thief and especially not someone who would steal from the dead. I'll call you with an explanation, I promise, and then I'll return the phone to you.'

'Thanks.'

There was so much more he wanted to say to her, but the words were like valuable jewels inside him themselves, and he knew this was not the time or the place to spend them. He had already blundered too much. He gave her a quick smile and walked out. She stood in the doorway and watched him go to his car. He waved. She nodded and closed the door.

As he started down the driveway, he wondered what he had accomplished. Evelyn had seemed genuinely surprised and at a loss to explain Barry Palmer's calling them. He regretted saying what he said about a baby in the coffin, but her reaction had convinced him she was innocent. She could have easily become very angry at his confronting her with the information and the proof. Of course, the insinuations hung in the air between them, but she was as calm about it as she was about anything. Now, he almost resented himself for bothering her.

How beautiful she had looked in that velvet robe. Any great artist would be motivated to capture her on a canvas. She was so elegant, so gentle. To him she was the personification of innocence and serenity. She looked like she belonged in that house, belonged in a castle. He had the urge to call her and apologize and tell her to forget it, toss the phone. He hoped he hadn't upset her and ruined her evening.

Was she preparing to go out? Perhaps she was seeing someone who was not from the area, a successful lawyer or businessman from New York City, someone like that. Surely, she didn't keep herself locked away in that mansion despite her revelation of loneliness. She was bright and intelligent. She had to be interested in traveling, going to shows, and going out to eat. It didn't matter that anyone he knew never mentioned her. Why would they know anything about her? No one he knew moved in her circles or could afford to attend the functions she and her brother surely attended.

After visiting her in her mansion on the crest of their property, a gated estate that to most people gushed its opulence and wealth, he felt like someone who indeed had been granted an audience with a princess. A part of him rejoiced in it, but another, more sensible part of him chastised him for permitting his schoolboy fantasy to blind him to what might be some horrible truth. Perhaps she was simply covering up for her brother and for her father.

His father never had to tell him to grow up or be more responsible. If anything, he would nudge him gently with a statement like, 'Open your eyes a little wider and a little longer, Randy.'

'Open your eyes,' he muttered to himself and drove on just as his cell phone rang. These roads were unlit and there was intermittent traffic to pay attention to so he pulled to the side and answered.

'Quinn,' he said.

'I thought I might hear from you today,' Scarlet said. 'Sorry I couldn't invade your space last night.'

'Yeah, me too,' he said.

'But you left me hanging with the possibility you had something else that might explain all this business with Barry Palmer. What's up with that?'

'I'm still following up on it. I think I'll be closer to an answer tomorrow. How are things with you?'

'I'm doing OK. The chief was here tonight with some man who looked like he could be a CIA agent or something.'

'Oh c'mon. I'm sure there's more going on than our graveyard mystery?'

'Siegman asked me how long you and I have been seeing each other.'

'Did he?'

'He made it sound very nonchalant, but his questions gave me a creepy feeling.'

'Questions. What else did he ask?'

'He asked if I had known Barry Palmer, for one thing. What were they after?'

'I don't know.'

He really didn't know or understand. Siegman had given him the clear impression he had no reason or desire to follow up on their story or Barry any more.

'Maybe I'm being paranoid.'

'No. It's understandable. If he comes back to ask anything else, let me know.'

'I'm leaving work early tonight. My mother is still not feeling well.'

'Oh, sorry. What's wrong?'

'Her back's been kicking up so she's on some meds and I don't like leaving her alone with Stacey when she's half out of it.'

'Understood. I'll call you tomorrow,' he told her.

After he ended the call, he headed for home. All sorts of questions were whirling around inside him; not least of all was why

Siegman had obviously gone to the diner to ask Scarlet questions. What was going on now? Did it have something to do with the missing baby? Had he found out something more about Barry Palmer?

The more he tried to unravel from all this, the more twisted he seemed to become within it, he thought. He was out of his league, reaching into areas beyond his expertise. Now he was positive that it had been a mistake to confront Evelyn with the phone. He should have done what he had first considered to do, go with it to Siegman regardless of how he might have belittled it. At least he would be able to comfort himself in the knowledge he had done what was right. After all, he was just a cemetery manager. He was no Sherlock Holmes.

He didn't anticipate Evelyn's phone call early in the morning, but he did expect it before noon. He had left her his cell number and kept the phone close, especially when he was working machinery and he might miss hearing it ring. Just before he broke for lunch, it finally did.

But it wasn't Evelyn Kitchen.

'Randy, Lou Siegman,' he heard.

'Yeah, what's up?'

'I need you to stop in the station.'

'When?'

'Right now.'

'Why?'

'We've got some questions for you,' he

242

said.

'About what?'

'Barry Palmer,' Siegman said. 'I figured you might be breaking for lunch. Can you come by?'

'Yeah, sure,' Quinn said. 'I'll be there in about twenty minutes.'

'Good,' Siegman said and hung up before he could ask anything else, but he felt good about it. His persistence with Siegman must have begun to pay off in some way. His tone of voice was different. He sounded more serious, even, should he dare think it, respectful, more formal like someone who was taking him seriously.

He was glad Jack wasn't around. He didn't think it would be too wise to let him know he was still on all this. Before he could run into him, he got to his truck and started out for the police station. After a little less than twenty minutes, he parked and walked in. Michele Williams, the dispatcher, moved instantly when she saw him enter. She knocked on the Chief's office door to announce his arrival. Michele had been a year behind him in high school and although he never had thought of her as someone with whom he could have a romantic relationship, she was a pretty girl and one of the few who were friendly and pleasant to him, unlike most of the others.

'Go right in,' she said.

'Thanks, Michele. How have you been?'

'Good, thanks, Randy.'

'How is your family?'

'They're all fine, thanks. Both my boys are in the junior high already.'

'That's great,' he said and headed for Siegman's office. As soon as he stepped in, he paused. The police chief wasn't alone. A tall, well-built man with short dark-brown hair sat across from his desk. He looked at Randy keenly without smiling. This must be the guy Scarlet thought was a CIA agent, he thought.

'Hey,' Siegman said standing up. 'Great. Thanks for coming so quickly. Have a seat,' he added nodding at the empty chair beside the man. 'This is Lieutenant Beck from the State Bureau of Criminal Investigation Unit.'

Beck gave him a slight nod.

'Really?' Quinn asked, impressed. A thought jumped to the top of the list. 'You guys found a dead baby's corpse?'

'No, no dead baby, Randy,' Siegman said.

'No dead baby? So then ... what's up? Why did you call me back? You found Kitchen's jewelry?'

'No, not yet.'

'Then what...'

'When did you last see Barry Palmer?' Siegman asked.

Quinn looked at Beck who was staring at him as if he were looking at something under a microscope.

'You mean before I saw him in the truck?'

'Yes.'

'I told you. I hadn't seen him since he left work that day. He didn't report the next day. The last time I saw him was when you saw him in the truck, dead.'

'But you were convinced he had dug up that grave,' Siegman continued. 'You were convinced he took Matthew Kitchen's jewelry off his corpse.'

'Are you kidding, Chief? If anyone knows that, you do. The last time I was in here, I asked you to save the dirt on the bottom of his shoes. What is this? Why have you asked me to come?'

'Was the robbery of one of the graves you had prepared really what made you so angry or did you want your share and were upset because he wouldn't agree to give it to you?' Beck asked.

The question came at him unexpectedly the way a pros-ecutor in a courtroom might ask a witness a question to stun him or her into revealing an important truth. Beck had a deep unusually resonant voice, the sort you might hear on the radio or on television behind commercials.

'Huh? What the fuck kind of a question is that? I'm the one who forced Jack to call you, Lou,' he said. 'Remember?'

'Jack never said you forced him.'

'Encouraged him, all right. What is this?'

'What if you helped Barry dig up that grave first? Helped him take the jewelry and then

245

when he took off with it and cut you out, you brought your girlfriend to the cemetery, pretended you realized someone else had dug it up, that someone being only Barry Palmer?' Beck asked. 'Barry had skipped with it and not given you your share. You were angry,' Beck said and shrugged as if it were so obvious, a child could see.

'That's nuts. If I had the police catch Barry, he'd implicate me, too, wouldn't he?'

'Who'd believe him? He was running off with it.'

'You would apparently. You just asked the dumb question, didn't you?' Quinn shot back.

'All right. Let me give you another scenario. More important perhaps, the jewelry is no good to anyone unless it's fenced and fenced jewelry has a tendency to announce itself often. You didn't realize how loudly this stuff would announce itself until after you two took it off Matthew Kitchen. The back of the watch read, *To MK from Governor Thornton*. Jack Waller said he never told you that. Only he and Curt Marcus knew about it. Once you saw that, you realized how dangerous it would be to fence it, but Barry didn't care. He was putting you at risk so you snitched on him.'

Quinn looked from Lou to Beck. He was familiar with all the players, even all the details. How long had he been on this? What had caused this new, intense investigation so quickly?

'It was a very expensive watch, Randy,' Lou Siegman said. 'Stuart Kitchen told us it had a street value of close to seventy-five thousand dollars if it were shopped out to fencers. That was about half its real value.'

'He wasn't wrong. It might even have fetched more,' Beck said.

'So if Kitchen told you that, why did he drop all charges and not have you pursue the theft?'

'That's another thing altogether. I don't even know how to begin to get into the Kitchen family issues,' Siegman said.

He looked from him to Beck and back to Siegman.

They really are considering me to be a suspect, he thought. Why?

'What about the baby Scarlet Moore and I saw in the coffin? Did you explain all that to him?' he asked nodding at Beck.

'I told him,' Siegman said with a smirk.

'Smoke and mirrors? Is that what you guys think?'

'There's a lot of confusion here, Randy. You promised Jack Waller you wouldn't mention the Kitchen jewelry to anyone,' Siegman said ignoring any reference to the baby. 'And according to you, first chance you get, you do.'

'I made a mistake. It was after a little too much partying the night before, and I trusted Barry to keep it to himself.'

'As I understand it, you hadn't seen him for years,' Beck said. 'And had no contact with him at all before he returned. Is that right?'

'He was just about my best friend in high school.'

'High school is a long time ago. I have no contact with anyone in my graduating class, matter of fact.'

'Not hard to see why,' Quinn said.

Beck almost smiled and then grew serious and intense again.

'Speaking of smoke and mirrors, you had the chief here follow up on some wild theory about that ghost baby, supposedly born dead on the road, Barry Palmer's baby.'

'First, it wasn't a ghost baby. Stop saying that. We saw it,' he said, raising his voice. 'Second, it wasn't Barry's baby. His wife had an affair and got pregnant. I told you all this, Chief. What I asked the Chief to do was logical considering the possibilities. You wouldn't have done it otherwise, Lou.'

'You were pretty much a pain in the ass. I thought it was the quickest way to get you off this.'

'So what the fuck is going on here, Lou? Why am I being questioned by a BCI investigator?' Neither of them replied. 'I've had about enough.'

They stared at him a moment and then Lou Siegman leaned forward.

'We don't have the sophistication for an

investigation like this so we call upon the BCI whenever something like this occurs. They have the forensics and the experience.'

Quinn pressed his arms to his side and turned up his hands.

'Something like what? You don't believe us about the baby.' He looked at Beck. 'You guys investigate grave robberies?'

'When it involves murder,' Beck said.

'Murder? Whose murder? Matthew Kitchen was murdered?' he asked quickly.

'No,' Siegman said. He looked at some papers on his desk. 'The full medical examiner's report was completed. Barry Palmer was struck in the right temple by a heavy, blunt object like a hammer. In fact,' he added, looking at the papers, 'they've centered in on a claw hammer.'

'Hit in the temple?'

'Yes and died before his truck went through the guard rail at Slauson's turn and down the slope into the gulch. Forensics can tell when traumas occur after death so there wasn't all that much confusion even though there were multiple body injuries because of the truck turning over and him not wearing a seat belt.'

'Did you use a hammer from the cemetery garage?' Beck asked.

'What?'

'The BCI team is over there examining your tools, Randy,' Siegman said.

'I don't understand. Why have I become

the number one suspect?'

'You have possible motive,' Beck replied. 'And we don't mean your act about taking the violation of one of your graves as a personal affront, although I won't completely discard it. I don't know what crawls under your skin. You could have believed Barry Palmer dug up the grave and took the jewelry. Maybe he said he didn't do it and you knew he did and the confrontation resulted in his death. Maybe you decided not to share the booty. Maybe you're sharing it with this girlfriend and the two of you came up with the dead baby story. Think she'll stick with it? She's in the other room with one of my interrogators.'

'You called Scarlet in, too?' he asked Siegman.

Lou raised his hands.

'The BCI have taken this over, Randy.'

'Maybe you'll save your girlfriend's ass,' Beck said.

'Maybe you're an asshole.'

Beck shrugged.

'Maybe, I am. But it's my asshole job to follow the motives and the leads.'

Quinn looked at Lou Siegman. He was buying into it, he thought, completely. He sat back. He thought he had better tell all he knew now.

'I just came from the Kitchen mansion.'

'Why? Beck asked.

'Earlier, I had visited Barry Palmer's aunt

Lily,' he said speaking only to Siegman now. 'She showed me Barry's stuff you guys brought her. One item was his cell phone.'

'So?' Beck followed.

Quinn closed and opened his eyes. He had hoped to get the answers himself and spare Evelyn Kitchen any discomfort. In his mind all the answers lay with Stuart.

'I looked at the phone and checked his recent phone calls because I suspected he might have tried to fence the jewelry. There was one local number called and someone from that phone called him the night you were at the cemetery investigating after Scarlet and I reported the dead baby,' he told Siegman.

'I repeat, so?' Beck asked.

'I took a shot and called the number on his phone. Evelyn Kitchen answered. I didn't say anything to her. I just ended the call, but I decided to follow up on it. I went up to their house and saw Evelyn Kitchen. Her brother was out. I showed her the phone and the recent call log and she said she would ask her brother about it.'

'Let me see the phone,' Beck said.

'I don't have it. I left it with her.'

'What are you suggesting that proves, Randy?' Lou asked.

'I don't know exactly. I thought it was very odd for Barry to have called the Kitchens,' he said. If he expressed some of his or Scarlet's theories, Siegman might totally discard anything else he said, especially after following the dead end on Barry's wife and baby.

'Maybe you scooped up that phone because you knew it would show his calls made to you and you to him,' Beck said. 'How you two planned all this.'

'He never called me and I never called him on his cell. Everything happened too quickly. Matter of fact, he never gave me his cell phone number. Here's my cell phone,' Quinn said digging it out of his pocket. 'You can check to see if I made any calls to him from it.'

Beck took the phone.

'Even if you erased it on here or made the calls from your home phone, we can find out, you know,' he said.

'Be my guest.'

Beck put his phone aside on Siegman's desk.

'I will. Thanks.'

'Look, just call Evelyn Kitchen, Chief. She'll confirm I was there and left Barry's phone with her.'

'We'll do that,' Beck said. 'But I'm still not sure of how that supports you in any defense.'

Quinn looked at Siegman.

'You back to accusing the Kitchens of putting a baby in their father's coffin?'

'Looks like anything I say will be ridiculed here.'

'Most of what you say cries out for ridicule,' Beck said.

'What now?' Quinn asked. 'Am I under arrest?'

Siegman looked first at Beck and then at him.

'Not at this time,' Lou Siegman said.

'However, we'd like you to wait in another room until I get the cell phone and we're finished with Scarlet Moore. It would save you having to come back,' Beck said suddenly sounding very reasonable and accommodating. Beck looked at his watch. 'We can send out for something for you to eat. Chief?'

'Sure. What would you like, Randy?'

'I don't want anything. Just go through this charade as quickly as you can.'

'We don't do anything quickly, Mr Quinn. We go through it thoroughly,' Beck said. 'You can be certain of that.'

'Contrary to what you might think, that makes me confident that you'll be owing me an apology.'

Beck shrugged.

'I never apologize for doing my job.'

'Sounds like something a good Nazi would say,' Quinn retorted.

Beck's face finally reddened. He stood up.

'I'll look in on Mrs Moore. You can show him the room in which to wait, Chief,' he said and started out.

'It's Ms Moore,' Quinn told him. 'She's divorced.'

Beck held the door open and smiled.

'Very good. You see how important it is to be thorough,' he said and left.

'I'm sorry, Randy,' Siegman said. 'But this is the way it's falling out right now. If you have anything more to add that would make it easier for both you and Scarlet Moore and her family...'

'I've told you the truth, Chief, and so has Scarlet. I'm cooperating because I know you're off in the wrong direction and will soon realize it,' he said and stood.

Siegman nodded and rose.

'Right this way,' he said and led him to another interrogation room that had only a desk and chairs. 'Sure you don't want a sandwich, something to drink?'

'Some water, thanks.'

'OK,' Lou Siegman said.

When he closed the door, the empty room and its accompanying silence came down like the hammer that had struck Barry Palmer's temple.

He sank to a chair and stared at the blank wall. A moment later, Michele Williams stepped in with a bottle of water and a plastic cup. She avoided his eyes and put it on the table.

'Thanks,' he said.

'You're welcome,' she replied as she quickly exited.

Just being a suspect already had made him a pariah with someone he had known and had known him for years, he thought and suddenly felt sorry for everyone ever arrested on suspicion of anything.

He poured some water in the cup, sipped it and then sat back with his arms folded across his chest.

How the hell did I get in this situation? he asked himself. And what about poor Scarlet being interrogated in another room? If he had only ignored Matthew Kitchen's grave and not become so indignant about it having been violated. His own son didn't care. What had he accomplished? In this case, opening that grave was really like opening Pandora's Box.

It was nearly forty minutes later when he learned just what more misery Pandora's Box had unleashed. Both Beck and Lou Siegman came in and without speaking sat across from him.

'So?' he asked.

'I didn't need to get the cell phone from her to learn that those calls were made,' Beck began, but he produced the phone anyway. 'Evelyn Kitchen contacted her brother about it. Wasn't too smart on your part. The guy's really pissed and,' he said looking at Lou Siegman, 'is coming in to press charges now for your illegally digging up his father, as well as declaring the jewelry stolen.'

Lou nodded.

'I'm afraid I will have to formally arrest you on that charge, Randy.'

'I don't care about that. Why did he say Barry called him?'

'He says Barry told him you had taken the jewelry, but he could get it all back for a price.'

Quinn looked at Siegman.

'I had taken the jewelry? That's bullshit. If he was told that, why wouldn't he have wanted the grave dug up then when we said we suspected the jewelry was stolen?'

'He had turned that request down before Barry called,' Lou said. 'Jack Waller told you Stuart Kitchen didn't want his father's grave disturbed only on the basis of your suspicion about jewelry that was already gone as far as he was concerned. It was six feet under, wasn't it?'

'But if I stole it, why would I have tried to get him to approve digging up the grave?'

'Possibly to show him it was missing so that when Barry called him, he'd believe him and pay to get it back,' Beck said.

'But Kitchen didn't do that, did he?'

'No, you killed Barry before he could,' Beck strongly suggested.

Quinn felt the sweat building on the back of his neck.

'Evelyn said nothing to me about that when I called to tell them what we found in his father's coffin. What about that?' Quinn asked. He hated the sound of his own voice now. He did sound a little hysterical. 'If I knew there wasn't any dead baby in there, why did I have everyone come to look?'

'To me it looks like part of your smoke and mirrors scheme. You came up with that, sent Chief Siegman checking on a woman and baby's death, everything and anything to keep the focus from falling on you.'

'That's nuts.'

'What's nuts is claiming there's a baby in a coffin,' Beck said. 'I think your girlfriend's going to realize that before you do.'

'Does Evelyn Kitchen believe this?' he asked Lou.

'We've only been talking with Stuart,' he said. 'What difference does that make, Randy? At this point you're the only one with any motive to do harm to Barry Palmer. He wasn't here long enough to piss off anyone else.'

'I spoke with his aunt,' Beck said. 'You made a point of searching his room when you paid that condolence call, didn't you?'

'So? I already told you, told the Chief, told everyone that I thought he stole the jewelry. I thought I might find it.'

'Did you?'

'If I did you'd know it,' Quinn said sharply.

Beck smiled.

Quinn shook his head.

'You're so fucking wrong, it's embarrassing to think you're the expert.'

'Really.'

They stared at each other like two hungry wolves.

'By the way, speaking of Scarlet, she was surprised about the story you brought me concerning Barry's wife and baby,' Siegman said to break the tension. 'You didn't tell her about the cell phone either. How come?'

'I didn't want to involve her in any more of this mess.'

'Does that mean she wasn't part of the conspiracy you and Palmer worked up to embezzle money from Stuart Kitchen?' Beck asked.

'Fuck you,' Quinn told him.

Beck shrugged.

'Two hammers from your garage at the cemetery fit the description of the type of hammer used to kill Barry Palmer,' he said. 'They're in the hands of forensics right now. We also are in the process of getting a warrant to search your home and the tools you have there. I don't think this will go on much longer, do you?'

Quinn took a breath, looked away and then at Lou Siegman.

'I think I should have a lawyer,' he said.

'First smart thing you have said,' Beck commented. 'Chief, read him his Miranda rights now that we're going to make things formal,' he added.

'What about Scarlet, Chief?' he asked Siegman.

'You mean, Ms Moore?' Beck asked with a smile. 'As soon as she owns up to the baby story being a fiction, we'll let her go home.

That will be the start of the collapse of your house of cards.'

He rose and walked out of the room.

Quinn turned to Lou Siegman who reached into his top pocket where he kept his copy of the Miranda statement and began to read it.

FIFTEEN

'Hey, Randy,' Cornelius Blocker said as he came into the room.

When the fact that he would need a lawyer settled in, Quinn immediately thought of Corny Blocker. He often read about him in the local paper. His father's firm was a highly respected one and Cornelius was cited as one of the most promising young attorneys in the Tri-State area. But the presence of a lawyer felt like that famous final coffin nail. There was no longer any denying that this was really happening.

Corny put his briefcase on the table and sat, brushing back the loose strands of his light-brown hair. He kept it shorter on the sides than Quinn recalled, but still let those strands float in a wave in front. He looked tanned, healthy and successful. Never a great scholar, Quinn wished right now that he had been more like him. People who do honest labor, even those who make out very well doing it, always seem to need the scholars one time or another, he thought. Lawyers, doctors and accountants were as much in their lives and as necessary as a good hammer and saw.

'Thanks for coming so fast,' Quinn said, actually surprised that he had.

'I make a special effort for fellow high school grads. So, what's this all about?' he asked. 'I mean I spoke with Sally Anderson, the assistant D.A., before I came in, but I want to hear it all from you.'

Where do I begin? Quinn wondered and decided to start at the beginning, when he had first heard the Kitchens talking to Jack about the jewelry they wanted buried with their father and then he brought it up to date, leaving out his feelings about and concern for Evelyn Kitchen. Corny listened, took some notes and then sat back.

'I was at the Kitchen funeral,' Corny said. 'My father couldn't be there so I attended for the firm, but I didn't hang around for the actual burial. I hadn't heard anything about the jewelry. No one was talking about it, and you could be sure they would have been.'

'Yeah,' Quinn said. Hearing that didn't cause him to feel any better. It emphasized his own mistake, confiding in Barry Palmer.

'I remember Evelyn well and Stuart, too. Can't imagine him stepping into his father's shoes. Never liked him.'

'Join the club. He was always an arrogant, snobby son of a bitch.'

'I wasn't all that much different from him sometimes,' Corny said smiling.

Quinn nodded.

261

'Yeah, but the difference was, you had some justification. He didn't.'

Corny laughed and folded his hands on the table.

'OK. First things, first. They can hold you tonight if they want, but let me see if I can get them to let you out. They have no hard evidence with which to pursue the theft of the jewelry. The one charge they've filed and will book you on involves illegally disinterring a coffin. The only time my father's firm had any experience with something like that involved teenage vandalism. Grave robberies aren't something we see often, at least around here, and certainly not often enough for a judge to deny you bail, especially with your motives. It sounds to me like you were just being overzealous and Stuart Kitchen is just being his usual horse's ass self.

'But I have to admit,' he added, 'that the story about a dead baby in the coffin makes you...'

'Makes me what?'

'Well, right now, I don't know what to make of that, Randy. According to Siegman, there's no report of a missing child and no one but you and a woman you're seeing, Scarlet Moore, saw any evidence of one at the site.'

'I don't care what they say. It was true. Scarlet Moore and I both really saw it. Someone took that baby out before we got back there.'

Corny stared at him a moment. Quinn sat back and tried to calm down quickly.

'Let's look at it this way,' Corny said. 'At the moment they don't have any real evidence connecting you to the grave robbery or the death of Barry Palmer. So let's stick with the one charge, illegal disinterment.'

'They won't stick with that. That state cop, Beck, said they were getting a warrant to search my property and the garage at the cemetery.'

'So what? You don't have anything to hide, do you, because if there's something you should be telling me, you should be telling it at the start of this, Randy.'

'No, I have nothing hidden at my home, but I don't like the idea of strangers traipsing through my father's house,' Quinn said. 'I don't care what they do at the cemetery garage. I'll fix it.'

'Well, let's see if we can get you out of here before they do too much damage. I'll speak with Siegman and Sally.' He rose.

'You never asked me outright if I had anything to do with Barry's death,' Quinn said.

'First rule for a good defense attorney is to assume your client is innocent until proven guilty, Randy. If you were going to confess to anything, chances are you would have done it already. We don't know each other that well. I remember you in high school. You were what? Two years behind me?'

'Yeah.'

'Well, my dad seems to know every family within a hundred square miles. I told him about you and he said you were a good bet. Let's see what I can do.'

'Thanks. Oh, if you can, can you see what they're doing with Scarlet Moore? I feel bad about her being dragged into all this. It was just her bad luck to be with me when I realized Barry had dug out that coffin.'

'Bad luck for both of you, it would seem. I'll check on her,' he said and left.

Quinn sat there, still feeling too stunned to think. It was all happening so quickly now. Overnight he had gone from a good whistle blower to a criminal. A few days ago, his biggest worry was a leaky bathroom faucet. Now, his frustration and rage churned up so hard and heavy inside him that he wanted to pound the table, get up and charge out of here. He hated to imagine what the disappointment in his father's face would have been like. How could he have been so stupid as to blunder into something like this?

When Corny stepped back in, Quinn looked up for a sign of relief and hope, but he didn't see it.

'They won't let Scarlet Moore go home, Randy,' he began. 'They're threatening to charge her with being an accessory to the illegal disinterment. She admitted to holding a lamp so you could see what to dig. And she admitted to knowing it was an illegal act.'

'I didn't want her to come along. Can you

help her?'

'She's hired Joel Barry. He can handle it, if it doesn't go much farther. He told me they're pressuring her to back off the baby story.'

'She won't,' Quinn said. 'But I'm beginning to wish that she would and go home.'

'I'm afraid I don't have good news for you either,' Corny continued, sitting again. 'Somebody put his foot on the accelerator here.'

'What do you mean?'

'They began investigating you sometime this morning and had that warrant a little before you had arrived here. They were playing with you a bit to let you believe otherwise.'

'I had a feeling,' Quinn said. 'I felt like I had been lured into some sort of a trap. So what's this all mean?'

'Siegman had a call from the field, which in this case means your property. They took three hammers that fit the pattern of the trauma on Barry Palmer.'

'What kind of hammers? Claw?'

'They didn't say. Whatever they took, they'll have no results on that this soon.'

'And there won't be anything they can use against me either,' Quinn said. 'So that's it. I'm out?'

'No, I'm afraid not.'

'Why not?'

'They found Kitchen's jewelry in a dresser

drawer in your bedroom,' Corny said.

For a moment Quinn thought he had imagined hearing it. Cornelius Blocker just sat there staring at him, studying him. When someone was waiting for your reaction to a fact like this and you were innocent, you couldn't help but worry that you would protest too much or maybe you wouldn't protest enough. Most of the time, just being accused, especially in a small community, was equivalent to ninety percent of the effort to convict.

'That's bullshit,' Quinn said in a measured tone. 'If any of that was there, someone planted it.'

'Don't you lock your house, Randy?'

'The front door locks automatically, but...'

'But what?'

'The back door isn't usually locked. I don't think about it. I mean, who'd come out there to steal from me?'

'It's not stealing from you that concerns me now,' Corny said.

'I didn't take that jewelry, Corny.'

Cornelius Blocker smiled.

'I haven't heard anyone call me that for years.'

'Well, I meant...'

'I understand. It's all right. I never minded the nickname. In fact, my father got a kick out of it.' He thought a moment and nodded. 'It's still within reason that someone planted the jewelry, although it will be on us

266

to provide a suspect. Obviously, no one on their side will care to follow up on that claim.'

'So now they'll charge me officially with Barry Palmer's murder?'

'They might not move so quickly to do that, as long as there are no hammers on your property or at the cemetery where you work with Barry Palmer's blood. It's one thing to accuse you of illegally digging up a grave and robbing the corpse, another to present a case for murder. If there is forensic evidence through one of those hammers ... well, then it might get a little tight for us. Then yes, you'll be charged with his murder.'

'And supposedly I did all this because Barry was running off with the jewelry and wouldn't share it? That's as idiotic as any of it. I told Siegman that I suspected Barry. Why would I put the law on him if I were in it with him? Ask Siegman or the assistant D.A. that.'

'I think you know their theory. They believe that was all after he had disappeared, so you were angry at being double-crossed. Besides, once Stuart Kitchen had dropped the charges, they didn't care where Barry was and that frustrated you. According to them, only you cared, cared enough to do your very best. However, I gathered there's another theory they're floating just to add some color so a jury would convict.'

'What theory?'

'They say you're anal about these graves you prepare. Jack Waller has been interviewed and confirms your ... how should I put it ... your high level of devotion to your work. I'm sure he didn't mean it to be something negative, but they'll try to make it sound like you're obsessive about the things you do, which helps give foundation to why you would react so violently to being betrayed.'

'That's all bullshit.'

'Nothing is bullshit in a court trial unless the judge disqualifies it for some reason. Siegman says you were more than just very upset for the dead Matthew Kitchen. He describes you as being over-the-top, taking it as if it were a personal affront that someone would tamper with your graves.'

'Why is that over-the-top? Because I have respect for the dead? Jack and his partner see this as solely a business thing. They could be burying bags of cement for all they care as long as they're paid for it.'

'Did you know Matthew Kitchen personally?'

'No. Never met him.'

'But you were so disturbed about his grave being disturbed that you disobeyed your boss and knowingly committed the illegal disinterment to pursue a possible theft even though his own children were letting it go and saw digging up their father as distasteful?'

'Yes, I was still very disturbed about what I was convinced Barry Palmer had done. It was solely because I opened my big mouth about the jewelry to him.' He leaned toward Corny. 'But we were far more disturbed because we saw a dead baby in the coffin! Why is everyone ignoring that fact?' he cried, raising his arms and his voice. He felt the blood rush into his neck and face.

Corny looked at him as if he were seriously considering an insanity plea.

'OK, relax. Right now, that sort of talk and that kind of emotional outburst is not going to help us convince people you wouldn't have killed Barry Palmer. If this gets into a courtroom, the district attorney will be a lot harder on you than I am and just so you'll react this way in front of a jury.'

Quinn looked down and then up quickly.

'All right. Tell me this,' he said as calmly as he could manage, 'If I had the jewelry hidden in my bedroom, why would I go after Barry or try to get anyone else to go after him?'

'They'll say you got it back when you killed him, Randy. No one can tell how long the jewelry was in that bedroom.'

'It was never in that bedroom!'

Quinn felt his throat squeeze closed as if a noose were tightening around his neck.

Corny looked at some paperwork to give him a chance to gather himself again. Quinn took a deep breath and looked down at

269

his feet.

'Bail costs a lot, doesn't it?' he muttered.

'For serious accusations, yes.'

'I have my whole inheritance in some basic stocks. It's about seventy-five thousand. Will that be enough?'

'Probably not if it's a murder charge, but you can go to a bail bondsman. You'll have to pledge your property.'

Quinn looked up.

'I could lose everything?'

'You're not going to run away so don't worry about it,' Corny said.

'Great. What a relief. I feel like they are the ones who are anal and crazy, not me.'

'Randy, look at this from their point of view. My father taught me always to do that. Look at it from your opponent's point of view as if you were your opponent. They don't have any other possible suspect right now. You were, according to witnesses, very angry with Barry Palmer. What you did and what you and Scarlet Moore claim about some dead baby in the coffin at minimum now looks like an attempt at an elaborate cover-up after you were betrayed. You sent the police on a wild goose chase looking into Palmer's dead baby while you possibly knocked off Palmer. The missing jewelry was found on your property. To be honest, if I were the prosecuting attorney, I'd feel I had a good case.'

'I didn't steal any jewelry and I didn't kill

Barry Palmer, but there was a dead baby in the coffin,' Quinn said in a quiet monotone.

Corny nodded.

'OK. This is enough for now.'

'So what happens now?'

'You'll be formally booked. They have enough to charge you with robbery as well as the illegal disinterment. The third shoe, if there is to be one, drops after forensics has a turn.'

'Can I see Scarlet?'

'She might have been moved to the county jail. That's what they'll do with you next. I'm afraid you'll have to be in there overnight. I'll get right on the hearing for a bail arrangement.'

'And Scarlet?'

'I don't know, Randy. As I told you, she has a different lawyer. Since she admitted to helping you dig up the coffin, they could charge her with accessory to the theft as well. But let's take it one thing at a time.'

Corny rose, gathered up his papers and closed his briefcase. If there had been any sense of camaraderie because they had graduated from the same local school, Quinn felt it had begun to slip away.

'Before I asked you if you thought I was guilty. What do you think now?'

Blocker thought a moment and then shrugged.

'Same answer, Randy. There have been

271

innocent people in worse situations.'

'Worse? Yeah, dead,' Quinn said.

Jack Waller gazed out of the window of his Spartan office at the two part-timer workers he had digging Ira Elmore's grave. They worked five or six minutes and paused to smoke or talk. Neither knew how to run a backhoe properly and he wasn't about to let some amateur gum up the machinery. More important, they could damage the grave sites on the right and left of Ira's. It was cheaper to pay them to dig with shovels.

A light rain had fallen in the morning and the clouds threatened a more dramatic follow up. If these two boneheads didn't dig that hole properly, half of it might cave in before the coffin was ready to be lowered, he thought. Randy Quinn had made this cemetery operation comfortable for both him and Richard. He was worth every dollar they paid him, if not more, even though Richard was always complaining about their overhead. As if Richard could hear him thinking about him, he appeared.

'What's going on?' he asked as he came into the office. 'Mary told me you said to get here quickly. Something else break in the case?'

Jack turned in his chair and held up an envelope with legal size paper.

'Something else broke all right.'

Valentine squinted and then took the

envelope and sat in front of the desk. After about a minute of reading, he looked up sharply.

'The bastard's suing us?'

'It's what you feared. Randy was our employee at the time. We're responsible.'

'How'd he get this filed so quickly?'

'People like Stuart Kitchen have their lawyers prepare paperwork to be instantly triggered. They don't care about the wasted expense if it's never activated, and besides, if you keep reading, you'll see his legal fees are part of the award they're asking.'

Valentine read on.

'Three quarters of a million?'

'Oh, they have their justifications enumerated, including irreparable emotional pain and suffering. Some suffering. From what I've been hearing, Matthew Kitchen was sorry he had never attempted to give Stuart away at birth. There was little love lost between them when Matthew Kitchen died.'

'Did you speak to our insurance company yet?'

'About to, but I've been reading our policy. There's this little escape clause for them if we committed a criminal or illegal act.'

'We didn't commit it.'

'I told you. Your employees are pretty much an extension of you when it comes to insurance claims and such, Richard. Don't act like you've never been in business.'

'I hope the bastard gets life.'

Jack shrugged.

'I don't know. I can't believe Randy would conspire to steal that jewelry and kill Barry Palmer. I've known him practically all his mature life. I'm not saying he wasn't obsessed about the place. Up until now it was a good thing. Look at how well everything's been kept. He'd hate the way the police went through his garage.'

'His garage?'

'He kept everything as if it did belong to him, Richard. You didn't know him and work around him as well as I did.'

'You really don't ever know anybody,' Valentine said. He looked up, slightly hesitant and then added, 'That's what your wife told Mary about you.'

'Yeah. Well, my love life is not the problem right now. I called Dwayne Petersen. We have an appointment at his office tomorrow at two to see what sort of a defense we can mount.'

'Christ, if Kitchen wins this award, he'll take the cemetery.'

'And the new parcel along with the government contract, if he wants.'

'I've got nearly three-hundred thousand sunk in this.' Valentine whined.

'And what do I have, chop liver?'

'Some simple business you got me into. Better than storage warehouses. I was leaning toward that, remember?'

'I didn't twist your arm, Richard. You had

274

the same information I had on all this, and you were just as excited recently about buying Mortman's property as I was, more so even. You found the investor.'

'Yeah. Imagine what I'll hear from him now.' He shook his head. 'That son of a bitch. I hope he gets convicted and gets life for putting us in this situation.'

'All things considered, I'd say he was in a worse situation, Richard.'

Valentine grunted.

Jack rose.

'I've got to get out there to supervise. Those guys are making a mess of it. We've got Ira Elmore's funeral this afternoon and the way they're going, Ira will have to help dig his own grave.'

'We should have invested in the vaults. I told you to add the building for the vaults.'

'People rob safes, don't they? It wouldn't have mattered,' Jack said and started out.

'Jack?'

'What?'

'Mary knows you had gotten Paula pregnant. And I didn't tell her,' he added quickly. 'I swear,' he added raising his right hand.

'Well, then how the hell did she find out?'

'Paula's talking is my guess. Maybe she's pissed at you. Where is she?'

'What are you, a reporter for the local version of the Inquirer now?'

'A lot of bad publicity for us at the wrong time,' Valentine said. 'Even if Kitchen does not win this lawsuit, we could be in for some bad economic hits.'

'Thanks, partner. You sound like a rat about to desert ship. You could drown, you know.'

'Rats can swim and hold their breath for about fifteen minutes under water.'

'Who told you that?'

'My grandson. He's doing a science project on rodents and rattles another fact about them nightly.'

'Your grandson is into rodents? Maybe you have more to worry about than you know,' Jack said dryly and left.

Valentine continued reading the lawsuit and cursing Quinn under his breath. After a few more minutes, he tossed the legal papers back on Jack's desk. He hated reading all this legalize and didn't understand half of it anyway. When he rose, he looked out the window and saw a light drizzle had started again. Jack had his shoulders hoisted and from this perspective looked like a giant hawk about to pounce on the part-timers who looked like two children being chastised, their heads bowed as Jack ranted and swung his arms wildly at the grave they had begun.

A feeling of deep, dark dread settled in his stomach. Mary had not been comfortable about their investing in a cemetery.

'I don't want to make money off other people's sorrow,' she had said. 'We should leave it for churches and synagogues.'

Wisecracks like 'It's a good business. People are dying to get into it,' didn't work with her.

Maybe she was on to something. Maybe it would serve Stuart Kitchen right to win ownership of this place. If only I hadn't invested so much, Richard thought. I would not even go to see our lawyer. I'd let it go by default.

But they did invest a lot and they were vulnerable. You didn't have to be a hotshot attorney to see that. Here comes another series of legal costs, lawyer bills, and ugly publicity in the local paper. It gave him indigestion and he hadn't even eaten.

'That son of a bitch better get life,' he muttered again and left the funeral home wishing he could be a rat deserting a ship.

At least rats got away.

SIXTEEN

'I have bad news and good news,' Corny told Quinn when he was brought into the court-room the next morning.

Sleeping in a jail cell had nearly broken his spirit. For him, someone who spent most of his waking hours outside, it was like being buried alive.

'What?'

'There was a hammer in your tool shed that has Barry Palmer's blood on it.'

Quinn felt his shoulders sink even lower. He had anticipated it and knew he was lying to himself to think nothing would have come of it once they had found the jewelry in his dresser drawer. Only the killer would have done that.

'And the good news?'

'The hammer does not have your finger-prints on it. The logical question is why would you rub off your fingerprints and put it back in your tool shed? If you were so concerned about a trail of evidence leading you to the murder, why not simply get rid of that hammer?'

'Yeah, but what's the but after asking that?

278

'I'm sure there's one.' Quinn said.

'It's a good question for us to ask, but the prosecution doesn't have to work hard on answering it, even in court. People who kill people make stupid mistakes all the time. Nevertheless, one of our arguments I will try to make will be that the hammer is not your hammer otherwise it would have your finger-prints somewhere on it.'

'That's not enough for anyone to believe in my innocence, is it?'

'No, but it's as true for the defense as it is for the prosecution that a murder trial is a puzzle, and all the pieces of evidence and witness testimony are pieces of that puzzle. They'll be trying to put it together their way and we'll be trying to tear it apart.'

'What kind of hammer was it?'

Corny opened his file and looked at it.

'Claw hammer, which fits the forensic conclusion.'

'What kind?'

'Kind?' He read. 'You mean the manufacturer?'

'Yeah?'

'Something made in China.'

'All my tools were my father's tools. I haven't bought anything new. He bought only quality stuff and he wouldn't buy anything but Craftsman. He liked to buy American. Every other hand tool in that shed is a Craftsman.' He thought a moment. 'You said they took three hammers to examine?'

'Yes, why?'

'I had only two claw hammers. If they took three, the third was definitely planted,' Quinn said.

'What about the hammers at the cemetery?'

'Same, Craftsman. My father helped set the place up.'

'Good to know,' Corny said making notes. 'Like any defense, we have to hammer, you should pardon the expression, home on reasonable doubt. But another obvious question is why would someone want to frame you for Barry's murder? Do you have any enemies on whom we can focus, perhaps?'

'I can't think of anyone who would want to go after me for personal reasons. I can't suggest anyone unless we can establish that the baby in the coffin is the key to all this,' Quinn said.

'A baby only you and Scarlet, who is now a defendant in two of the three charges, saw. At this point not an easy thing to establish,' Corny reminded him.

They rose when the judge entered. As they expected, the prosecution pushed to have bail denied, now that they were adding murder to the charge of robbery and illegal disinterment, but Corny did a beautiful job of drawing up the picture of a man to be trusted, a lifelong resident, a man with solid employment. He had Jack Waller's affidavit

280

attesting to Quinn's reliability and not only his assurance he would be continually employed, but very much needed. Quinn had no record, not even a traffic citation. Corny had a file full of letters attesting to Quinn's character, letters written by businessmen, his doctor, accountant, and even his old school teachers. When Quinn saw the file, he thought Corny had not left a stone unturned.

It worked. The judge set bail, but the amount took up every available dollar Quinn had inherited as well as required him to put his property on the line.

'Maybe I should have stayed in jail,' he muttered, depressed.

'You won't come to trial for quite some time, Randy,' Corny told him.

Scarlet got off much easier because of the lesser charges and was out hours before he was. His first thought was to call her when he got his truck back and was on his way home. It wasn't until then that he remembered Beck had taken his cell phone and the police had not returned it. He made a mental note to have Corny get it back for him.

Right now he was eager to get home to see what Beck's people had done to his house during their search. When he arrived, he was surprised to see it so pristine, not a cabinet or a drawer left open and nothing tossed to the floor. It was almost as if they had come in and gone right to the drawer that had the jewelry.

His tool shed was a different story. Every cabinet was left open and every drawer emptied, with nothing put back. All of his tool cases were turned over, the contents left on the floor. He had to step around scattered equipment. Before he started on getting it all put back, he went to the phone.

Scarlet answered after the first ring. He imagined her sitting there and waiting for his call.

'How are you?' he asked and immediately felt it was a stupid question.

'I'm OK, Randy. I don't understand what's happening. Why didn't you tell me about the death of Barry's wife and baby or his cell phone having the Kitchens' number on it? How could the jewelry be in your house and that hammer?'

'I can explain only the cell phone and the story I learned about Barry's wife and baby. I didn't want to involve you any more than I had. I tried to find out what went on by myself and got bitten in the ass.'

'I told you to leave it for the police, that you weren't a professional detective.'

'Yep, you were right,' he said.

'I thought I couldn't have more of a nightmare than we already had seeing that baby, but now...'

'Listen, Scarlet. Do what you have to do to protect yourself and don't worry about me,' he said, perhaps a little too harshly, but he wasn't in the mood for lectures, even if the person doing the lecturing was dead on right.

'You know that's a waste of words, Randy. Despite the evidence they claim to have now, I don't believe you're guilty of anything more than caring about what happened at that cemetery and what happened to that infant. You were just as surprised and disturbed at the sight of it.'

'I know. I appreciate that. Sorry about my tone. You going back to work?'

'Not this week. Gordon told me to take it off. I'm afraid it might be forever.'

'It won't be forever. I'll figure this out,' Quinn said.

'I know you will. Just please, please don't get into any more trouble.'

He didn't know what else to say. He wasn't going to propose they do anything recreational. That was for sure.

'I'll call you very soon.'

'I hope so,' she said.

The moment he hung up, his phone rang.

'I was expecting you'd come directly here,' Jack said.

'I had to see what sort of mess they made in the house.'

'Bad?'

'Not the house, but my tool shed looked like it housed a small tornado. How did the Elmore funeral go?'

'Rough. Something shorted out in the chapel and we couldn't use the microphone. There were more people than I expected. I had a feeling some came because of our situation. Sick curiosity seekers.'

'The sound system failure is probably just a breaker. I'll check on it.'

'I hate to remind you of this, but there's the Palmer grave ... needs to be ready tomorrow.'

'His aunt Lily still wants to go through with it at Sandburg?' Quinn asked with surprise.

'She's still a fan of yours. She had me on the phone for nearly twenty minutes relating stories about how good a kid you were and how all this has to be some mistake.'

'I was a good kid. I still am. And this is some mistake,' he said.

'The irony can't be lost on the district attorney ... you're preparing the grave for the man they are accusing you of killing.'

'I'll get on it, Jack. Thanks for giving my attorney the affidavit. I'm not sure I would have gotten out without it. My lawyer called it the *piece de resistance*.'

'All of it is true or I wouldn't be calling you so soon after you got out.'

'I know. Thanks. I'll be right over,' Quinn said and went to take a fast shower. Sleeping in the jail made him feel dirty inside and out.

It felt strange driving over to the cemetery to work, and not only because of what he had to prepare. It was almost as if all that had happened during the past few days was only a dream. In a moment he would blink and forget it. He'd have one of those second chances to save himself like that lawyer at the end of The Devil's Advocate movie.

But that didn't happen, of course. This was all coldly real. Although it was a very sunny day with only a dab of a cloud here and there, it still looked dull and dark to him. It was as if what had happened and what he had been through had placed a gray film over his eyes and the world would never look bright and hopeful again.

When he arrived at the cemetery and parked, Jack came out of the funeral home quickly. He waved toward the garage.

'Same as your place. They took the place apart and I'm sure messed up things for you in there,' he said.

Quinn gazed into the garage and saw where drawers had been left opened, some contents sprawled over counters and the floor. He saw immediately that his claw hammers here had been taken and were still not returned. Jack stood beside him as he looked it over.

'I'll take care of it,' Quinn said.

'Right. First things first. Let's look over the plot Lily Palmer took for her nephew.'

'Sorry about all this, Jack,' Quinn muttered.

'No, I'm sorry for you, Randy. I hope it all

works out. Just get back into your work for now and don't do anything else to rile up Stuart Kitchen. He's suing us, you know.'

'I figured he would do that, but I didn't know it had actually happened.'

'Well, like I said, let's take care of first things first. Plenty of time to deal with the devil,' Jack said.

Quinn followed him out and up to the cemetery to look at the plot Jack had assigned for Barry Palmer. It was off to the right and close to the edge of the property, some distance from plots already taken. Jack said he had described it to Lily Palmer and she had approved.

'She's taken the one beside him for herself,' Jack said.

Quinn nodded.

'I'm not surprised. His aunt Lily always treated him more like her son than her nephew,' he said. 'What time's the funeral tomorrow?'

'Ten. She's not using our chapel. They should be here about noon with the casket. Curt just got the body today. I don't suppose you want to see it.'

Quinn looked at him as if he were crazy.

'Well, regardless of all this, he was, you said, your best buddy once.'

Was Jack testing him, trying to see if he was afraid of looking at his victim or something?

'I'm not afraid of looking at him, but once is a long, long time ago, Jack,' he said.

286

'Yeah, I suppose so.' Jack looked up at the sky. 'Weather report is good for tonight and tomorrow. When do you want to dig the grave?'

'I'll do it now,' Quinn said.

He returned to the garage to get his equipment. When he brought the backhoe up and began, he couldn't help but recall his initial conversation with Barry and how timid he was or pretended to be about working in a cemetery. It had bothered him to learn about Nick Reuben, their high school classmate killed in Iraq. Despite what he had told Scarlet about desperate people doing desperate things, he still couldn't get over Barry returning at night to dig up a grave and open a coffin. Had he found and taken Matthew Kitchen's jewelry? And if he had, and had discovered the dead baby, would he risk Stuart Kitchen finding out just to blackmail him? He already had the jewelry. Was he that greedy or that stupid?

No, Quinn thought as he manipulated the backhoe, what's more logical is he probably had opened the coffin, found no jewelry in there, and, in the course of doing that, discovered the dead baby. That was the only explanation he could imagine for why Barry would have called the Kitchens. Barry knew it also explained why Stuart made a big deal of burying his father with expensive jewelry and wanting to be responsible for the final closing of the coffin. The jewelry was just an excuse.

Afterward, Stuart Kitchen had surely killed Barry and planted the evidence in my home, Quinn concluded. He had wanted to describe all this to Corny, but was afraid that without any proof of the baby, Corny would see him as reaching for straws, creating a scenario just the way someone guilty and desperate might. Right now he still saw no way of proving it.

As he worked, he tried to envision Barry Palmer approaching Stuart Kitchen to blackmail him. Despite how much he detested Stuart, he had to admit he was five times Barry's intellect. Originally, when Barry dug up the grave, saw there was no jewelry, but saw the baby and then refilled the grave, he must have felt he had his gold mine six feet under despite there being no jewelry to steal. Kitchen couldn't come over and uncover the grave and remove the baby. Barry had him over a barrel until I uncovered the grave and Scarlet and I saw the baby, Quinn thought. He couldn't come to me with his discovery. He knew how I would react to his attempting to steal from a coffin, and he certainly knew I wouldn't go along with any blackmail scheme.

No, Barry had to keep going on his own. Stuart must have agreed to pay Barry to keep his mouth shut, but with the baby exposed because he and Scarlet had seen it, Barry no longer had anything to use for blackmail and Kitchen was in great danger of being caught. The only way out for either of them was for Barry to return before the police had arrived and take out the baby. That was the purpose surely of the call Kitchen had made to Barry's cell phone, and now that he thought back over all of it, why Stuart Kitchen had delayed looking at the coffin to see the baby.

New questions kept him thinking. How did Stuart Kitchen know there would be enough time between when he called Barry and told him to get the baby out of the coffin and when Lou Siegman and his patrolman had arrived? How did he know Jack would come first and decide to look at the coffin without the police?

He looked back at the funeral home for a moment and then jumped off the backhoe to march down the path. He hurried in and to Jack's office. Jack was at his desk, his head lowered as he spoke softly into the phone. Quinn heard him say, 'Paula, will you calm down.'

He looked up when he realized Quinn was there.

'Hold on,' he said into the receiver and covered the mouthpiece. 'What's up?'

'I have to ask you something important. The night I called you to tell you what Scarlet and I saw in Matthew Kitchen's coffin...'

'Randy, man...'

'No, listen. I told you I had called the

Kitchens first. Did you call them or did Stuart call you before you arrived?'

Jack stared at him a moment and then said, 'I'll call you right back. I promise,' into the receiver and hung up. 'What is this now?'

'Really, why didn't you call Lou Siegman first, Jack? I had told you something horrendous.'

'You're blaming something on me? After what I did for you?'

'No, no, I'm not blaming you for anything. I'm just trying to fit a piece into a puzzle. Stuart Kitchen called you right after I did, didn't he?'

'Yeah, he did,' Jack admitted. 'I didn't see any reason to bring it up with you. It didn't seem to matter once we saw there was no baby in that coffin, Randy.'

'It was his idea for us to go up and look into the grave without the police first, right?'

'Yeah. He said if the police were there, too, when such a disgusting accusation was made, he would have no choice but to sue us for a whole arm long list of things. He advised me to go slowly and confirm what was happening for our own good as well as his. I didn't see how it would matter all that much since as far as I knew nothing dead has gotten up and left this cemetery,' he added dryly.

'You don't see how that matters now, Jack?'

'Randy, why don't you leave this up to your lawyer, to the professionals? Otherwise, I'm sure you'll do something to violate your parole and end up back in the can.'

'Don't you see? The delay gave them so much time to get the baby out of the coffin.'

'What do you want me to do?'

'Nothing,' Quinn said. 'But when you're asked in court, just tell the court what you just told me.'

'You think that'll happen?'

'I hope so.'

'Don't screw around and force me to have a lawyer too,' Jack warned.

'I don't want anything more from you, Jack.'

Waller looked at his phone.

'I wish that was true for everyone I spoke to this morning. I gotta get back to this call.'

'OK. Thanks,' Quinn said and left.

He returned to the grave site, feeling he had opened a curtain just enough to let in some daylight, but what he would do with that light was still part of a bigger question. He started up the backhoe again.

Using Corny's metaphor, Quinn believed all this was a logical alternative to the puzzle the prosecution was putting together to convict him, but unlike their puzzle, his was made of invisible pieces. How in hell can he make them visible? He had said it before and would continue to say it until it became his mantra for survival. Everything was explained when you included the baby.

Quinn had no definite idea about whose

baby it was, but as he shaped the gravesite, his suspicions closed on it having been Matthew Kitchen's. However, if he told Corny that Stuart used the jewelry story to give him access to a coffin so he could include the baby's corpse with his father's, Corny's logical question would be why not just find another simpler way to dispose of an unwanted infant corpse? These were people of great means. Alternative solutions were easily available. How could he explain that?

Further, for any of this to make any sense, that baby would have had to have died just about the same time Matthew Kitchen had died. If he had died much earlier, why would they have kept the corpse this long? What were the chances of something like the two of them dying at the same time happening? He could just hear the prosecutor or even Corny ask, 'What, did the sight of his illegitimate child and the illegitimate child's sight of him kill them both simultaneously, give them both heart failure?'

He paused and looked around the graveyard. Perhaps the baby had been buried somewhere else first, but Stuart Kitchen had dug it up and put it in his father's coffin. But then he was back to the why? Big piece in his invisible puzzle, he thought. Could he propose any sort of sensible answer?

Maybe. Maybe Stuart found some ugly revenge in doing this. It was pretty much well known that his father didn't have much respect for him. Up until his death, he hadn't given Stuart very much authority with his business interests. It would be just like Hit and Run Kitchen to look for a grotesque way to get back at his father when his father could do nothing to protect or defend himself. He could just hear Stuart thinking *let your sin rot with you in your grave*.

And now that he thought of it, hadn't Barry gone through a somewhat similar thought process contaminated with anger and revenge when he dragged his pregnant wife out of Arizona, punishing her by having her give birth in the back of a truck? Maybe he didn't expect it would turn fatal. Maybe all he had hoped to do was make her suffer, but that didn't change the outcome.

He could hear his father's voice: 'Anger and vengeance are probably the two most powerful human motivations or reasons for doing bad things.' How many of the graves his father and he had prepared were graves to house the victims of violent crimes? His father never made much of a distinction. He'd comment, but in the end, he'd say or imply that Death was still the same dark host, the only place to get your ticket to any afterlife. Death didn't discriminate and certainly didn't turn away a victim.

He mulled all this as he worked the backhoe. The baby wasn't cloned, he thought. Who was the woman who had given birth to him? Where was she? Was she paid off and gone forever? He would need the help of a real detective to track someone like that, and where would he get the money to hire a professional detective now?

Evelyn Kitchen had told him that she had spent most of their time traveling with her father, working with her father. She surely must know of his sexual assignations, but how much of what he suspected about Barry and Stuart did Evelyn Kitchen really know? When he showed her Barry's cell phone, she looked surprised about Barry calling them. Did she buy into the story Stuart gave the police, his explanation of why Barry had called him and why he had returned the call? Did she now completely believe that he, Quinn, was guilty of conspiring with Barry to rob her father's coffin? She had said she didn't believe it when he was at her home, but now, now that all this evidence against him was revealed, she surely thought he was guilty. That sickened him as much if not more than anything else.

He shut off the backhoe. While he was down in Barry's grave doing his detail work, he was suddenly overcome with the same feeling he had experienced in the jail cell. Despite all these real possibilities and explanations, he was still as helpless as a corpse in a coffin, weak and frustrated and unable to dig himself out of the trap that Death had set. Throwing tantrums, screaming, nothing like that would help or make the slightest difference. No one would hear him. He was as good as buried in this same grave with Barry when Barry was lowered in here tomorrow. What he really felt like now was one of those people forced to dig his own grave just before being shot.

He pulled himself up and sat on the edge staring at the woods.

Corny had told him to return to work and keep his nose clean after he had been released.

Jack had told him not to do anything else that would infuriate Stuart Kitchen.

Scarlet had said don't do anything that would get him into more trouble.

All three of them were trying to help him, but he knew in his heart that the bottom line was he was the only one who could help himself.

He had been in Barry's grave. Now he had to get into Barry's mind. If Barry had tried to blackmail Stuart Kitchen and Kitchen had called him back to tell him if he didn't get the baby's corpse out of the grave before the police arrived, they'd both be in trouble, then Barry would have done it. But if he showed Stuart the corpse or turned it over to him to dispose, he would lose the only leverage he had. What he had to do was dispose of the baby himself and in a place only he would know and continue to hold that over Kitchen. He would certainly not have driven off with the baby in his truck and just dumped it somewhere, Quinn realized now. If he had done that, how could he threaten Stuart Kitchen?

And he wouldn't have the baby on him when Kitchen met him. That would be too great a risk. Kitchen could stick a gun in his ribs and force him to hand the corpse over to him. No, Kitchen figured Barry had the baby's corpse hidden in a way that only he knew where it was. If Barry was dead, no one would find the baby's corpse and for him everything would be solved, especially after framing me for the murder, Quinn thought. Proving all this would do much toward filling in the pieces of his invisible puzzle.

What was the logical place for Barry to hide something like a baby's corpse where he knew it wouldn't be accidentally found and, in fact, it would be guarded? Obviously, in a cemetery, but not in an unused plot because that would eventually be dug up and the baby's corpse found.

Excited now, he stood and gazed over the monuments. Except for the first twenty, he was personally responsible for the rest of the occupied grave sites in this cemetery. He pruned and combed the grass and kept the monuments clean. What had Barry called it, his garden of the dead? Yes, it was. He planted and nurtured it to reap peace and tranquility.

Slowly, he toured the grave sites close to

Matthew Kitchen's. He realized that Barry would be in a hurry, actually nearly in a panic. It was dark, too. What did it matter which grave site he chose? He certainly wouldn't have worried about defiling any of them after what he had done to Matthew Kitchen's grave.

The ones to Kitchen's immediate left and right were clearly undisturbed. He must have worried they would be too close. Quinn lifted his eyes slowly and fixed his gaze on the monument just behind the one to Kitchen's left. Barry knew who that one was and maybe in his desperate, now manic state, he thought there was some comfort in the choice.

Irony of ironies, Quinn thought and stepped forward, his heart racing as he approached Nick Reuben's grave. Even without kneeling down to study the grass, he could see the clumsy attempt to cut away a portion of it, dig quickly beneath it, and then put the grass back in clumps.

He got to his knees and carefully pulled the clumps of grass back. Then he began with his hand shovel. Daylight was already waning and the air taking on the chill of early fall nights. It enhanced the darkness inside him as he uncovered the still softened earth. He stopped when he saw the baby's fingers and stared for a moment before he started to dig harder and then stopped after he had uncovered most of the baby's arm. He looked back toward the funeral home and then down at the makeshift shallow grave.

I've got to look at this from every conceivable angle, he thought. My problem's been that I've been too impulsive, too anxious and desperate to make things right again. I've got to anticipate, to do what Corny said he does, think the way his opponent might, even become his opponent.

So we turn up the dead baby we said was in the coffin. What if it has nothing to do with the Kitchens? What if there's no DNA tying Stuart or his father to the dead infant? Although that's unlikely now, it was still a possibility. If that turned out to be the case, could he somehow be blamed for this as well? This discovery in and of itself won't discount the jewelry being found in his house and the murder weapon being found in his shed. He wasn't sure how he might accomplish it, but that Lieutenant Beck could somehow twist something to add the dead baby to the list of reasons to convict him of murder.

Don't be in too much of a rush to turn this over to the police yet, he told himself and sat back on the ground to think.

After a minute or so, he had a better idea.

Stuart Kitchen would never admit to putting a dead baby in his father's coffin if no baby was discovered. But now he had discovered it and perhaps when he confronted him about it, he could get him to admit to killing Barry and trying to frame him for the murder. Just like Barry, however, he couldn't reveal where the baby's corpse was. For all Stuart Kitchen knew, he could have been in cahoots with Barry and might even have put him up to attempting the blackmail.

He nodded to himself and quickly re-interred the baby's hand and arm. Then he put the grass back as neatly as he could and returned to Barry's grave site to start up the backhoe and return to the garage. As he turned in, he saw Jack hurrying to his car. Usually, he said goodnight or told him he was leaving and wasn't returning until morning. He didn't even glance his way. He got into his car and hurriedly backed out of his parking spot and drove off.

Quinn had much left to do to restore the garage, but for now he just cleared enough space in it to park the backhoe.

There will be time for the rest of this later, he thought, or really hoped.

For he was about to set out on either his own rescue or his own demise.

Whatever it was to be, it was at least to come about because of his own doing.

A man should have control of his destiny, he thought. There's more comfort in blaming others for our disasters, but there's no honesty in it.

'It's easy to deceive yourself,' his father told him once, 'but it's hell to live with it and believe me, it weighs heavily and stands out when you're down to your final thoughts. It makes death that much harder to face.'

He was determined not to let it happen to himself.

SEVENTEEN

He smiled to himself thinking how Scarlet would call this déjà vu all over again and entered the funeral home. By now he had the Kitchens' number in memory. He went directly to Jack's office and sat behind the desk. He formulated his strategy depending upon who answered the phone, Evelyn or Stuart, and then he carefully poked out the numbers and waited as it rang. He was determined to tell Stuart what he had figured out and then inform him he was calling the police. That should get him spinning for a change, he thought. Of course, he was betting on the baby being tied to Matthew Kitchen.

'Pray for DNA,' he muttered as the phone began to ring. Just as he thought an answering service would cut in, she picked up. For a moment, he hesitated, disappointed, and considered hanging up and calling again in a few minutes, but she repeated, 'Hello.'

'Evelyn, it's Randy Quinn.'

For a moment he thought she had hung up. Then she spoke.

'I don't think it's wise for you to call here,

Randy, or for me to speak with you. I'm sorry.'

'Ordinarily, I would agree, Evelyn, and I would understand, but this isn't ordinarily now.' She was silent. Now he did expect she would just hang up, so he hurriedly said, 'I did see a dead baby in your father's coffin, Evelyn. Barry Palmer did return to take it out while we were waiting for the police, and I figured out where he buried the child. He buried him in the cemetery, the Sandburg Cemetery.'

She didn't speak, but she didn't hang up either.

'I wanted your brother to know this, Evelyn. Is he there?'

'We've been through this with you before, Randy.'

'I know, but...'

'No, my brother's not here.'

'This time I'm sticking right with it, Evelyn. No one is going to get here and hide him again. I'm going to call the police.'

'I see. So you are at the cemetery now?'

'I am. I'm not going anywhere,' he said.

'You can show me this child?'

'Show you? Yes.'

'I'll be there in twenty minutes or so,' she said. She didn't sound horrified to him as much as sad.

'I'll wait for you in front of the funeral home, Evelyn, but I want you to know that after I show you the baby's corpse, I will call

302

the police.'

'No you won't,' she said. 'If what you say is true, I'll call them.'

He heard her hang up.

And for the first time in a long time, he felt he had made the right decision.

He decided to call Scarlet. This time he wouldn't leave her out of his discoveries and his plans. From the sound of her voice when she answered, he knew she was having a bad time of it. Her mother had probably been at her for getting involved with him in the first place. Of course, he couldn't blame her.

'I have some good news,' he said.

'What?'

'I found the baby we saw in the coffin.'

'You did? Where?'

'Barry buried it a row back in Nick Reuben's site. Nick was a classmate of ours.'

'Oh, this is fantastic, Randy. How did you figure that out?'

'I know my garden,' he said.

'What?'

'Barry once called this place my garden of the dead.'

'Oh. Well, are the police there?'

'Soon.'

'Should I come over?'

'No,' he said too quickly and too hard. She was silent. 'I mean, I don't expect to be here that long, and there's nothing for you to do.'

'I have to confirm that's the baby, too, I imagine.'

'I doubt the police or anybody would doubt it. We don't have infants buried a few feet down on other people's grave sites. Besides, once they do the DNA work, I'm sure what you suspected first will prove true. The baby belonged to Matthew Kitchen.'

'My head is spinning,' she said. 'I know I should be happy, but my god, Randy, the horror of it all.'

'I know. Let me spare you some of it. I'll call you as soon as it's over here, and I learn what is next for us to do from a legal standpoint.'

'This is going to sound crazy to you, Randy, but I feel closer to you now because of all this than I did before it had started.'

'It's not crazy,' he said. 'I'll call you as soon as I have something concrete to say.'

'I'm as happy for you as I am for myself, Randy,' she said. He could hear the tears coming.

'Likewise,' he told her, hung up and went outside to wait for Evelyn Kitchen.

As he looked around the property, a property he had been caring for with as much concern and pride as he had his own home and grounds, he felt a great weight being lifted from his neck and shoulders. The events, the depth of the mess he had been in, his own mistakes had not only dragged him down mentally and spiritually, but also affected him physically. He lacked energy, walked with his head down, his shoulders slumped. If he gazed at himself in a mirror, he would see only defeat.

All that had happened had not only injured him and foretold his demise, it also meant this place would suffer. He had seen a number of old, neglected cemeteries when he worked with his father. They weren't gardens of the dead; they had become burial grounds for the forgotten. Their tombstones were practically illegible, tilted or partially sunken. The grounds were overrun with wild grasses, broadleaf weeds and tall fescue grass. There was either no money for maintenance or no interest since the dead were not very recent and relatives had lost concern or had moved away.

Cemeteries die, too, he thought. We kill our loved ones many times over.

Was there something abnormal about someone as young as he was worrying about such things? His youth flashed by him. He saw a teenage boy who was far too serious and yes, maybe too old too quickly. The things he took pleasure and satisfaction in were boring if not distasteful to his peers. He did try to find a middle ground, joined the football team, attempted to have a romantic relationship here and there, and pal around with Barry. But that darkness that settled on things morbid, things most people rather keep tucked away in closets or under other possessions in drawers and cartons, never seemed to lift from him. To so many it was as if he walked in perpetual gloom, lived under cloudy skies.

Evelyn Kitchen had been aware of him and at least intrigued enough to reveal some curiosity. Perhaps it was his own fault for not being more persistent, for idolizing her so much that he belittled himself, actually thought of himself as unworthy. She was a princess and he was plebeian, common and ordinary. He so lacked her sophistication. He was too quick to accept failure when it came to her, he thought.

Of course, he couldn't imagine her thanking him for what he was about to do. He could easily see her hating him, perhaps. After this was over, she would never look at him or hear his name without thinking of the ugly, unpleasant things that were about to ensue.

No one likes to see their idols reduced to common and ordinary status. What was that line in *Mrs Robinson* ... where have you gone, Joe DiMaggio ... it's in our nature to create heroes, gods and goddesses. We need to know there are people who can be better than we are, more beautiful, more intelligent, and more talented. They help us strive to rise above our own meager skills, give us motivation and hope.

The Kitchens, despite Matthew Kitchen's wealth and power, were not to be idolized after all, and Evelyn wasn't a goddess. She was trapped in a world her father and brother had made. He actually pitied her and almost regretted allowing her to come see the dead infant.

It would be the last wish he would grant her, he thought, and then he would bury his glorification and reverence for her out there in his garden of the dead. And after he had done that, he would walk straighter and with more confidence. What it would do is release him so he could fall in love with someone like Scarlet Moore and put to rest impossible dreams.

He would, at last, be happy.

The approaching car's headlights seemed to unfurl the darkness before it. He recognized the Kitchens' Mercedes as it entered the jurisdiction of the cemetery's driveway lights. He saw her silhouetted at the steering wheel, her hair down. He imagined she had just thrown on something and come as quickly as she could. He decided to walk to the car and not wait for her to approach. She parked and turned off her lights, but didn't get out immediately.

She sees me coming, he thought and hurried his steps.

Just as he reached the vehicle, she stepped out and with her left hand, slipped off her wig and in an instant, became her brother, Stuart. Quinn paused, shocked. Stuart Kitchen had a forty-five in his right hand.

'Rarely have I considered being a twin an advantage,' he said and smiled. 'This is obviously one of those times.'

'Where is Evelyn?' Quinn asked.

'Home. Crying, but she'll get over it. Now we can do two things here. Up to you. Take me to this infant you claim to have found. I'll handle that and you can take your chances again with the courts and jury, or I shoot you here and now and claim you were blackmailing my sister. I came to confront you and you threatened my life. With all that's against you at the moment, I don't expect too much doubt or skepticism. I have a better lawyer than you do anyway.'

'How do you know I haven't left the baby uncovered?'

'Oh, I intend to check every grave in the cemetery and make sure before I leave,' Stuart said and showed Quinn his flashlight. 'Well? What do you choose? Door number one or door number two?'

Quinn glared at him for a moment.

'I'll need to get a shovel,' he said and then turned and headed for the garage. Stuart remained close.

'I wouldn't attempt anything, Randy,' Stuart said. 'I not only took lessons from a gun expert for this pistol, but practice often. Guns have always been fascinating to me. It's so much less of an effort to use a gun than to learn all that self-defense, karate crap my father tried to get me to learn. It was why I usually avoided confrontations in school.'

'Hit and Run Kitchen,' Quinn muttered

loud enough for him to hear.

'Oh yes. I knew they called me that, but I never considered anyone's friendship in the public school important enough to care. Fortunately for them, no one got me angry enough for me to be more than Hit and Run.

'I must say,' he continued, 'I appreciated the fact that you never participated in that juvenile humor. There was a time when I even considered the possibility of becoming friendly with you. It seemed we both despised the idea of socializing with the gang, although I was disappointed to see you become so buddy-buddy with Barry Palmer. What a loser he was.'

Quinn opened the garage door.

'Watch it,' Stuart Kitchen warned.

Quinn flipped on a light and then took a shovel off the wall and turned. Kitchen backed up carefully.

'I don't intend to be within reach of that so if you don't need it...'

'I need it. He buried the kid a good four feet down.'

'Let's go,' Stuart said waving the pistol. Quinn started out in front of Stuart and turned toward the funeral parlor. 'We can walk a little faster than this.'

They began up the path to the cemetery proper.

'How did you kill him?' Quinn asked, glancing behind.

'Barry Palmer? Oh, you figured that out,

I'm sure, when you showed my sister his cell phone and the calls. He tried to blackmail me and I got him to get the baby out of the coffin. We rendezvoused not far from where he went over the cliff. I thought the hammer was a clever touch, don't you? It was the perfect modus operandi for framing you after you made such a big damn deal of finding the infant's corpse. It was truly like killing two birds with one hammer,' he added and laughed.

'So there was never any jewelry in your father's coffin then, was there?'

'Please. Put all that six feet under? He's lucky I buried him in a good suit and an expensive coffin.'

'How much does Evelyn know?' Quinn asked pausing.

'What difference does that make?' rejoined Stuart, pausing too to remain a safe distance behind.

'I'd just like to know.'

'Forget about Evelyn. She's of no concern to you. Move,' Stuart ordered waving the pistol. He was clever enough to remain a good ten feet back. Lunging at him before he was able to get off a shot was impossible, and Quinn knew what sort of damage a forty-five would do.

Quinn continued and then paused at Barry Palmer's opened grave.

'Your victim's final resting place,' he said nodding at it.

'Oh. Very nice. I'll be sure to stop by here when I visit my mother's grave.'

'Not your father's?'

'I'll give him a glance, just about the same interest he gave me. Where is the infant?'

'Over there,' Quinn said. 'Behind your father's and mother's,' he added and kept walking until he reached Nick Reuben's site.

'Here?'

'Yes,' Quinn said.

'So you didn't leave it uncovered. I find calling everyone's bluff is usually ninety percent safe. That's a bit of wisdom for you when you're in some maximum security prison and some other killers threaten you.'

'Thanks,' Quinn said and began to dig deliberately in the wrong place.

His mind raced, chasing possible solutions. He could risk throwing a shovel full of dirt into his face, but if Stuart sidestepped it or wasn't blinded enough by it, he would surely get off his shot. Maybe he should uncover the baby. Afterward, there might be a better opportunity, but another very real possibility occurred to him. He paused and turned to Stuart.

'What are you doing? Dig it up.'

'I was just wondering, Hit and Run, what's to stop you from shooting me after I show you the baby?'

'Now what would be the sense in my doing that, Randy? You're practically dead now with the case built against you, and I would

311

only have to revert to the story of your trying to blackmail us. I would have to bring my sister into it. Why would I want to put myself through so much unnecessary hassle when the state is going to do it all for me?

'Now, uncover the baby. We'll get it down to my vehicle, put it in my trunk and you can go home. Dig!'

'Turn your flashlight on here,' he said. 'I'm not sure I'm in the exact right spot. There's not enough starlight.'

Stuart smirked and then flipped on his light. He directed the beam at the grave site. Randy pretended to test the earth with the edge of the shovel.

'Before you ask, I'm not coming closer with the flashlight, Randy. And I can tell you now that I had better see some evidence of that corpse in the next minute or so. I'm not particularly fond of being out here.'

'Too close to your father?'

'Shut up and dig!'

Quinn put the shovel in the right spot and gingerly removed the grass clumps. He dug a little more around the arm he had first uncovered and paused.

'This is it,' he said.

'Step back,' Stuart ordered. 'Back more.'

Quinn moved to his right. Stuart Kitchen came forward and directed his flash light at the uncovered area. Then he smiled.

Just as he started to step back, they both heard a shrill voice call, 'RANDY!'

312

Surprised, Stuart turned just enough for Quinn to lunge forward and swing his shovel flat so that the blade caught Stuart Kitchen turning back and sliced through his Adam's apple. He managed to get off a shot, but the gun was pointed downward. He gasped, dropped the pistol and brought his hands to his throat. The blood gushed over his fingers. He gaped in astonishment, looked at Quinn and then folded to the earth slowly, floating like a sheet of paper someone had released. He landed on his back with his legs twisted. His body shuddered badly, his legs jerking until all movement stopped.

Randy stood over him with the shovel raised to strike him again, but he relaxed when he clearly saw he was dead. After a moment he heard footsteps and looked up to see Scarlet running toward him.

She paused at the sight of Stuart Kitchen's body sprawled at Quinn's feet.

'Is he dead?'

'Yes.'

'I heard the gun go off. You didn't get shot?' she asked.

'No. What are you doing here?' Quinn asked. 'I mean, how did you know to come now?'

'I didn't know when to come. I just knew I should come,' she said stepping closer to him. 'Something in your voice when you said "soon" after I asked about the police told me you were up to your old tricks.'

He felt his body relax some more, the steel in it soften and turn back to flesh and bone. Then he smiled and dropped the shovel.

'Lucky I'm so obvious,' he said.

'Maybe only to me.'

He looked down at Stuart Kitchen.

'Only you is enough, especially this time,' he replied and stepped forward to embrace her.

EIGHTEEN

'Why didn't you call us first?' Lieutenant Beck asked Quinn.

It looked like every available cop in the township, sheriff's office and BCI in the area was gathered there around Stuart Kitchen's body. The medical examiner was supervising the retrieval of the baby. Lou Siegman stood next to Jack Waller, who even in the illumination from all the extra light, perhaps because of it, looked pale white. Richard Valentine as usual was just arriving, huffing and puffing his way to the scene. Scarlet was still at Quinn's side.

'I had to do something that was personally important to me first,' Quinn replied looking at the uncovering of the baby's corpse.

'What? Kill Stuart Kitchen?'

Quinn turned to him.

'You doubt this was self defense?'

'No, but there's self defense and there's self defense.'

'What the hell's that supposed to mean?' Scarlet asked before Quinn could. 'I was here. I saw him pointing the gun at Randy.'

'All I'm saying is if he had called us first,

Kitchen wouldn't be here pointing the gun at him and he wouldn't have had to kill him. You can bait someone into a situation, you know.'

'From what well of stupidity did you draw that pail?' she asked.

Quinn smiled.

'You think Randy wanted to be seconds away from having himself shot and killed?'

'I think, Scarlet, that our Lieutenant Beck is simply upset that his solid, thorough investigation turned into fertilizer,' Quinn said. Even though Beck was somewhat in the shadows, Quinn could see his face redden.

'What the hell's going on here?' Richard Valentine asked. It seemed like perfect timing for comic relief. Everyone looked at him as if he were the dumbest man on earth.

Jack came to life.

'Randy figured out that his high school buddy, Barry Palmer, the one he hired to work here, did dig up Matthew Kitchen's coffin. There was no jewelry, but there was a dead baby in there. He also figured out that Palmer tried to blackmail Stuart Kitchen with the discovery and when Randy found the baby, too, and called the Kitchens first...'

'Which was his first dumb mistake,' Beck muttered. Jack ignored him.

'Stuart told him to get the baby out of the coffin. He did and then Stuart killed him when they met for him to pay off Palmer. Kitchen tried to frame Randy and Randy figured out where Palmer had buried the baby.'

'How did he get dead?' Richard asked nodding at Stuart Kitchen's body.

'Randy decided to call the Kitchens and let Stuart know what he had found. He says he expected Evelyn to show up to see it and he says she and he were going to call the police, but Stuart showed up instead.'

'Well, what does she say about it?' Richard asked.

'I'm heading over there now,' Lieutenant Beck said. He nodded at the two agents who were with him and then glanced at Quinn before starting away.

'Well, I don't get it, Jack,' Richard continued. 'Whose baby is this?'

'The medical examiner will tell us in about three or four days,' Lou Siegman said. 'But you can risk a few bucks on it being tied to Matthew or even Stuart Kitchen.'

Everyone turned as the ambulances arrived

'I thought cemeteries were supposed to be peaceful, tranquil places,' Richard muttered.

'It will be that way again very soon,' Quinn told him.

'Yeah, right. I'm going to be a nervous wreck every time we bury someone. I may live forever. It's too risky to die.'

That seemed to crack the ice and everyone smiled.

'I need you to come to the station, Randy,'

Lou said. 'We'll need to do a formal full report. You can call your lawyer now. You have his home phone number or do you need me to get it for you?'

'No, I got it. I'll just stop in Jack's office and use the phone. Beck never gave me my cell phone back.'

'He left it in my office. Sorry. You can get it now,' Lou said.

'You don't need to stop in Jack's office, Randy,' Scarlet said. 'I'm going with you and I have my cell phone.'

'Right. I'm not going anywhere without her, Chief,' he said and took Scarlet's hand.

On the way to the parking lot, they passed the paramedics who carried the stretchers.

'I thought people are dead before they come here,' one quipped. 'We usually don't take the bodies from a cemetery.'

'Oh, don't worry. They'll be coming back,' Lou Siegman said.

It was the second opportunity to smile.

'We'll take my truck,' Quinn told Scarlet when they reached the parking lot. 'We'll get your car in the morning.'

'Oh?'

'I'm not going to sleep alone tonight,' he said.

'Any port in a storm?'

'Oh no. I know when I've found my home port,' he replied and she pressed her body closer to him.

Quinn was hoping that before they left the

police station, he would learn about Beck's interview of Evelyn Kitchen, but whatever conclusions were arrived at were apparently being kept under tight wraps. Even Corny couldn't find out anything. On the way out, Quinn did see Beck on the phone in another room. They glanced at each other and then Beck nodded at one of his agents and the agent closed the door.

'You've got to be running on fumes,' Scarlet told him when they got into his truck and started away from the station.

'I'm too tired to notice or feel anything,' he replied.

'I hope not everything,' she said.

'Well ... I'm around graves enough to know how to resurrect,' he said and she laughed.

They were quiet most of the way, but when they reached Sandburg, she turned to him.

'Why didn't you call the police first, Randy?' she asked. 'You really didn't need to confront Stuart Kitchen to get to this place.'

'I wasn't expecting Stuart Kitchen.'

She was quiet for a few moments.

'Did you know her in high school?'

'Oh, not like you think. I knew of her, of course. She was, how should I put it ... unapproachable? But for me most of the girls were.'

'Yes, but for you she was different, wasn't she?'

'I'm sure there was someone like that for you,' he offered as an answer.

319

She said nothing more about it until they had made love and now both fully exhausted began to turn away from each other to go to sleep.

'I never asked you why you kept all these comic book heroes on your walls.'

He paused and looked at the posters, pictures and covers dimly lit by the moonlight piercing the veil of thin clouds and streaming in through his bedroom windows.

'Maybe men never stop being boys at heart. When you're younger, you can't wait to stop being a child, and when you're older, you regret you're not.'

'Because you lost your heroes, your dream girls?'

'I suppose that's part of it, but the good thing is you also finally realize what's really important, substantial. Cemeteries aren't simply places filled with the dead. They're places full of regrets, full of people who missed the point.'

'What is the point?'

He reached for her hand.

'When you find something or someone real, you hold on to it. In the end it's the only thing that will give your life any meaning.'

'Are you holding on to me?' she asked.

'Just try to get out of this grip,' he told her and they fell asleep holding hands.

NINETEEN

There were only ten people at Barry Palmer's internment around noon the next day. Unlike every other burial, Quinn joined the group at the grave site and stood beside Lily Palmer. By now it was pretty much known throughout the community that Quinn had not killed Barry. News spread that fast at breakfast in the small restaurants, phone gossip and the local radio stations that had picked up enough detail to develop the story as a lead. Quinn knew that from the lack of any surprise on the faces of the group of mourners when he stepped up beside Barry's aunt and took her hand.

'I knew you couldn't do him any harm,' she whispered. 'Not Spike's boy.'

That brought tears to his eyes. Others thought he was crying for Barry. He was in the same way he cried for his own lost youth. When he looked at the coffin, he recalled their Huck Finn days together. It was good that Barry had changed so much since he had left the area. The man he thought about now was not the same man he had known. This man's body he would soon lower into the grave and cover was a stranger. The Barry Palmer he knew was still out there, hovering in the company of all of his other memories from his teenage years.

The whole community was different in so many ways, too. It once had a faster heartbeat, an aura of excitement and energy which filled the faces of its citizens with hope and joy. He felt sorry for the kids growing up here now who never had known it in its heyday, but he imagined that was true for so many places, not only in America, but in the rest of the world. Being nostalgic might feel good when you first yearn for the return of things you once loved, cherished, and enjoyed, but as soon as that journey back was over, you were overwhelmed with too much self-pity. It was better to bury and forget perhaps.

He took no joy in plowing the dirt into Barry's grave and putting up the marker. He was still that angry at his friend's betrayal. For a few moments he stood there trying to come up with a final thought, a goodbye, but he could think of nothing satisfactory.

Jack approached before he got back on to the backhoe to park it in the garage.

'That's one you won't forget so soon,' he muttered gazing at the marker with him.

'Don't know how to figure it, Jack. If I didn't give him the job, he wouldn't have dug up the grave. If he hadn't dug up the grave, we wouldn't have found the dead baby.'

'Maybe we're not supposed to figure it out,' Jack said. 'I don't know if it was all this or the way events took shape for me and Paula, but my wife and I are seeing a counselor and talking reconciliation.'

'Oh? That's good, Jack.'

'I'll tell you in a few months or maybe a few years if it was good or not.'

Quinn laughed.

Jack followed him back and went into his office.

Quinn spent every available free moment with Scarlet that he and she could manage over the next four days. For most of it, they included her daughter. He wanted to get to know the child more for reasons that became more and more obvious. He was amused by how friendly and hospitable Scarlet's mother became toward him. Everyone was seeing everyone else in the mix as each other's salvation.

He was also very busy that week working out the layout for the parcel Jack and Richard and their investor had bought to expand the cemetery and compete for county welfare business. There was a lot of clearing to do and leveling of the earth. They rented a good size bulldozer and he hired four more part-timers to assist.

Toward the end of the week, just as he was shutting down his equipment and preparing to lock up tools, he saw Lou Siegman drive up, park and start toward the garage. He put the wrench in his hand down and grabbed a towel to wipe his palms. Siegman stepped into the garage. He looked even more hunched up and slouched than ever.

'Damn, it's getting cold,' he said.

'No surprise,' Quinn replied.

'I'm getting too old for this. I should have retired first chance I had.'

Quinn waited. He knew Siegman wasn't here to chat.

'The report's in on the baby,' he began, leaning against a counter. 'She knew it was coming, but she held out as long as she could.'

'Evelyn?'

'Yeah. There's a team coming here tomorrow to disinter Matthew Kitchen.'

Quinn held his breath a moment and then asked, 'Why?'

'The baby was Matthew Kitchen's, but also Evelyn's,' Siegman said. 'What a mess. Stuart Kitchen not only hated his father; he had a incestuous affection for his sister. Neither were gay it seems. From what we can tell, nothing ever happened in the incestuous brother-sister relationship. She didn't share his unnatural passion.

'But Matthew Kitchen had a ... what should I say ... overzealous relationship with Evelyn for some time. It happens,' Siegman said. 'I can't tell you for sure if it was a mutual thing. I suspect it wasn't, but she was abused and that abuse eventually resulted in her pregnancy. She kept it secret from her brother as long as she could. Result was, she had the child.

'The baby died three days after it was born, and Stuart was taking care of it. We think he also took care of his father.'

'Murdered him?'

'The heart attack might have been initiated. There are a number of drugs that could have been used. No forensic toxicology was done, but Evelyn Kitchen suspects it. She was, from what we can conclude, initially unaware Stuart had put the baby in her father's coffin. She was obviously trapped after you called because pursuing the revelation would lead to the revelation of what had happened to her. She is obviously ashamed of it. Whatever,' Siegman said. He put his unlit cigar into his mouth and spoke through the corner of his mouth as he often did. 'That's it for now.'

'Why bother digging him up to find out?' Quinn asked.

'That part is out of my hands. You met Beck. He's leaving open the possibility that Evelyn was involved in her father's death, that she might even have killed him.'

'He's crazy.'

'Who knows, Randy? A month ago, if I came in here and proposed any of this, you'd say I was crazy. Frankly, I don't think he's going anywhere with it. Any good lawyer would keep her out of it, but you saw how passionate Beck is about his work.' He smiled. 'Maybe she'll hire your guy.'

'Thanks for coming over to tell me all of it,' Quinn said.

'Figured you had a vested interest and should know it before it hits the street. Anyway, I had to prepare you for the disinterment tomorrow. I imagine you can handle it.'

Quinn nodded.

'You know, Chief, I had a nagging feeling that I would be doing it again.'

'Whatever. Hopefully, you'll bury him for the last time this time.' He turned to leave and then turned back. 'Oh ... guess who you'll have to prepare in a day or so when his body's released.'

'That one I will enjoy,' Quinn said.

Lou Siegman laughed and then hunched up his shoulders again.

'I knew I should have taken that job in Miami.'

Quinn watched him hurry to his vehicle. Then he returned to locking up.

When he picked up Scarlet an hour later, she looked like the light at the end of a tunnel.

She took one look at his face, then asked, 'The DNA results are in?'

He nodded.

'More nightmares?'

'Not for us,' he said and began to explain.

EPILOGUE

He saw Evelyn Kitchen at her brother's internment, of course. The funeral itself was not held in their chapel as her mother's and father's funerals were. She apparently wanted as little to do with the Sandburg Cemetery as possible, but the grave sites were there, and of course she decided her brother should be beside her parents. Toxicology revealed Matthew Kitchen's heart attack was not the result of any drug. Perhaps if it had, she wouldn't have buried her brother near her father. Quinn was happy to hear that was the result of the investigation, not only because it rid them of Lieutenant Beck, but because it truly brought Evelyn Kitchen's ordeal to an end.

To prevent any chatter or disturb the ceremony at the grave, Quinn kept out of sight, but from where he was, he could watch and saw Evelyn Kitchen carried herself as dignified as possible. Most of the sordid details had gotten out by now. There was little she could do about it.

After it was all over and everyone had left, he started up his backhoe and began to fill in

Stuart Kitchen's grave. He concentrated on doing a good, clean job of it and pushed all other thoughts from his mind. When he was finished, he put up the marker as usual and headed back to the garage. It had been an unusually warm day for this time of the year. He knew it was an anomaly and would probably not last for more than thirty-six or so hours at most. Winter here was not to be denied. At least Lou Siegman was happy today, he thought.

Later, he didn't hear the car come up and park in the cemetery parking lot and wasn't even aware that someone had entered the garage. When he turned to put his gloves in a drawer, however, he saw her standing there. For a moment he thought she was a figment of his imagination. He didn't speak. She stepped more into the light.

'I'm sorry I was unable to be honest with you from the beginning, Randy,' she began. 'I hope you understand.'

'I do,' he said.

'I wanted you to know that I did not send Stuart here to harm you. I had to tell him what you said and he decided he would take care of it. He insisted I should not come along. I didn't know he had taken one of my fashionable wigs to use to fool you at the start, but you see, Stuart always felt it was necessary to protect me. I have no other excuse for his behavior. I hope you believe me.'

'I see no pleasure or benefit for believing otherwise, Evelyn.'

'You may or may not believe this, but I never believed you were guilty of the things you were charged with and Stuart claimed were true. Before this happened here, I was struggling to find a way to help you.'

Quinn nodded.

'No point in belaboring it now,' he said. 'I appreciate your coming here considering what happened and what I had to do.'

'We're all victims of actions and events beyond our control eventually,' she said.

'No doubt about that.'

'I'm not sure why I feel I need to tell you all this now, Randy, but maybe it's because we were both caught up in something that seriously affected our lives.'

She paused and stepped farther in and to the right. He could tell she was thinking carefully about what she was about to say, so he remained still, silent.

'For as long as I can remember, my parents slept in separate bedrooms, as did Stuart and I. When my father was home, it was always he who came to kiss me goodnight and always he who came rushing to my room when I was frightened or sick. Our mother favored Stuart, but that never seemed to bother me because I had so much more of my father's love.

'His closeness to me never lessened as I grew older, and I never thought much of it, even when I was a teenager. He never missed an opportunity to have me with him. There were many trips during which we shared one bed.'

'You don't have to...'

'I know, but I also know everything is out and probably the lead story on everyone's lips. It eases my pain to talk to you about it now. Sometimes ... sometimes, I blame myself as much if not more than I blame my father. Can you understand that?'

'I suppose. Yes.'

'It's so much more convenient to play the role of the sexually abused daughter. It helps me live with all that happened, too.'

'I understand.'

She smiled

'Somehow, I believe you do. I really don't know very much about you, but there was a kindness in your face that night we met here, a kindness that helped me get through it.'

'I always admired you, Evelyn ... from afar.'

She nodded.

'Maybe in a different life...'

He shrugged.

'As far as I know, this is it.'

She laughed.

'I wish you luck, Randy. I think you're strong enough to put it all behind you.'

She started to turn away to leave.

'Evelyn?'

'Yes?'

'What are you going to do now?'

She smiled.

'I think I would be happier somewhere else. I have an aunt who lives in London and she's found me a town house. It's always wise to return to your roots at times like this, not that there are many who get into times like this especially. I'm putting the estate up for sale and negotiating the sale of much of the property and businesses my father established. I'm looking for a new start. Maybe there is one out there.'

'Oh, I can't imagine there isn't one for you,' Quinn said.

'Thank you.'

She gave him another one of those soft, angelic smiles and then she walked off. He stepped up to the doorway to watch her go to her car. Before she got in, she turned to him and for a moment, she looked just the way she had looked that first day when she and her brother had come to the funeral home to make her father's arrangements. Just like then, he thought she was asking for something from him, and just like then, he wasn't sure if she was or what it could be.

Perhaps, right from the beginning, she was asking for forgiveness, he thought.

He didn't have the power to grant it completely. He could forgive her as regards himself, but she would have to go elsewhere for the rest of it.

She drove off and disappeared around a

turn.

He left about twenty minutes later. Before he did, he walked up to the cemetery. It was still light enough to look out over the monuments. Once again, it looked quiet and tranquil. The trouble that had been in the hearts of those buried here was asleep, forgotten.

It wouldn't be all that long before they would all be forgotten just the way they were in less expensive cemeteries everywhere. That was OK, he thought. The earth never forgot them.

'What is a grave anyway?' his father once asked when they were finished working for the day and the sun was on its way to the other side of the world. 'A hole or a door?'

'I don't know, Dad. What do you think?'

'I think it's a door. Or at least I like to think it is. Makes me feel better about it. How about you?'

'Yeah,' he said. 'It does.'

His father laughed, scrubbed his hair and put his arm around his shoulders as they started for home.

In the end that was the best place to be and always would be.